IRON HORSES

Annabel Claridge was born in 1955.
Her working background is in journalism and design.

IRON HORSES is her third book about the adventures of Bo, the time travelling poodle. The story is set in North America during the 1860's and 1870's. The railway has arrived. Soon, its Iron Horses, or trains, will be chugging across The Plains. Two things stand in their way. One is the native Sioux Indians, and particularly their strange but brilliant warrior, Crazy Horse. The other is the very lifeblood of the Sioux - the buffalo herds.

By the same author

STORM DOGS

MORTAL GODS

IRON HORSES

Annabel Claridge

Hemington Publishing

First published in 2010
by Hemington Publishing Limited
18 Magdalens Road, Ripon, HG4 1HX

www.hemingtonpublishing.co.uk

ISBN 978-0-9558142-2-8

© Annabel Claridge 2010
Cover design © Annabel Claridge 2010

Printed in Great Britain
A CIP catalogue record is available for this book from
The British Library

For Mat and Ol

The following story is based on actual events

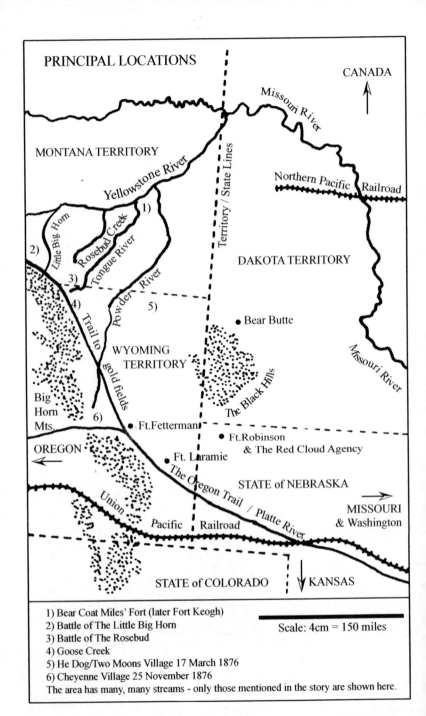

PRINCIPAL LOCATIONS

CANADA

Missouri River

MONTANA TERRITORY

Yellowstone River

Northern Pacific Railroad

Little Big Horn

Rosebud Creek

1)

Tongue River

2)

3)

Powder River

4)

Trail to gold fields

5)

DAKOTA TERRITORY

Bear Butte

WYOMING TERRITORY

The Black Hills

Missouri River

Big Horn Mts.

6)

Ft.Fetterman

OREGON

Ft.Robinson & The Red Cloud Agency

Ft. Laramie

The Oregon Trail / Platte River

STATE of NEBRASKA

Union

Pacific Railroad

MISSOURI & Washington

STATE of COLORADO

KANSAS

1) Bear Coat Miles' Fort (later Fort Keogh)
2) Battle of The Little Big Horn
3) Battle of The Rosebud
4) Goose Creek
5) He Dog/Two Moons Village 17 March 1876
6) Cheyenne Village 25 November 1876
The area has many, many streams - only those mentioned in the story are shown here.

Scale: 4cm = 150 miles

CHAPTER ONE

Walnut Creek, Kansas, North America.
April, The Moon of the Birth of Calves, 1867

'I hope I'm wrong about this,' the raven chattered to himself. 'I really hope I'm wrong.'

He tapped his beak against his beaded ankle bracelet, beat his giant wings and launched himself from the side of the creek. He was flying to investigate a sinister-looking black cloud. He knew the cloud was smoke. He could smell it. When he saw movement on the ground below him, he spiralled downward and hovered. Fifty or more women, children and old folk were struggling through the waist-high grass. A few wore buckskin shirts. Others had shawls of animal skin. Many were naked.

'Oh, no. Not again,' he sighed. 'Please. Not again.'

He flew on, towards the cloud.

A mile or so later, he passed another group of people. Then another, and another. All were similar to the first. All were struggling and poorly dressed. None were riding ponies, as they would usually do. None had strong young men to protect them.

And then, all of a sudden, he spotted the absent ponies. There were hundreds of them. A whole herd of ponies, grazing quietly and encircled by well-armed Cheyenne Indian warriors. The warriors were sitting cross-legged

1

with guns on their knees and quivers of arrows on their backs. These were the strong young men that the wandering women, children and old folk were missing. Something, or some*one,* had separated them from each other.

'Well, at least the ponies are safe,' thought the raven, 'and the Indians will soon reunite. What worries me is that there are so few warriors. There should be many more than this. So where are the rest? Oh, my! What have we here?'

Four-hundred horses were approaching. The raven landed on a solitary tree and settled down to wait for them. He could pick out their brands; the letters U and S on their shoulders, the number 7 on their flanks. Their riders had blue shirts and trousers, black felt hats, a sabre on their left-hand side, and a pistol and rifle on their right.

'As I thought,' the raven cawed. 'The United States 7th Cavalry.' He cocked his head and trained a sharp black eye on the cavalry's commanding officer. 'Good morning, Mr Custer!' he squawked.

Lieutenant Colonel George Armstrong Custer stood out from his men like a raven in a flock full of sparrows. He seemed to like it that way. Not for him, the standard issue ankle-boots. His boots came up to his knees. He wore a toothbrush in his top pocket, and a bright red kerchief and a pair of field glasses around his neck. His nose was sharp and beaky, and he had bright blue eyes that seemed bluer still against his florid complexion. Most distinctive of all were his long blonde curls and flamboyant matching moustache.

Yes, Custer stood out, all right.

'Does he know about the Indians?' the raven wondered. 'Is he looking for them? Because if he is, he has *no* chance. He'll never find them, now. The women and children have scattered, the pony herd is guarded by warriors, and the rest of the tribe is who knows where.'

The raven knew, everybody knew, why Custer was here on the plains. He'd been sent here to hunt for Indians, any Indians, and move them away from the white man's roads, especially their iron roads.

They were strange things, these iron roads. The raven had never seen their like. He'd thought the prairie grass grew fast, but it had nothing on the iron roads. An iron road could grow two whole miles in a single day. Its tracks were dragged and hammered into place by thousands of men who worked in searing heat and incredible noise. The eagles had reported the identical thing happening way out west, in California. Another iron road was being built there. It seemed to be heading east. Supposing it met up with those the raven had been watching? If that were to happen, the roads might be joined. The Atlantic and Pacific Oceans would be joined. The iron road would run all the way from one to the other and back again, and the vast beasts that travelled it would huff and puff and belch their way right across America. The Indians called these beasts iron horses, but the white men said they were trains.

The raven stretched his wings.

'I should go,' he told himself. 'That smoke cloud's getting bigger by the minute.'

Just then, though, Custer raised his field glasses. Something had caught his eye.

'What's he spotted?' the raven muttered. 'Is it the Indians? If so, I must fly to warn them.'

He swept over Custer's head and aligned himself with the glasses. There wasn't an Indian in sight. What Custer had seen was a pair of antelope. Custer dropped the glasses to his chest, raised an arm and spurred his horse. Then he peeled away from the cavalry and galloped, full pelt, towards his quarry.

The raven followed.

Custer rode well and his horse was beautiful. It sped through the grass like streaked lightning, but the antelope were too clever and too agile to be caught on home ground. They bounded away, zigzagging and prancing over the tall grass. Custer gave up, pulled his tiring horse to a halt, and peered through his glasses again. He was focussing on a lone bull buffalo.

'Don't even *think* about it,' the raven warned.

Buffalo were the most dangerous animals on the plains. They made the local wolves and coyotes seem like shy kittens. They were massive and powerful and could halt without warning and spin on a coin. Buffalo were unpredictable, and the most unpredictable buffalo of all was a lone bull.

There was a whoop and a shout and the raven glanced down. Custer was galloping towards the buffalo.

'Is he *trying* to get himself killed?' the raven gasped. 'No one *ever* pursues a lone bull. Those things are *lethal*. Hunting buffalo is a skill, it takes teamwork...'

Custer galloped on. His horse was already flagging.

Its sides were heaving, its chest and shoulders were white with sweat, and its mouth was foaming with effort. Custer whooped and shouted. The buffalo looked at him lugubriously, made a little buck and hared away. It plunged and swerved through the grass, but Custer caught up with it, drew his pistol, and waved it in the air. He urged his horse some more and laid his gun against the bull's enormous head, but he didn't shoot. He was enjoying the chase too much.

'Enough!' the raven screeched. 'Can't you see your horse has had enough?'

It was true. Custer's beautiful mount was beginning to flounder. Custer levelled his gun with new determination. The buffalo stared down the barrel and snorted. Its beady eyes rolled white in its deep brown fur. Custer aimed. The buffalo shifted its weight and spun. Custer pulled the trigger. There was a crack of fire, the buffalo swerved violently, and Custer and his horse were thrown to the ground. The buffalo looked bemused. It pawed at the grass and bellowed, then took off at the gallop. Custer stood up, rubbed his sore bottom, glanced at his rapidly receding target, then looked for his horse. It was lying at his feet, stone dead. Custer had accidentally shot it through the head. He was alone in the middle of nowhere. He had no horse, no water and no food, and his cavalry was miles behind him.

'Hah!' the raven chuckled with glee. 'Good luck with the hunting, Mr Custer!'

CHAPTER TWO
Pawnee Fork, Kansas.
A little later

The raven's high spirits were short-lived.

As he approached the smoke cloud, he saw more soldiers. There were about a thousand of them, the largest number the raven had ever seen on the plains. They were marching on foot and accompanied by mules and wheeled guns. One of the soldiers was carrying a Cheyenne Indian lance. Another had a beautifully decorated baby's cradleboard, a third had a puppy in his arms, and a fourth was brandishing a warrior's shield.

The raven darted sideways and ducked beneath the smoke cloud. Below him were the miserable ruins of what had once been the Cheyennes' village. The soldiers had taken what they wanted and burned the rest to the ground. There was no sign of life in the stinking, blackened heap, but no dead bodies, either. The Cheyenne had seen the soldiers coming and managed to escape. They'd saved their ponies, but they'd been so frightened and in such a hurry that they'd had no time to pack their possessions. They'd left with nothing, and nothing remained of what they'd left. Everything they'd owned had been destroyed.

It wasn't the worst thing the United States Army had

done to an Indian village, but the raven had a horrible feeling it wouldn't be the last. As his lungs began to choke with the acrid stench of burning, he turned sadly in the sky and headed for home. He knew, now, where the missing warriors had gone. They'd gone to seek revenge.

'They'll hold up the stagecoaches, rip down the telegraph wires and pull up the tracks on the Kansas railroad. They'll kill a few white men. It might not be many, but that's not what the papers will say. The reporters will write with gusto and exaggeration about the terrible things the Indians do, but they won't explain *why* they do it. Oh, no. They won't mention the villages burnt to dust. They won't mention the women and children who ran for their lives. Oh, no. They won't mention *that!*'

CHAPTER THREE

The Oregon Trail, Wyoming Territory, North America.
One year later, June 1868

The wagons were strung along the trail, their cream canvas covers gleaming in the sunshine. From the raven's eye view, they looked just like a necklace of ivory beads.

The raven saw a small black nose push between one of the wagon's rear flaps. It was followed by a pair of eyes, round and black and shiny as coal, and two neat little paws. The bird cawed a greeting to the dog, and the dog, a young poodle, glanced up and blinked against the bright blue sky. She saw the raven turn, its dark wings casting a long shadow on the pale road. Then the raven and its shadow were gone, and the poodle blinked again.

'Nearly there,' called the driver of the wagon behind her. 'Nearly at camp!'

The poodle withdrew her head and slipped back into her own wagon. Inside it were two children, a boy and a girl. They'd been sleeping for most of the afternoon, but now their patchwork quilts were beginning to stir. The children were waking up.

'Are we there yet, Kal?' the little girl yawned to her brother. 'Are we in Oregon?'

'No, stupid,' Kal replied. 'We're barely a quarter the

way. Don't you listen to *anything*?'

'Where are we, then?'

'*I* don't know, but I think we're pulling in for the night. What shall we have for supper, Effie?' he asked more kindly. 'What would you like?'

'Tinned oysters and catsup,' said Effie firmly.

'That's what you always say.'

'Because we never have them, even though I *know* we've got them. I've seen them in the dry stores box. There's six tins of oysters and three catsup bottles.'

'I think they're being saved for something special.'

'Like my birthday?' Effie offered.

'I hope not. You won't have another birthday for nearly a whole *year*. You already had one, remember? That's why you got the puppy.'

'No, it isn't. I got the puppy because we left our house in Missouri and now we're going to Oregon.'

'Well, anyway, we're not having oysters and catsup today. We're having *antelope*! The MacCauleys brought it in. They'll have it cut up by now. It'll be delicious. We've stopped. Come on, Effie. Let's get out.'

The children's wagon was one of thirty. Its journey would take several weeks and cover three-thousand miles, from one side of America to the other. Now, just on four o'clock, it was swinging off the road to find its place in the already half-formed circle in which it would spend the night.

'All right, you lot,' said a man's voice. 'Jump off.'

Jack Irvine opened the wagon's flaps and helped his children down.

'Go get the basket, Kal. There's plenty of lovely dry

chips out there. Put the doggy on her lead, mind, and remember to stamp your feet as you go.'

Chips were dried up lumps of buffalo dung and the best, sometimes only, source of fuel on the Oregon Trail. Collecting chips was a highlight of the poodle and the children's otherwise tedious days on the road. Even more exciting was having to stamp the ground to clear it of rattlesnakes, then watch them shoot from the shade and side-wind away.

Whilst some people searched for snakes and chips, others washed clothes or made bread dough, or led horses, oxen and mules to drink and cool off in the lazy waters of The River Platte.

At six o'clock, the chips were in, the fires were lit and the antelope was roasting; lines of clean washing were strung between the wagons, and the Dutch ovens were bursting with rising dough. Come seven, the bread and antelope were ready to eat, and the travellers were pulling up stools or spreading blankets on the ground. By eight, supper was over, Effie and Kal were back in the wagon and sound asleep, and the poodle was sitting with Mr and Mrs Irvine and the MacCauley brothers, Pip and Luke.

Pip and Luke were just two of about twenty lone riders in the party. These lone riders were expert horsemen and crack shots. They had no wagons of their own, no families to care for, and few possessions, so, in return for food and company, they helped out along the road. They guarded the dairy herd, fixed and mended things, hunted for supper and searched for water and suitable campsites.

Mrs Irvine dragged her stool closer to the fire and hitched the poodle onto her lap.

'The stars are beautiful tonight,' she said as she cradled a mug of coffee.

She tipped her face and pointed skyward.

'Did you see that?'

'Yes. Yes, I did,' her husband replied.

'A shooting star. I love them.'

'You saw a shooting star? I missed that,' said Luke. 'But look over there. Do you see? It's a fire of some sort.'

'A campfire?'

'No. That's no campfire. The flames are too high, too fierce.'

'Where is it?'

'Down on the railroad, I think.'

'Is it Indians?' Mr Irvine asked. 'I hear they've been setting fires. Torching the railroad towns, ripping down the telegraph wires.'

'I thought that was last year,' said his wife.

'This year, too.'

'Last year's trouble was with the Cheyenne,' said Pip. 'That was in Kansas, a long way from here.'

'Well, that fire sure isn't in Kansas,' Mr Irvine replied. 'How far d'you reckon it is, Luke? Five, six miles?'

'Hard to tell. The ground's so level, these parts.'

'Where's the railroad?'

'Not far, but it might not be the railroad. And the Indians, if that's what they are, aren't interested in us.'

'But they'll know we're here?' asked Mrs Irvine nervously.

'Of course,' Luke replied. 'There's been white settlers camped along this road every night for a generation. But the Indians'll be set on the railroad and the telegraph wires, not us. Now then, who's in charge of the coffee? My mug's empty. One last cup, and Pip and I'll go to bed. See if we can't rise early and get more on those fires.'

CHAPTER FOUR
The following morning

As they'd promised, Luke and Pip left camp at first light and rode to the nearest town. When Mrs Irvine saw them returning, she whispered to her husband.

'The boys are coming back,' she said hastily. 'I'm going to make them something to eat, so could you put the children in the wagon for me? I mean *before* you take the horses to water. I don't want Effie and Kal hearing about Indians, especially not if Spotty's around. You know what he's like. He'll put the fear of God in them.'

Spotty, so-named because of the smallpox scars on his face, was the party's elected leader, their captain. His job was to make the final decision about where, when, and for how long the wagons could stop, and to ensure that everyone was treated fairly and kept safe. Mrs Irvine couldn't deny that Spotty was a good captain, she just didn't like him very much.

Spotty wandered over to listen to what Pip and Luke had learned, and Mrs Irvine handed the brothers a hunk of bread, some bacon and a mug of hot coffee.

'Thank you, ma'am,' they raised their hats.

'Any news?' asked Spotty.

'Yup,' said Luke as he dropped his reins to tear at the bacon with his teeth. 'Those fires were set by Indians, all right. The fellow we spoke to says there's hundreds of them round here. They've been robbing the railroad depots and running off with things.'

'Including scalps, I've no doubt,' Spotty growled.

'What's a scalp?' a small voice asked.

Effie had climbed down from the wagon.

'Nothing,' said Mrs Irvine. 'It's nothing. Go back to the wagon, please, Effie.'

'A scalp is what Indians take,' said Spotty. 'They get a sharp knife…'

'Go back to the wagon, Effie. Run!'

'…and then they do this,' Spotty bunched the hair at the crown of his head and circled its base with his finger, 'and then they cut through the flesh...'

'Be quiet!' Mrs Irvine screamed as she ran after her daughter.

'…and then they tug hard,' Spotty shouted as he jerked his head back, 'and rip everything clean away! *That's* what a scalp is! *That's* what Indians do!'

'Don't know about that,' Pip tried to hide his shock, 'but they've certainly been ripping up the railroad tracks. They used to derail the trains, but they've given up on that of late. Seems a few too many got their calculations wrong. Trains ran them over, or caught them up in their wheels and dragged them along behind.'

'Well, what the trains don't get, Colonel Custer will,' Spotty cackled.

'Custer? Hah!' Luke laughed. 'We met a trooper. Said he'd been months with Custer, eating biscuits six-years-old, riding all day long and never even *seeing* an Indian.'

14

'Custer's not catching any Indians,' said Pip. 'They're running rings round him. Killing settlers, driving off stock, stealing horses, robbing stagecoaches, tearing down the telegraphs.'

'Red-skinned devils,' Spotty spat. 'Custer should kill them all. Kill them all's what I say. General Harney was right. Those Indians are lice. Kill the squaws. Kill the children, too. Get them whilst they're young. Nits make lice.'

'Well, there's plenty white lice too, let me tell you,' said Luke. 'Where we've just been,' he jabbed a thumb over his shoulder, 'there's all sorts. That trooper we met? He told us he's seen white men dressing up as Indians. They go making trouble, big trouble. They do terrible things and the Indians get the blame.'

'There you go, Spotty! It's not just Indians that do terrible things!' interrupted a furious voice.

Mrs. Irvine was on the warpath.

'Fortunately for you, Spotty,' she smouldered, 'Effie didn't hear what you said about scalps, and neither did my husband, since he's watering the horses. The Indians aren't saints. I know they do terrible things, but so do the whites. None more so than your precious army.'

'They're the army. That's their job.'

'I don't think so. I don't think it's anybody's job to murder innocent people. Three years past, the army attacked some Indians at a place called Sand Creek. The Indians were taken by surprise, but their warriors fought back. Forty-seven soldiers were killed.'

'And?' asked Spotty. 'What's your point?'

'Forty-seven soldiers were killed, but more than a

hundred Indians died, mostly women and children. The soldiers hacked them to pieces and scalped them. They took the scalps to Denver, to the theatre, and then, during the interval, they strung them across the stage. And do you know what the audience did? They stood up in their seats and cheered. They gave that hideous display a standing ovation.'

'Nonsense,' said Spotty. 'White men don't scalp. Only savages do that.'

'Oh really? There was an investigation, Spotty. One of the officers had refused to attack. He testified to Congress. He told the truth about what had happened.'

Spotty swallowed hard.

'Well, that was some time ago,' he said lamely. 'Things are different now.'

'How? How are they different?' Mrs Irvine asked.

But Spotty didn't reply. He picked up the camp bell and swung it rigorously.

'Gather round, folks!' he hollered.

At least one adult from every wagon stopped what they were doing and hurried to hear their captain's instructions.

'We need to move on quickly,' Spotty told them. 'Pip and Luke have been into town and it seems there are Indians about. No need to worry. They won't bother us. Just stay close, please. No spreading out on the trail. Those of you with dogs, keep an eye on them. Better still, keep them on your wagon.'

'Why's that?' a man asked.

'Indians eat dogs, is why,' replied another.

Even Mrs Irvine gasped at that.

'Where's…? Oh, there you are, little one,' she said as the poodle pawed at her skirts.

'I was thinking more about us not needing any delays,' Spotty continued. 'Such as the one we had last week, when the Jones' dog went bounding off. If that happens today, we won't be hanging around waiting. Any dog that goes missing today is on its own. Understood? Those of you with oxen or mules, keep them moving. Horse teams? No running ahead. Any questions? Good. Hitch those wagons! Let's roll!'

The wagons pulled out of their circle and formed an orderly line on the trail. This was always the best time of day. Everyone was refreshed, the animals were raring to go, and the travellers were optimistic about ticking another twenty to twenty-five miles off their journey to Oregon.

The poodle and the children spent the morning looking out of the rear of their wagon, but at midday they let down the flaps and crawled inside, where boredom and the rocking motion soon sent them to sleep.

The poodle was first to awake. The heat inside the wagon was stifling and the air was stale. She moved away from the children's clammy bodies, pottered over to the flaps and pushed her nose outside. There was barely a breeze, her mouth was dry and her water bowl was empty. She wanted to stretch her legs, see something other than the dim interior of the wagon and have a long, cool drink.

She heard a distant shout, and then another, closer

one.

Her wagon slowed and jolted to a halt.

The jolt woke Kal and Effie, and they sat up just as their mother appeared.

'Why've we stopped?' Effie asked.

'Is it lunchtime?' offered Kal.

'Nearly,' Mrs Irvine replied, 'but that's not why we've stopped. Something's happened up front. Luke and Pip'll come tell us what it is.'

'A loose tire, I think,' said Kal.

'Probably,' his mother agreed.

'Can we get down, then?'

'No. Wait 'til we hear what the matter is.'

'Why?'

'Don't ask so many questions, Kal,' Mrs Irvine snapped. 'Just stay where you are for the moment, please.'

Kal shrank away.

'Why's she so cross?' the poodle wondered. 'And why *have* we stopped? I hope it's not Indians. No. It can't be. Can it?'

When two sets of hooves thundered up to the wagon and skidded to a halt alongside it, the poodle raised her eyes nervously, but it was only Luke and Pip. They removed their hats and leant out of their saddles.

'Someone's sprung a tire,' Pip explained.

'Told you,' muttered Kal.

Mrs Irvine ruffled her son's hair.

'Yes, darling, you did,' she laughed.

'The wheel's just shrunk a bit in the heat, that's all,' Luke added. 'I'll give it a soaking with water. The tire'll

18

soon fit snug again. Shouldn't take long, but Spotty says this is a good time to have lunch. We'll stay for an hour, then move on 'til the end of the day.'

Mrs Irvine hesitated.

'Is it…safe?'

'Yes, ma'am,' Luke replied. 'There's been no sign. Enjoy your lunch.'

'No sign of what?' asked Kal as the brothers trotted away.

'Snakes,' said Mrs Irvine, quick as a flash. 'There's been no sign of snakes.'

'Good,' said Effie as her mother lifted her to the ground. 'I *hate* snakes.'

'Kal,' Mrs Irvine turned to her son, 'could you… where are you going?'

'To collect chips,' Kal replied.

'No, darling. We don't need any chips just now. We're having a cold lunch.'

'But there's *hundreds* of them,' Kal protested. 'I can see them from here. We can save them for tonight, and the boys said there weren't any snakes, so…'

'We don't need chips,' said Mrs Irvine firmly. 'Why don't you help me get the lunch things out?'

The poodle didn't really feel like eating. She was too hot. She managed a handful of biscuit and tinned sardine and had a lap of milk and water. She was about to crawl under the wagon for some shade when Mrs Irvine hauled her onto her lap, pulled Effie alongside, and opened a well-thumbed copy of McGuffey's Reader.

'Lesson time, Effie.'

'Aw,' Effie wriggled. 'Please, no. Not lessons.'

'Yes. Here we go,' Mrs Irvine said as she pointed to a letter A with a drawing beside it.

'A is for?'

'Ax,' answered Effie.

'Good. B is for?'

'Box.'

The poodle sighed. She'd been hearing this drivel for weeks. She knew it off by heart.

'C is for cat, D is for dog, E is for elk, and F is for fan,' she recited to herself. 'Wish *I* had a fan.'

She noticed a large boulder a few paces off the road. Beyond it was a mound of earth with a crude wooden cross and a posy of wild flowers on top. The Oregon Trail had hundreds of such mounds. Some were old and sunken, others were newly dug, like this one. Kal and Effie had once asked what they were, and Mr Irvine had said they were graves.

'Whose graves?' Kal had asked.

'People's. People who've died along the way,' his father had replied.

'Why?' Kal had persisted.

'Because they were old,' his mother had said quickly.

'No, they weren't. I saw one yesterday and its cross said "Elijah. Died aged 7 years." Was he killed by Indians?'

'Indians? Whatever makes you say that?'

'Because I saw another one that said, "Killed by Indians".'

'Well, Elijah wasn't killed by Indians, Indians don't kill small boys.'

The poodle slipped from Mrs Irvine's lap and padded over to the boulder. It was covered with letters and numbers. Some had been carved into the stone, others had been painted on its surface, sometimes with paint, more often with grease. She picked out a C for Cat and an F for Fan, and the numbers 1,8,5 and 4.

'C.F.1854,' she mouthed.

She walked around the boulder and examined more of the marks.

'W.J.K.'

'M.M. '49.'

So many people had passed this way. So many had stopped at this very spot. The poodle wondered what had become of them, whether they'd made it to Oregon, and why they'd been going there in the first place.

She reached the space between the back of the boulder and the grave. The grave was still fresh. Even its posy of flowers was fresh. She stood on her hind legs and placed her paws on the arms of the cross.

'AMY,' she read. 'Aged 9. R.I.P.'

She felt sad for AMY and R.I.P. They'd never get to Oregon now. She lay down and put her nose on her paws. It was cool here, in the shadow of the boulder. The poodle was cooler and more comfortable than she'd been for days. She closed her eyes and fell into a deep sleep.

Her dreams were about the journey so far. She relived the river crossings, the animal sightings, the loose tires and the broken wheels. She saw the tall grasses, the rushing streams, the bright stars and the campfires glowing orange in the dark. She heard her name being called, heard Spotty ring his bell and shout 'Let's roll!' Her name was called again and she heard Effie sobbing, Kal chastising and the comforting voice of Mrs Irvine. She dreamt the wagons were starting to move. Their iron tires were vibrating on the dry ground, disturbing the dust and sending it billowing. She twitched in her sleep, made a little stretch and extended her paws. She expected to feel Effie's soft body, but her paws pressed instead against something hard and unforgiving. The inside wall of her wagon, perhaps. She flipped over and stretched again. Sure enough, her paws met with something soft and warm. She lay for a moment, but the warmth turned cool and damp. She sat bolt upright and looked down. The soil at the edge of Amy's grave had been disturbed. *That's* where her paws had been. Not pressed against Effie, but pressed into Amy's grave. She raised her head, expecting to see the Irvines, the wagons and horses, the oxen and mules, but there was nothing there. She scrambled onto the boulder and stared ahead, a long way ahead. She could just make out the tops of the wagons. Luke and his horse were closer. They were stationary and hesitant, searching for her, looking straight at her. She barked, but they didn't hear her. She leapt from the boulder and hurtled towards them. She hadn't ever moved so fast, hadn't known she could. She tried to keep barking, but when Luke raised his reins, turned his horse and cantered away from her, she stopped barking and put all her effort into running. Her paws were drumming, pounding the hard earth as she bounded over ruts and holes. She began to gain ground. She was catching up.

Suddenly, though, her paws began to sting and her vision blurred. Her head was throbbing, her legs were weak and she was desperate for water. She stumbled. Picked herself up. Galloped some more. The wagons were fading into the horizon, disappearing to a point she couldn't hope to reach. She stumbled again, buckled, and fell sideways onto the verge.

CHAPTER FIVE

Bo's House, somewhere in England.
The 21st Century

Almost a hundred-and-fifty years later, a poodle named Bo was lying in her garden in England. The tip of her nose was pressed against a daisy stalk, and she was fast asleep and dreaming in the sun.

She felt something touch the top of her head. It crept through her fur and tickled her skin. She snapped awake. Hovering in front of her was a silky cream paw with chestnut-brown freckles.

'Cavendish,' she sighed. 'I might have known it was you.'

'So why didn't you?' her spaniel friend asked.

'Because I was asleep. I thought you were a beetle or something.'

'Were you dreaming?'

'Yes! I dreamt I was a poodle.'

'You *are* a poodle.'

'This was another poodle. She belonged to an American family. They'd been farmers in a place called Miz...Miz...'

'Missouri?'

'That's it. Missouri. But then they packed up all their possessions, loaded them into a wagon and left on this

24

long, long journey to the other side of the country.'

'Did they follow The Oregon Trail?'

'Yes. Why would they do that? Why would they leave their home and travel so far?'

'To look for a better life. To go out west and buy a bigger farm. Thousands of Americans did that very same thing. Did your family pack their poodle, too? Was she with them in the wagon?'

'She *was*. But she got left behind.'

'And? What happened then?'

'I don't know because just as I was about to find out, some idiot came along and woke me up.'

'Are you certain it was a dream, Bo?'

This was a leading question. Until that moment, Bo hadn't considered the poodle's adventure to be anything *other* than a dream. Yet now the spaniel mentioned it, it had all seemed very real. Too real for a dream. Too detailed. How had Bo known that buffalo dung can be used to build a fire? Or that stamping your feet scares rattlesnakes? She'd never even *heard* of buffalo. Or rattlesnakes.

'No,' Bo replied. 'I'm not certain it was a dream.'

'Well, then. Perhaps it wasn't,' said Cavendish. 'Perhaps you really *were* that poodle.'

Bo sat up sharply.

'Could this be what we've been looking for?' she asked.

'I do believe it could,' Cavendish smiled, 'I do believe it could.'

Bo was an ordinary dog with an extraordinary gift. She

could time travel. Better yet, wherever she went, and for however long, her present life remained on hold. The secret of these powers was both magical and unique. That secret was Cavendish the spaniel.

Often evasive, sometimes pompous, always charming, wise and kind. That was Cavendish. He was Bo's best friend, and her mentor and advisor on all things time travel. It was he who sent her to interesting places in interesting times. It was he who decided which real-life person's pet she would be. For this latest adventure, he'd decided on a North American Indian. But, being Cavendish, he wasn't going to settle for any old Indian. Oh, no. The man that Cavendish had chosen to be Bo's master was one of the greatest warriors in history. His name was Crazy Horse.

All that remained was to find him...

'You said the poodle got left behind?' Cavendish mused. 'What did you mean by that, exactly?'

'That she fell asleep in the shade and the wagons moved off without her,' Bo replied. 'Spotty had warned everyone not to let their dogs run free, that the wagons couldn't wait for them, and then someone said...Oh! Oh, no!'

'What? What is it, Bo? Who's Spotty?'

'The party captain. Spotty's the party captain. He said the wagons had to keep moving because there were Indians nearby.'

'Indians?'

'Yes. They'd been ripping up the railway tracks, and then someone said...'

'Perfect,' mumbled Cavendish. 'The railways suggest our timing is perfect...'

'Could you stop interrupting? I'm trying to tell you what someone said. They said that Indians ate dogs.'

'*Some* Indians *did* eat dogs. They had dog feasts. *Puppy* feasts on special occasions.'

Bo swallowed. She was feeling sick.

'Hold on a minute,' she rasped through the bile in her throat. 'You told me about Crazy Horse, and I agreed to try to find him. At no point did you mention he might eat me.'

'He won't. There were hundreds of Indian tribes. Some ate dogs, some didn't. Anyway, he's not going to eat you if you're his *pet*. Look. We've been talking about Crazy Horse for months, and now all of a sudden you've discovered this poodle, this *lost* poodle. She's on the Oregon Trail, the railways are being laid *and* there are Indians nearby. That puts her in exactly the right place, at exactly the right time. It's too much of a coincidence, Bo. Trust me. I think this poodle's the dog we've been looking for.'

'Suppose you're wrong?'

'I'm not,' said Cavendish. 'Why don't you give it a go? See what happens. You can always come home if you don't like it.'

'All right,' Bo sighed. 'I'll give it a go. How should I start?'

'Try lying down. Like you were before. Good girl. Now put your right paw on my left one. Imagine the wagons, the road...you're feeling sleepy... Bo? Close your eyes...'

'Hold on…'

'What's up?'

'I need something to remember from my own time. Something from Bo's time, so I can get back here when I want to.'

'No, you don't. You only needed that when you were a beginner at time travel. You're an expert at it, now.'

'Still. I'd rather have something, just in case. How about that crow? The one on the tree?'

'It's not a crow,' said Cavendish. 'It's a raven.'

28

CHAPTER SIX

The Oregon Trail, Wyoming Territory, North America.
June, The Moon of Berries, 1868

When the poodle came round and opened her eyes, the first thing she saw was a hoof. It was pale and small and unshod, tipped forward and resting on its edge. It made her think of Kal's little pony, the one he'd had to leave behind in Missouri. She raised her head and tracked upward. The hair around the hoof was long and untrimmed, and the leg above it was patched in brown and white. Not Kal's pony, after all, but a pinto.

The pony stretched its neck and snorted through its pink muzzle, and the poodle heard a voice. It was young and male, and it spoke in a language the poodle couldn't understand.

'He taku hwo?' it asked.

'Shunke,' another voice replied.

They sounded curious, almost bemused.

The poodle tried to put faces to these strange sounds, but all she could see was dark silhouettes. There were four, at least. Men astride ponies, carrying long sticks. The sticks were perpendicular to the ground and had sharp ends with many things tied to them, things that were fluttering. The poodle's ears were fluttering, too. A breeze was picking up. The sun was going down.

Something touched the top of her head. At first it did no more than tickle her fur, but then it began to prod. The poodle yelped and tried to sit up, but she was too weak. She'd chased after wagons, lain all day in searing heat, and had nothing to eat or drink for hours. Her legs gave way, and she flopped to the grass. The prodding stopped and someone asked again, 'He taku hwo?'

The reply was the same as before.

'Shunke.'

The poodle felt something slip beneath her pompommed tail and raise it off the ground.

'Masteencala! Ha, ha, ha!'

The men slapped their thighs and whooped with laughter.

'Hoppo!' said one, and their ponies spun, kicked up the dust and cantered away.

Their going left a sudden, terrible silence. The sun had set completely now, and the vast and endless prairie had turned an inky, moonlit blue. The poodle began to shiver.

'Someone's out there, heading my way,' she whimpered softly to herself. 'All I have to do now is survive the night.'

She knew that come morning there'd be people on the road. They'd missed her today because she'd been lying on the verge. From the seat of a wagon she'd have looked like nothing more than a discarded blanket or a piece of clothing. There were many such things on The Oregon Trail. The poodle had seen pots and pans and pieces of furniture. She'd even seen a piano. Tomorrow, though, she would *not* be a discarded thing. She would *not* be forlorn. She would be standing in the middle of the road. She would stand and bark at every wagon that came her way. Someone would be bound to pick her up, rescue her, give her food and water. They'd lift her onto their wagon and take her into their hearts. Then, one day soon, she'd catch up with the Irvines.

She lowered her head to her paws and thought about her family. She thought about the evening they'd spent without her. Kal collecting chips, Mrs Irvine kneading dough, baking bread, washing Effie's pinafore. Mr Irvine milking the family's cow, leading his horses to water. Effie with her legs dangling over the rear of the wagon, kicking absentmindedly as she leafed through her ABC.

'A is for Ax, B is for Box,' the poodle recited.

The drivel was of comfort until she heard a distant howl.

'Mmmwooh! Oohoogurru-amoo! Amwoo-hoolooh!'

A wolf.

She sat upright in the dark and heard another noise.

A soft, lolloping gait.

It was coming towards her.

'Who's there?' she barked.

She was trembling.

The lolloping slowed.

'Three Legs Running,' came the reply.

'A dog! You're a dog! Where are you? I can't see you!'

'I'll move into the moonlight. Can you see me now?'

She could.

Three Legs Running was not a dog.

He was a wolf.

His fur was silver, and he had iron-brown hackles and a long, bushy tail that was tipped with white. His eyes were of palest blue, almost grey, and were circled with black, as if he were wearing make-up.

The poodle wanted to run, but she was rooted to the spot. Frozen like a rabbit, or a deer in the headlamp of an oncoming train. The distant howl came again, 'Mmmwooh! Oohoogurru-amoo! Amwoo-hoolooh!' and the wolf glanced over his shoulder.

'Go on then,' the poodle said shakily. 'Call your friends.'

'Friends?' the wolf growled.

His gums glistened like wet coal.

'Yes,' the poodle answered. 'I know I can't escape, so call your pack. You can *all* rip me to shreds. It'll be quicker that way.'

'They're not my friends,' said the wolf. 'They're not even my kin. They'd probably rip *me* to shreds.'

He turned sideways and the poodle saw that one of his hind legs was missing.

'I wouldn't have a leg to stand on,' he chuckled. 'Now you know how I got my name. Three Legs Running. Legs for short. Pleased to meet you.'

He held out a paw, but the poodle didn't reciprocate.

She was staring at the stump of his leg.

'Did the wolves do that?' she asked.

Legs shook his head.

'I owe this to a fur trap,' he said. 'I was just a cub. I could have died, but luckily the scouts were out that day.

32

They found me and took me to Worm. Have you met Worm?'

'*Worm*?'

'No, of course you haven't. He's a medicine man, and a bit of a magician. He couldn't save my leg, but he saved my life. He's saved other animals, too. They've gone back to the wild, but it's hard out there for a three-legged wolf, so I stay around camp and help where I can.'

'Whose camp?' the poodle asked incredulously. 'Who keeps a wolf in their camp?'

'Indians do.'

'Oh,' said the poodle lamely. 'Stupid question. Silly me.'

'I was here with them earlier,' the wolf continued.

'I didn't see you.'

'No, the sun was going down. Anyway. I came to tell you that one of them is coming back.'

'That was kind of you. I'll go now, before he finds me.'

'Why? Why would you want to go?'

'So he doesn't eat me, of course.'

'Eat you? He doesn't want to eat you. He wants to keep you as his pet. He's already given you a name. He calls you Pte Masteencala. It means Buffalo Rabbit in his language. Pte for buffalo, because you have a coat like a buffalo, and Masteencala for rabbit, because your tail's like a rabbit's.'

The poodle laughed despite herself. She was intrigued.

'Who is this man?' she asked.

33

'Crazy Horse. He's a warrior. He comes from the Oglala tribe of the Lakota Sioux. Warriors are two cents a piece around here, but Crazy Horse may turn out to be one of the finest ever.'

'He's young, then? Is he kind? Will he be kind to me?'

'Very kind. He comes from a kind family. But he's a solitary soul. I think he's lonesome. He has no wife and no children. He still lives with his parents. His father is Worm, the medicine man I told you about. But listen, I hear hooves.'

He tipped his head and pricked his ears.

'Yes,' he said. 'That's Crazy Horse, all right. He'll be here in a second. What do you want to do?'

'I have a choice?'

'Of course you do. You can hide, but you can't run. Do that, and he'll track you. He'll lay his ear to the ground and detect your vibrations. But if you hide and stay still, I can mask your scent with my own. I'll have to pee on you, of course, but it'll confuse him. He'll soon lose interest. It'll confuse the wild wolves too, by the way.'

'Will *they* lose interest?'

'No.'

The hooves had come closer. Now they were walking, picking over the ground.

'Quick, Rabbit. Make up your mind.'

There was a soft thud, and the poodle realised that Crazy Horse had dismounted from his pony. She could smell him, now. He had a scent of wood-smoke, animals and grass.

'I'll stay,' she whispered.

'Good,' said Legs. 'You won't regret it. I promise.'

Crazy Horse crouched, ruffled the wolf's fur, and lifted the poodle onto his knee.

'Cante chante sica yaun sai ye,' he said gently.

'Don't have a sad heart,' Legs translated.

Crazy Horse took a leather bag from a belt at his waist. He held out his cupped palm, filled it with water from the bag, and offered it to the poodle. She lapped at it gratefully and Crazy Horse poured her another helping.

'Micaje, Tashunke Witko,' he whispered as she drank. 'My name, Crazy Horse. Your name, Pte Masteencala.'

'Told you,' said Legs.

'He speaks English?' the poodle asked.

'A bit,' said Legs. 'He grew up not far from here. The white men were more friendly then. He's going to put you on his pony now, but don't worry. You'll be perfectly safe.'

'Are you coming, too?'

'Of course,' said the wolf. 'I'll be right alongside.'

Buffalo Rabbit began the journey in Crazy Horse's arms but, when she awoke the next morning, she was in a pouch on the side of his pony. The pouch was the size of a small pillowcase, and was made of the skin of an animal, furry side in. Buffalo Rabbit tried not to think too hard about what sort of animal it might have been. It was barely past sunrise, there was a chill in the air, and she was cosy. She would have liked to continue dozing, but Crazy Horse unhitched the pouch and set it on the ground.

'Hau,' he smiled.

He slid the pouch from under Buffalo Rabbit's feet, and she stood up and shook herself. For the first time ever, she was up-close to an Indian in daylight, and what she saw surprised her.

Crazy Horse was what the white men called a redskin, but he didn't have red skin. He didn't look any redder or more brown than Mr Irvine or Pip or Luke, or anyone else who'd spent a life out of doors. He did wear fewer clothes than them. All he had was a blanket over his shoulders, a belt around his waist, and a piece of soft leather between his legs. He'd flipped this leather under and over his belt, and it hung down in panels at front and back, panels that were decorated with tiny, coloured beads. His eyes were almond-shaped and almond-brown, and he had a long, narrow nose and broad cheekbones. A pebble on a leather cord was hanging from his neck, and another pebble was tied behind his left ear. It was threaded into his hair, which was hanging loose and long, almost to his waist, and had a brown and white feather tucked into the crown.

He squatted beside her.

'Wasna,' he said, as he waved something in front of her nose.

Wasna looked like a dried-up old shoe, but it smelled delicious and was studded with fleshy red lumps. Buffalo Rabbit gripped a corner of it in her teeth, tore away a hefty chunk, and realised that wasna was some type of dried meat with added fat and berries. It *was* delicious. She gobbled it up until she was full.

'Ota wayata hwo?' Crazy Horse asked her.

He curled his right hand into a fist and moved it up and down in front of his mouth. Then he made a V shape with his thumb and index finger and stroked upwards from the base of his neck to his chin.

Buffalo Rabbit wanted to help him, but she didn't know what he was doing, or saying, so she just stared back.

'He's asking if you've eaten enough,' said Legs from over her shoulder. 'He's talking in Lakota and signing in Plains Indian. All of the tribes speak Plains. They have different languages, but they all understand Plains. That way, they can communicate with each other. They can also speak in silence. Like when they're hunting. They can creep up on animals, speak in Plains, and never give themselves away.'

Crazy Horse reached for more wasna.

'Ota wayata hwo?' he repeated.

'I have,' Buffalo Rabbit replied. 'It was delicious.'

'Good,' said Legs. 'Turn your head away if you don't want any more. He'll understand you, then. We need to leave. We're still a long way from home.'

When Buffalo Rabbit was safely back in her pouch and hooked onto Crazy Horse's saddle, she and her new master set off at a steady trot, with Legs lolloping alongside.

The land was wild and undulating, and covered with short, tough grass and millions of flowers. There was a range of craggy, inhospitable-looking mountains to the left, and some smaller, more friendly looking hills to the right.

'What are they?' Buffalo Rabbit asked Legs.

'The Big Horn Mountains and The Black Hills,' the wolf replied. 'The hills are very beautiful. They're ancient and sort of magical. The Indians believe they are sacred. They call them Paha Sapa.'

He drew breath.

'Jump coming up,' he said. 'Hold on tight!'

The wolf leapt a stream, and Crazy Horse's pony leapt after him. There were many such streams. The narrow ones could be jumped, but the wider ones had to be splashed through, which sprayed everyone with refreshing, ice-cold water. Every so often, a creature would bark an alarm, or an antelope would vault across the path. Eagles soared, birds sang and animals called, but there were no people, no wagons, no houses, and certainly no railroad tracks.

They stopped only twice, both times at creeks, where they drank from the sparkling water, and Crazy Horse gathered wild fruit and threw it into his mouth by the handful. Other than that, he ate on the move, pulling pieces of wasna from his bag and tearing at them with his teeth. Once, when Buffalo Rabbit looked up at him, she saw that his eyes were closed. She went on watching him for a while, but his eyes never opened, and she realised he was riding in his sleep.

Buffalo Rabbit was too excited and too nervous to sleep. She wanted to see where Crazy Horse and Legs were taking her. Then, just before sundown, they climbed a ridge and Crazy Horse hoisted her out of her pouch and onto his lap.

Below her was a wide, level valley and a winding

river. Along the river's nearest bank was a sweep of conical tents. These tents were glowing with orange light, and the figures inside them were flitting in shadow, like dark moths. The peaks of the tents were criss-crossed with interlocking poles which had plumes of gentle grey smoke rising between them. More smoke was rising from campfires on the ground. Buffalo Rabbit could see people sitting around these fires. They were laughing, eating and talking.

'Wow,' she gasped.

'Wicoti,' said Crazy Horse.

'Village,' Legs translated. 'We're home. Tiyatani, Rabbit.'

CHAPTER SEVEN

The Powder River Country, Wyoming Territory.
The following morning

Buffalo Rabbit opened her eyes.

She was inside one of the conical tents, but she didn't remember arriving there. She didn't remember falling asleep, though she clearly had. It was daylight outside. She could see a patch of bright blue sky. It was high above her, peeking through a criss-cross of poles. The poles had been stacked in a pyramid and wrapped with a circle of animal hide. Her eyes moved down these splaying walls. The centre of the floor had a freshly laid fire. More hides were spread about this fire, and there were stacks of beaded bags, brightly coloured boxes, and a pile of cooking utensils, including an iron pan. Beyond the fire was a wooden frame, a type of chair with a high back and a low, elongated seat. The chair was draped with furs, and a collection of objects was hanging on the wall behind it. There was a rifle, a shield, and several bows and quivers of arrows. Kal had had a bow and arrows. He'd also had a shield, though it hadn't been quite like this one. This one was decorated with pictures of ponies, bunches of feathers and locks of hair. Buffalo Rabbit sniffed. The tent had a cocktail of odours. Here, the scent of Crazy Horse, there, the scent of others, of people she hadn't yet met. She smelled wood-smoke and tree bark, grass and meat, human sweat and animal fat, ponies and fur, berries and herbs. She tipped her head and listened. She could hear low voices, soft footsteps, and the occasional whinny of a pony.

A hand appeared through a break in the hides and pushed them apart.

'Hau!' said Crazy Horse as he ducked into the cone. 'Hau, Pte Masteencala! Tiyatani!'

He raised his hands and pressed his index fingers together.

'Tipi,' he said. 'This, tipi.'

'Tipi!' Buffalo Rabbit barked. 'Pte Masteencala tiyatani tipi! Buffalo Rabbit is home in tipi!'

'Good,' Crazy Horse laughed, 'but no bark, please,' he added in English. 'Bark not good. Bark tell soldiers and Crow that wicoti is here. You come now. Come with Crazy Horse. Hoppo!'

Buffalo Rabbit followed her master through the village. The sun was already hot and most of the tipis had their sides rolled up and propped with forked sticks. She could see people snoozing inside them. Those who weren't snoozing were sitting on the ground in small groups. Women and girls were chatting and threading beads or scraping the flesh from animal pelts. Young men were making arrows or sharpening knives, and older ones were talking quietly and puffing at pipes.

Crazy Horse spotted a man sitting under a tree and began to walk towards him. The man was fanning himself with an eagle's wing, and Buffalo Rabbit thought he looked very serene and rather important.

'Ateh,' said Crazy Horse. '*Ateh*. Father.'

'Ah!' Buffalo Rabbit murmured. 'So this is Crazy Horse's father. This is the famous Worm, the medicine man who saved Legs from the fur trap. I recognise his scent, now. It was one of the smells in the tipi, but I still can't believe anyone's called *Worm*, especially someone as distinguished as him.'

But then the man spoke loud and clear.

'My name, Worm,' he said. 'I am happy to meet you. Iyeshkinyan wanchenyanke*loh*!'

Buffalo Rabbit and Crazy Horse walked on until they came to a group of women, and many dogs. Buffalo Rabbit took a swift, wary glance at these dogs. They were lean and tough and watching the women closely. It wasn't hard to see why. The women were guarding a row of washing lines but, rather than being hung with clothes, the lines were hung with strips of meat.

'Ooh,' one of the dogs snarled. 'Look at the mincing *poodle*!'

'Ooh,' growled another. 'Look at her silly *tail*! Make a nice bit of jewellery, that would. My master could wear it round his neck!'

'Good one, Thunder Cloud,' a third dog chuckled.

'Get her tail! Get her tail!'

Buffalo Rabbit began to tremble.

She edged sideways, putting Crazy Horse between her and the dogs, but they bunched together and inched towards her. Crazy Horse and the women seemed oblivious. One of the women even took a piece of meat from the line and swung it in front of Buffalo Rabbit's nose.

'Eat,' the woman said softly. 'Good.'

'I'm sure it is,' Buffalo Rabbit whimpered. 'But right now there's a pack of dogs…'

She felt a paw on her back and whipped round. Her teeth were bared. She was ready to snap.

'Steady on,' growled Legs. 'It's only me.'

He tipped his head towards the dogs.

'Don't worry about them,' he said. 'Watch.'

He flattened his ears, raised his nose and tail, and stepped towards the pack. They were already retreating.

'Move back and lie down!' he ordered. 'I want heads on paws and tails tucked in. DO IT! NOW!'

The dogs dived to the ground.

'Now listen up,' Legs snarled at them. 'We have a new one among us. Her name is Buffalo Rabbit and you are not to bully her. She is good medicine and Dog of Crazy Horse. Understand?'

'Yes, yes,' the dogs replied. 'Three Legs Running has told us not to bully Buffalo Rabbit.'

'*And*?'

'And Buffalo Rabbit is good medicine. She is Dog of Crazy Horse.'

'Well then, don't you forget it.'

'Don't we forget it,' chorused the dogs.

'Thanks,' said Buffalo Rabbit when Legs returned to her side.

'No problem,' the wolf smiled. 'They're good sorts, really. You won't have any trouble with them now, but come to me if you're worried.'

He raised a front paw and cupped it over his snout.

'Best to avoid having puppies, though,' he whispered. 'Know what I mean?'

Buffalo Rabbit nodded. Nothing had been further from her mind.

'Whoa!' she shied sideways.

A huge black bird had landed beside her.

'Oh, dear. Did I bark?' she muttered as the bird shook out its giant wings. 'I hope not. I'll be in *so* much trouble, and it's only my first day.'

'What are you talking about, Rabbit?' the wolf asked.

'Crazy Horse told me not to bark. He said it would tell the crow that we're here.'

'Ah! I see. No, Crazy Horse meant the *Crow,* not the crow. The Crow are an enemy tribe. Anyway *this*,' Legs added with a tip of his head to the bird, 'is not a crow, it's a kangi tanka, a raven. His name is Maka Mani. He's another of Worm's rescues. Worm found him in The Black Hills. His wings were broken, so he couldn't fly. All he could do was hop about, hence the name. Maka Mani is Lakota for Walk On Foot. Worm mended the wings, and one day Maka Mani flew up and kept flying as if he'd been doing it forever. He goes all over the place, now. Crazy Horse has seen him way down south, but his home is with us. He always comes back to us.'

'He's wearing a beaded ankle bracelet,' Buffalo Rabbit observed.

'Yes,' said the wolf. 'Crazy Horse's mother made that. She slipped it over his foot when he was still very small. I don't think he could get it off now. He's a good bird. He's good medicine. He's also excellent at back scratching.'

Legs stamped a paw and lay down, and the raven hopped onto his back and trod and raked with its talons. The wolf's eyes were glazing over with pleasure.

'Ooh, up a bit,' he moaned. 'Down a bit. That's it. Just there.'

CHAPTER EIGHT
Bo's House.
The 21st Century

Bo was still in her garden. Her right paw was still resting on Cavendish's left one, and a raven was still sitting in the tree above her.

'Are you good at giving back scratches?' she barked.

'*What*?' Cavendish asked.

'Not you,' Bo giggled. 'I'm asking the raven. There was a raven in the village. He's called Maka Mani, and Three Legs Running said he was excellent at giving back scratches. You could tell he was good. Legs' eyes were glazing over.'

'You've lost me,' sighed Cavendish. 'What village? And who's Three Legs Running?'

'Oh, come on,' Bo protested. 'You can't fool me. You know I'm talking about Crazy Horse's village. You also know that Three Legs Running is a wolf.'

'I do?'

'Yes. You do.'

Whenever Bo had gone back in time, the spaniel had come along, too. He'd been there in the days of King Charles I, and been there again in Cleopatra's Egypt.

'I think you and the wolf are one and the same,' said

Bo. 'I think you are Three Legs Running.'

'Fine,' Cavendish grinned. 'As you please.'

He gave his friend a sideways glance.

'Interesting that Maka Mani should have an ankle bracelet, don't you think?' he asked. 'It puts me in mind of Sioluc.'

'Yes,' said Bo. 'That *is* interesting, now you mention it. I hadn't thought about it really.'

'Clearly not,' Cavendish smiled to himself.

Sioluc had been a raven in the time of King Charles. She, too, had worn an ankle bracelet, although hers had been made of diamonds, rather than beads.

'So!' the spaniel said out loud. 'Start at the beginning. You said you were in Crazy Horse's village, but did you find the man himself?'

'Not exactly,' Bo replied. 'He found *me*. He rescued the poodle from The Oregon Trail and adopted her. She's got a really cute name. She's called Buffalo Rabbit because her tail's like a rabbit's and her fur's like a buffalo's.'

'That's quite a compliment. The Lakota revered the buffalo.'

'I'm not surprised. You should taste their meat, Cavendish. It's fantastic, much better than beef.'

'Buffalo were more than just meat. They were walking department stores. The Indians carved their bones to make weapons, sledge runners, toys and tools, they boiled their hooves to make glue, made candles from their fat and paint from their blood...'

'Shields, tipi covers, moccasins, dresses, shirts, bowstrings, saddles and big furry rugs were made from their hide...'

'Twine from their gut, bridles and halters from their beards, fly swats and fringes from their tails, bags for food or tobacco from their unborn calves. For so long as the Indians had buffalo, and the ponies to follow them, they didn't need much else. Oh, trees. They needed trees for their tipi poles.'

'There was plenty of fruit and water,' added Bo. 'There was plenty of everything where we were. They called it The Powder River Country.'

'Ah, yes,' Cavendish sighed. 'The Powder River Country. It was the perfect place for Indians. The Lakota were lucky to have it. Other tribes had lost their lands to the white man, but the Powder River Country had nothing the white man wanted...'

'Until?'

'Until someone discovered gold.'

'*Gold*?'

'Yes. Tons of gold. It wasn't in the Powder River Country itself, but the best way to reach it was. There was this old track, you see. It was only used by fur-trappers and antelope, but it crossed The Powder River Country and then led over The Big Horn Mountains. The gold was on the other side of those mountains, so all of a sudden this little-known track became a famous short-cut. It was flooded with white men, wagons and mules, all rushing to the gold fields.'

'I didn't see any white men,' said Bo. 'All I saw was Indians and wildlife.'

'That's because you got there too late...'

'Go on.'

'As long as the miners kept moving and didn't disturb the buffalo, the Indians let them pass. The miners were fairly safe until some bright spark decided otherwise. The government moved in, built forts along the trail and filled them up with soldiers. It was complete rubbish, of course. The miners didn't need protection, they were just an excuse.'

'To do what?'

'To show off the white man's strength. The government thought the Indians should stop living like savages and learn to be civilised. The Lakota didn't know this, of course. All they knew was that their hunting grounds were being invaded by soldiers.'

'So what did they do?'

'They attacked the forts. They had a war leader named Red Cloud who was very good at tactics and organisation. They also had their brilliant young warrior, Crazy Horse. He proved to be a natural at arranging quick, in-and-out ambushes. The soldiers didn't even see him coming, half the time.'

'Well, it obviously worked,' said Bo.

'The soldiers achieved nothing,' Cavendish nodded, 'except to get themselves killed. The miners were worse off because the trail became so dangerous. Meanwhile, down south, the Cheyenne were ripping up the railway and tearing down the telegraph. *That's* where the army was needed. They knew they should leave The Powder River Country and rescue the railways, but they didn't want to admit defeat. So they agreed, somewhat reluctantly, to try another tack. If the Lakota couldn't be bullied into changing their ways, then maybe, just maybe, they could be bribed. Buffalo Rabbit got to The Powder River Country just after the soldiers left it. A few months later, the bribery began.'

CHAPTER NINE

Fort Laramie, Wyoming Territory, North America.
November, The Moon of the Hairless Calves, 1868

Fort Laramie didn't look like a fort at all. It had no moats or ditches or high stockades. It was just a motley collection of mismatched buildings in a flat, barren landscape.

Amongst these buildings was a large canvas tent. The rear of this tent was open to the elements, and the one-hundred Indians who were sitting on its floor were huddled in blankets. In front of them was a table and chairs and five officers of the United States Army.

Maka Mani darted over the Indians' heads and landed on the table. The officers tried to shoo him away, but he stood his ground and gaped his beak. The Indians laughed.

'Leave the bird be, if it lightens the mood,' said one of the officers nervously. 'What harm can it do?'

'None,' Maka Mani cawed, 'except to see what you're up to.'

He cocked his head and examined the scrappy-looking sheets of lined paper that were laid out on the table. They were dog-eared and grubby, and covered in scrawly writing and ink spots.

'The Indians may not be able to read,' he chattered,

'but I can. Although, quite frankly, I'd be surprised if *anyone* can make sense of *this* mess. Still, I'll do my best.'

The papers may not have looked like a legal document, but that's exactly what they were. It was also how they were worded. Maka Mani's blood boiled at the very sight their self-important lawyer speak.

'Hereby agrees and stipulates?' he squawked. 'Any portion of the same? Except as hereinafter provided? What turkey gobble! How are the Indians supposed to understand this? There isn't an interpreter on earth who could translate this into Lakota. Let's see, though. What's it actually saying? Ah yes. The Lakota are to be given their own hunting grounds. Good. They may keep Paha Sapa, The Powder River Country and The Rosebud Country. No white person may settle on those lands. Good, good.'

He read on.

'Bla, bla, bla. Oh, now *this* is useful. The Indians are to have physicians. Hah! The white man *deliberately* gives out blankets infected with smallpox, waits until hundreds of thousands of Indians die, and *then* sends in the physicians. Still, better late than never, I suppose. Maybe the physicians can treat the other diseases the white man brought on his sailing ships. The measles, the cholera, the tuberculosis... But what's this? All Indians over the age of four are to be given a pound of flour and a pound of beef per day. *Flour*? What are they supposed to do with *flour*? And why beef? They don't need beef. They have buffalo. Why are they getting blacksmiths and carpenters? And millers? Why millers? Oh, *I* see.'

Maka Mani stared at the Indians nearest him. Here were Thunder Man, Iron Cane and High Eagle. Here, too, Red Cloud, the war leader who'd led the fight against the soldiers in The Powder River Country.

'Do you understand this?' he screeched at them. 'Do you *really* understand this? They want you to be like them. They want you to wear a suit, like they do. They'll give you a pair of oxen. Do you know what oxen are for? No, of course you don't. Well, I'll tell you. Oxen are for pulling things. Things like ploughs. They want you to be farmers! They say you can keep your hunting grounds, that you will have your own land, but have you read the small print? You can't *live* on that land. Not if you want to visit their physicians and collect their rations of meat and flour. If you want those things, if you want *any* of the things they promise, then you have to live in their agency. And do you know where that agency is? It is three-hundred miles from here!'

The raven drew breath.

He had the Indians' attention now. They could see he was furious.

'By the way,' he spat as he pranced on the table. 'You can hunt only "for so long as the buffalo may roam" which may not be long, because it also says, right here, Article XI, Paragraph 6...'

He drummed his bill into one of the papers.

'...that if the government decides to build a road, or a railroad, or anything else that crosses your hunting grounds, then they can go right ahead and do so! What will the buffalo think of that? Are they going to roam over railroads? Dodge iron horses? I don't think so!'

Maka Mani was in such a temper that his talons were beginning to rip through the papers. The officers shooed him again, and this time gladly left the table.

He settled on Red Cloud's shoulder.

'Don't sign this treaty,' he pleaded. 'Don't sign this trash. Don't put an X beside your name. The white men think you're important, that you're a big chief who speaks for all the Sioux. But no one can do that. No one can speak for all the Sioux. This treaty won't help your people. It will divide them. It will bring them nothing but misery.'

'You will touch the pen?' one of the officers asked Red Cloud. 'You will sign for peace?'

Red Cloud crooked a finger and stroked Maka Mani's throat.

'NO!' Maka Mani screamed. 'No! Listen to me! Touching the pen will not bring peace! Keep your people together! You must fight this thing together!'

'Yes,' Red Cloud told the officer. 'I will touch the pen. I will live in your agency. I want peace.'

CHAPTER TEN

The Powder River Country, Wyoming Territory.
April, The Moon of the Birth of Calves, 1869

Crazy Horse's mother was sewing at the fireside.

A large buffalo hide was spread across her lap. The hide was lying fur-side down, and the upper, skin-side, was decorated with beadwork and a border of porcupine quills. Crazy Horse's mother sighed, raised her buffalo-bone needle to her lips and snapped its buffalo-gut thread with her teeth.

'There,' she said in Lakota. 'It is finished at last!'

Her work had taken her most of the winter. Her fingers were calloused, her eyes were puffy with strain, but it had been worth it. The finished robe was the most beautiful thing that Buffalo Rabbit had ever seen.

Crazy Horse stepped into the tipi. He had a bow, arrows and a rifle over one shoulder, and several bags over the other.

'Is the robe ready, mother?' he asked. 'The ponies are waiting. We must go.'

'Yes. It is ready,' replied his mother.

She held the robe towards her son, and he knelt to run his fingers over the beads.

'It is very fine,' he smiled. 'It will fetch a good price. Have you thought of anything else you want?'

'No. It is just as I told you. Do not forget your father's coffee.'

'I will remember,' said Crazy Horse as he lifted the robe. 'Come on, Rabbit.'

Legs was waiting on the outskirts of the village with six ponies. Five of these ponies had been roped together in a line and loaded with embroidered buffalo robes. The sixth was Crazy Horse's riding pony. Crazy Horse added his mother's robe to one of the loads, placed Buffalo Rabbit across his riding pony's withers and jumped up behind her.

'Where are we going?' Buffalo Rabbit asked Legs as they trotted away from the village.

'To the trading post,' the wolf replied. 'We're taking the robes to the trading post so we can swap them for other things.'

'Swap them? We can't swap them!' Buffalo Rabbit protested. 'They've taken months to make. Crazy Horse's mother only just finished hers.'

'That's the whole point,' Legs replied. 'These robes are special. They're not for us to sleep in or throw on the floor. They're for trading. Indians have always loved to trade.'

He paused.

'Have you ever been to the sea?' he asked.

'No, never.'

'Me, neither. I'm told it's a lot of water but it does have these very pretty things called shells. The tribes who live by the sea used to collect these shells and take them inland to the tribes in the south. "Give us some of your pottery and turquoise," they'd say, "and we'll give you some of our shells." The tribes would swap. Now both tribes had both things, but neither had anything made from buffalo. So the southern tribes would come here to the plains and say, "Look at these lovely shells. Look at our lovely pottery. Will you trade them for some buffalo hides?" The plains people would agree, take some shells and pottery, and hand over some hides.'

'The hides would be taken south. And when the shell people next visited, they could choose from pottery, turquoise *and* buffalo hide…'

'Exactly,' said Legs. 'Everything was passed around, and every tribe had new things.'

'So are we going to swap the robes for shells?'

'Sadly not. We mostly trade for white man's things, nowadays.'

'What sort of things?'

'All sorts,' the wolf replied. 'Crazy Horse has a whole long list in his head.'

'Coffee for Worm,' Buffalo Rabbit remembered.

'Yes. Sugar. Beads. Lots of beads. Blue ones, yellow ones, white ones, red ones. Ribbons. Blankets. Kettles. Knives. Pots and pans. Bullets. Guns.'

Buffalo Rabbit shivered and licked a snowflake from her nose. Spring on the plains was unpredictable, warm and sunny one moment, cold and snowy the next.

'The early bird catches the worm,' grinned the wolf. 'Crazy Horse wants to reach the post before anyone else does. That's how you get the best price. But better weather's on its way. Maka Mani went out a couple of nights ago and hasn't come back. That's always a good sign, weather-wise.'

'Where do you think he's gone?'

'Oh, just scouting. He's barely been out all winter. He'll be flying around, seeing what's what. He doesn't know we're going to the trading post, but I dare say he'll guess. He'll probably come and join us.'

Maka Mani reappeared on the afternoon of the third day. He landed noisily on the leading pack pony and flapped his wings furiously.

'What's up with him?' Legs wondered. 'Not the weather. The weather's fine.'

Crazy Horse was also wondering what the raven was trying to say. He pointed at the clear blue skies, held out his palms and shrugged. The raven flapped some more, gathered the pack pony's rope in his beak, and flew sideways. The pony turned obediently and so, almost, did its four companions.

'He's trying to make us go home,' said Buffalo Rabbit.

'He is tangling my ropes,' said Crazy Horse. 'But it is good to stop. We will camp the night here. If we go much further, we will come close to the white man.'

'You can see what he means,' Legs told Buffalo Rabbit. 'Look over there.'

Buffalo Rabbit followed the wolf's gaze. A row of cream-coloured dots was moving east-west along the horizon.

'Is that what I think it is?' she asked.

'Yup. That's The Oregon Trail, all right. We can drop you off, if you like.'

'No, thank-you,' giggled Buffalo Rabbit, 'I'm very happy where I am.'

They spent that night as they'd spent the previous two. Crazy Horse gathered some brushwood, constructed a makeshift corral and hobbled the ponies inside it. He made a fire from buffalo chips, then shot and cooked a squirrel, which he shared with Buffalo Rabbit and Legs. Maka Mani picked at the bones. When everyone was full, Crazy Horse prepared his bed. He laid more brushwood on the ground, then shook out his blankets and sleeping robes and placed them on top of his brushwood mattress. Then he climbed beneath the blankets, pulled Buffalo Rabbit up close, and patted the space beside him.

'Lie here, Legs,' he whispered, 'Maka Mani will roost beside you.'

Just after dawn, they all awoke at once. They'd heard something. Maka Mani squawked, Buffalo Rabbit growled, and Crazy Horse reached for his rifle. Legs stood into the wind, ears pricked, nose and tail raised, then sighed and flopped down.

'Lakota,' he said. 'He's Lakota.'

Crazy Horse got to his feet.

The Lakota was walking towards him, huddled in a blanket and leading a line of ponies.

'Hau!' Crazy Horse greeted him.

'Hau!'

'Tokiya la he?' Crazy Horse asked.

'Home,' the man answered. 'I am going home.'

'Will you join me for wasna?'

'It is kind of you,' the man smiled, 'but no. I have eaten.'

'You did not take your robes to the traders?'

'Oh, yes. I took my robes. I rode three sleeps from home to take my robes. I was told that trading has closed.'

'Closed?'

'Closed. Finished. We can trade there no longer. If we want to sell our robes we must travel to the agency. In the east,' the flung his arm sideways, 'over The Missouri River.'

'But that is five sleeps from here,' Crazy Horse groaned.

'More, if the weather does not hold.'

'Who has told you this news?'

'A horse soldier. He told me kindly. He did not lie. This raven is a friendly bird…'

Maka Mani had flown to the Lakota's shoulder. Now he was preening the man's braided hair.

'Maka Mani knew the trading post had moved!' Legs exclaimed. *'That's* what he was trying to tell us!'

'This soldier,' said Crazy Horse. 'Did he tell you why we must travel so far?'

'Yes,' the man nodded. 'He said that it was written in the white man's treaty. The treaty that Red Cloud put his mark upon.'

CHAPTER ELEVEN
The Big Horn Valley,
Montana Territory, North America.
May, The Moon of the Strawberries, 1870

Buffalo Rabbit had been living with Crazy Horse for two years. That was many times longer than she'd lived with the Irvines. She'd been a puppy, then. Now she was a grown-up dog, an Oglala Lakota dog. She didn't miss the white man's world. She wanted nothing to do with it, and neither did Crazy Horse.

He hadn't signed the treaty at Fort Laramie. He didn't want to live in an agency. He didn't need the white man's handouts. He didn't need ploughs and oxen and cow meat, mouldy blankets and sour bacon. He could live without flour that was heaving with weevils. He was happy to trade the women's robes, but he wouldn't be told where to do it. That was not the old way. The old way was what he would follow, and part of that way was raiding the Crow.

The Crow had once lived where the Lakota were now, along The Powder River and up towards The Yellowstone. But as the white man had pushed further and further west, the tribes had also moved west, and the Lakota had claimed the Crow country for themselves. The two tribes were sworn enemies, yet also admired one another. At one point they'd even talked about joining forces to defeat the whites, but the Crow had touched the pen instead. They'd given up the fight. Some of their warriors had even been hired to work as scouts for the U.S. Army.

Which made raiding them all the more fun.

Buffalo Rabbit had raided the Crow before, but this raid was going to be different. Crazy Horse had organised things in the old-fashioned way. The women would come along, too. They'd already loaded the pack ponies with ladies' saddles and travois. Travois were the Indian way of carrying things. They were made from two lodge poles and a stretcher of buffalo hide. The poles were fixed to the ponies' saddles like the shafts of a wagon and then angled to drag along the ground. The hide was then piled with possessions and, sometimes, people who were too sick or old to walk or ride. Whenever Buffalo Rabbit saw pack ponies and travois, she was glad the Lakota had moved to the plains. Before that, they hadn't known about ponies. Their travois had been pulled by dogs.

Buffalo Rabbit wandered closer to the travois. They weren't carrying the entire village, but they *did* have everything needed to make a comfortable home from home. She could see buffalo robes, pillows, blankets, cooking utensils, pegs, ties and tipi covers. She nodded her approval, then stood well back.

The warriors were coming out.

Each man was sitting on one pony and leading another. The ponies being ridden were sure-footed, long-distance riding ponies. Those being led were war ponies. These were fighting animals. They were highly skilled, highly trained and very feisty, and they were squealing and nipping as they jostled for position in the line. Buffalo Rabbit took another step back. She didn't want to get kicked and have to stay behind.

At Crazy Horse's signal, the raiding party left the village and began to move towards the Crow country. Buffalo Rabbit started the journey on foot, trotting alongside Legs. After a few miles though, she decided to hitch a lift. She raced up to Crazy Horse and he reached out a hand to give her a leg up. Then she settled herself across his riding pony's withers, front paws dangling over one side, back ones over the other, and fell fast asleep.

They travelled all day. Then, just as the light was fading, they reached the place they'd been heading for, an old and trusted camping ground on the banks of The Little Big Horn River. The travois were unloaded, the tipis were raised and the fires were lit. The ponies were untacked, taken to water and hobbled to graze. Within an hour of their arrival, everyone had their own spot in a cosy, well-furnished tipi, and the cooking pots were bubbling with a supper of hare, berries and herbs.

Buffalo Rabbit tucked herself between Crazy Horse and Legs and gazed across the fire. Sitting on its opposite side, and preparing themselves for tomorrow's raid, were Crazy Horse's best friends, He Dog, Young Man Afraid and American Horse. All three were from Crazy Horse's tribe, the Oglala Lakota, but they looked very different from him. They were much more typically Lakota.

Crazy Horse's hair was brown, loose, and sun-bleached on the ends. Theirs was black and heavy and braided with strips of fur. His clothing was simple, theirs was highly decorated. His only jewellery were his pebbles; one on a cord around his neck, the other behind his left ear, their jewellery was both colourful and plentiful.

He Dog had a whetstone in front of him and was whipping arrow heads back and forth across its surface to sharpen them. Like all Indian males, he wore a piece of soft leather, a breechcloth, between his legs, and a belt around his waist. Attached to this belt were two leggings. These were separate, not joined at the top, and were made of dyed blue buckskin. The buckskin was patterned all over with beaded stars and cut into fringes along the seams. He had a silver cuff on one arm and a row of bangles on the other, and his earrings, a string of silver discs, were so long and dangly they reached to his chest.

Next to He Dog was Young Man Afraid, full name Young Man Whose Enemies Are Even Afraid Of His Horses. He was making arrow shafts. He'd polished and notched some slender willow stems and was now painting his mark on their ends. His leggings had once been a cavalry trooper's trousers, but he'd dipped them in yellow dye, cut out the seat of the pants, and then studded the legs with brass tacks.

American Horse was trimming feathers for fletchings. His leggings were decorated with porcupine quills and an assortment of military buttons. He, too, had dangly earrings, but most amazing of all was his necklace. It was fashioned from chunks of fur, a dozen fearsome claws, and twenty extremely large teeth.

'From two entirely different, but equally enormous, grizzly bears,' Legs had informed Buffalo Rabbit. 'He killed them both.'

Supper arrived, and Buffalo Rabbit politely waited her turn. The night guards, which included Legs, must eat first. They needed to hurry to their posts and keep a look out for Crow.

Legs was handed a chunk of something squishy and steamy.

'What's that?' asked Buffalo Rabbit enviously.

'Um. Let's see now,' pondered the wolf as he smacked his lips and swivelled his tongue. 'Hare brain. Hare-brain.'

'Very funny. I'm starving.'

'Yours'll come soon. You'll get all the gooey bits at the bottom of the pot. And then you'll fall fast asleep, all snuggled up by the fire whilst I spend my night at the top of a termite mound.'

'Remember to check it's abandoned.'

'I don't want it abandoned. That's the whole point. I need the occasional nip to keep me awake.'

'Off you go then. See you tomorrow.'

When everyone had eaten, they had an early night. They were too exhausted and too close to the Crow for singing and dancing. Sound carried far in these otherwise silent places, and rule number one for attack was surprise.

Rule number two was preparation.

Before a warrior set off to a fight, he went through a pre-battle ritual. He believed his life depended on this. He believed he must wear his favourite clothes and lucky amulets and charms, and paint himself and his pony in his own, very personal and particular way. Some of these ways harked back to experience. A warrior might mark the day he killed a Crow, rescued a friend or recovered from a nasty wound. These ways were important, but the most important ways of all were those of the spirits.

When an Indian boy reached a certain age, he asked the spirits to show him what he would grow up to be. He did this by seeking a vision, a sort of dream, and whatever he saw in that dream, he followed for the rest of his life. Not every boy could be a warrior, but there was no shame in that. Everyone had a role to play in Lakota society. The dreams told the boys how to be good at whatever they did, whether it be warrior, medicine man or horse-catcher. It also showed them things that would help and protect them. For future warriors, those things included the all-important preparation for battle.

When Buffalo Rabbit shot out of bed at daybreak, that preparation had already begun. Every corner of the camp was alive with painting, plaiting and preening. There were pouches of pigment, piles of feathers, bundles of necklaces and heaps of bangles, ribbons and pelts. Bowstrings were being waxed, arrows sharpened, fletchings smoothed. Clubs were being examined, lances inspected, quivers filled, water and wasna packed.

Buffalo Rabbit wandered through the camp until she

found He Dog, Young Man Afraid and American Horse. They were standing together, putting the finishing touches to their war paint.

He Dog had already smeared his lips and chin with black. Now he was dipping a stick into red powder. He turned to the mirror that was hanging from the tipi next to him and pulled his forehead taut. Then he painted a broad red stripe along the central parting in his hair and all the way down to the tip of his nose.

'Akicita,' Buffalo Rabbit reminded him.

Akicita were special clubs. Membership of these clubs was by invitation only, and you had to be brave and sensible to be asked. Then, once you were a member, your job was to break up fights in camp and stop warriors from rushing in too fast and spoiling things on raids and hunts.

He Dog nodded and smiled, picked up another stick, and drew two vertical black stripes on his right cheek.

Buffalo Rabbit danced in approval.

Now everyone would know that He Dog was one of today's akicita.

He puckered his lips and kissed his reflection.

'Washteh,' he laughed. 'Good.'

'Washteh!' Buffalo Rabbit wagged her tail.

She glanced at American Horse and Young Man Afraid.

They, too, had finished their face painting. They, too had the black stripes of the akicita.

'Ponies, now!' squeaked Buffalo Rabbit. She grabbed one of American Horse's leggings in her teeth and tugged. 'Come on! Hoppo! Let's go!'

Buffalo Rabbit and the three friends wandered over to a cluster of war ponies, women and warriors. The pony's tails were being knotted and bound with ribbons and weasel pelts, and their manes and forelocks were being combed and intertwined with eagle, hawk and owl feathers. Symbols of good fortune were being drawn on their hooves, and their coats were being polished, ready for painting. Being the centre of so much attention had made them dopey. Their heads were bowed, their lower lips were floppy, and their eyes had glazed over. It was hard to believe that these soppy, soporific creatures were hardened fighters, but they were, and they had the scars to prove it.

Buffalo Rabbit watched as American Horse delved into his pouch of coloured pigments and painted circles around his pony's eyes. These would sharpen its sight. He painted a bolt of lightning on the pony's chest, to give it speed and strength, and added a bear's paw to its shoulder, to give it bravery and ferocity. He blackened the palm of his hand and made an imprint on the pony's hindquarters to represent victories won, and made another palm print, this time in red, to show that he had killed a man in hand-to-hand fighting. Meanwhile, He Dog and Young Man Afraid were doing similar things to their own ponies. They were serious about their task, but they were also flicking paint, laughing and cracking jokes.

Buffalo Rabbit left them to it and padded out of camp to look for Crazy Horse. Jesting and joking was not his way. He liked to carry out his rituals alone and in peace.

Sure enough, he was down by the river.

He was dressed in plain blue leggings and a breechcloth. He'd painted his face with a red zigzag that ran from his hairline, over his nose, and down to his chin. His chest and shoulders were dotted with white, and he wore a pebble round his neck, another behind his ear, and a single hawk feather at the back of his head. His pony was unpainted. It had no marks from previous battles, no birds' feathers, no ribbons, and no weasel pelts. Its only decoration was a third pebble, which was threaded into the hair of its long, unknotted tail.

All of these things had come to Crazy Horse in his boyhood vision. To seek the vision, Crazy Horse had gone out alone, found an isolated spot and hobbled his pony. Then he'd lain down on a bed of sharp stones and put more stones between his toes, to keep himself awake.

After three days like this, and with no food or water, he'd seen his pony break away from its tethers and gallop towards him. Its tail had streamed out behind it, and its coat had changed colour with every stride. There'd been a rider on its back, and a hawk had flown above its head. Every so often, there'd been a flash of lightning, and hailstones had dropped from the sky. Shadowy enemies had reached out and tried to touch the rider, but he and his pony had darted away. The rider's own people had been there, too. One of them had tried to catch him and hold him by his arm. He'd shaken the man off and continued riding, but somehow the man remained, still trying to catch him and hold him by his arm.

When the vision had faded away, the young Crazy Horse had gone home to tell his father, the medicine man, Worm, what he'd seen, and Worm and another medicine man, whose name was Chips, had interpreted the dream.

They'd said that Crazy Horse would become the rider he had seen. That rider was a great warrior, but his pony was unpainted and its tail flowed free. Therefore, they said, Crazy Horse must never paint his pony or knot its tail. The rider had galloped through lightning and hail, so Crazy Horse should prepare himself for battle by painting lightning across his face and hailstones on his body. A hawk had flown above the pony's head, so Crazy Horse must wear a hawk's feather in his hair, but only a single feather, never a full war-bonnet. He should also always carry two pebbles, one behind his ear and another around his neck. These pebbles would be given to him by Chips, along with a third, which Crazy Horse should thread into his pony's tail. Finally, Crazy Horse should never go into battle without first throwing a handful of dust over himself and his pony.

'Do these things,' Worm had said. 'and you will be protected. You will never be injured or killed in battle.'

'Not in battle,' Chips had warned. 'You will not be killed in battle. But there is danger. The vision warns of danger. Unknown enemies will try to hold you back. One of these enemies is amongst our own people. This enemy will take you by the arm. You will shake him off, but he will never be far from you. He may try to catch you by the arm a second time. Do not allow that. Do not allow anyone to catch you by the arm.'

Crazy Horse had followed his vision to the letter. He'd grown up to become a great warrior, one of the best. Not only had he never been injured in battle, but he was known for rescuing those who were, even at risk to his own life. The truth of his vision and the magic of his pebbles was so powerful that even the Crow were in awe of him. They believed he was bullet-proof. As for the Lakota, they would always choose him over anyone else to lead them on the warpath.

Buffalo Rabbit waited on the embankment whilst Crazy Horse scooped a handful of dust from the river's edge, sifted it over his pony's back, then scooped another and sifted himself. The wishes of the spirits had been fulfilled. He was almost done, almost ready to fight. There were just two more things still to do. He picked up a pillow-sized pouch. The pouch was one of a pair, one for hunting and one for fighting. Both were exquisitely beaded with the shape of a black dog flying through the air. Both belonged to Buffalo Rabbit.

Crazy Horse flipped the pouch's straps over his pony's withers and knotted the ends tightly behind its forelegs. He checked that all was secure, then took something from the pouch and beamed Buffalo Rabbit a smile.

Buffalo Rabbit trotted down the embankment and leapt onto the pony.

'Ohan,' said Crazy Horse. 'Wear this.'

Buffalo Rabbit raised her chin, and Crazy Horse lowered a leather cord over her head. Threaded onto the cord was a small pebble, a present from Chips. Crazy Horse adjusted the pebble until it rested, just so, on Buffalo Rabbit's chest.

'There,' he said. 'Let's go find us some Crow!'

71

CHAPTER TWELVE
A little later

Buffalo Rabbit had seen many war parties since she'd joined the Lakota, but she still gasped and drew breath at the sight of them. Men she knew, whom she loved or liked or didn't like, with whom she spent lazy, ordinary days, and who cooed at their babies, whispered to their wives and played with their children were suddenly transformed. Most were barely recognisable. All were terrifying.

Each individual was a unique combination of symbolism, colour and costume. There were circles, paw prints, hand prints, spots, stripes and zigzags; shades of yellow, red, black, blue and white. There were brown feathers, black feathers, white feathers; long ones, short ones, curved ones, straight ones and fluffy ones. There were beaver tails, weasel pelts, hanks of yarn and bunches of ribbon; silver cuffs, beaded bracelets, cat's claws, bird's feet and bear's teeth. There was buffalo hide, rawhide, tanned hide, dyed hide, buckskin and doeskin; hatchets, clubs, rifles, quivers and bows. There were bridles of horse hair, locks of human hair, fringed sleeves, bare chests and painted faces. The sky was spiked with lances and coup sticks, war-bonnets fluttered in the breeze, and the earth was a frenzy of prancing hooves.

The war party headed for a rise in The Big Horn Valley.

When they reached it, they gathered quietly at its base. Then two of the warriors dismounted and ran, crouching, to its top. Buffalo Rabbit could see the soles of their moccasins as they lay on their stomachs and spied on the Crow village in the valley below. They were memorising its layout, estimating its number of warriors and, most importantly, establishing the size of its pony herd.

The spies wriggled back and reported to He Dog and Crazy Horse, who had a short discussion before waving everyone forward. The warriors spread out and walked their ponies up the slope. From the top of the rise, they looked down. The Crow children were playing in a stream. Dogs were snoozing in the shade. Ponies were grazing the rich spring grass. Smoke plumes were rising from the tipis, meat was drying on the lines, and women and warriors were going about their work. It was a happy, peaceful sight.

The Lakota shouted and waved their weapons. The Crow glanced up. Children screamed, dogs barked. Warriors dashed to and fro, gathered their weapons and hollered at their wives and mothers to fetch them a pony and be quick about it. The Lakota laughed and shouted some more. They geed up their ponies in full view of the Crow. They galloped from a standing start, made U turns, and swept the ground for imaginary fallen arrows. They were warming up for battle, but they were also showing-off. They knew the Crow could see them.

Crazy Horse and He Dog levelled their lances.

'Yip, yip, yip!' they screamed. 'Wahi, wahi, wahi!'

'Yip, yip, yip!' Buffalo Rabbit joined in.

She saw her warriors divide, some to the left with Crazy Horse, the rest to the right with He Dog. She saw the Lakota women slide from their saddles and settle on the ground, saw Legs lie down beside them. She manoeuvred herself into her pouch and felt her stomach lurch as her pony plunged fearlessly over the edge of the rise and charged towards the village.

She heard someone shout her name. A Lakota named Little Big Man was galloping beside her. His dark eyes were flashing with excitement. He reached out his hand and touched her head.

'First coup! First coup!' he laughed.

'Ha, ha,' Buffalo Rabbit muttered sarcastically.

Counting coup was the most dangerous, and therefore the bravest, thing a warrior could do. To be able to count a coup, you must be the first man on the field to touch the enemy. You could use anything to do this; a hand, a coup stick, a lance, a rifle butt, anything. Then, assuming you were still alive, you could claim the day's coup and notch it onto your stick.

Little Big Man's joke wasn't just stupid, it was also very risky. He'd have done better to concentrate on what he was doing, which was galloping flat-out, downhill and towards the notorious Crow. But there again, Buffalo Rabbit wasn't surprised. Little Big Man had a reputation for recklessness.

'Be careful down there,' Crazy Horse shouted after him. 'And do as I say. This is not a day to die!'

'Not listening,' Buffalo Rabbit sighed.

After counting coup, the next bravest thing a warrior

could do was to rescue a friend from under the enemy's nose or, if needs be, recover his dead body. Crazy Horse was famous for this. It was one of the reasons the warriors loved him as a leader. They knew they could trust him to look after them. Buffalo Rabbit was proud of that, she just wished that certain people would stop taking it for granted.

Whilst Crazy Horse and his men worked to distract and confuse the oncoming Crow warriors, He Dog and *his* men rounded up the Crow pony herd. There'd be no attempt to enter the village. These raids were not about burning possessions or killing women and children. They weren't even about killing warriors. They were about speed, bravery, horsemanship and, most important of all, stealing ponies. Buffalo Rabbit could hear these ponies. They were already squealing in panic as the Lakota surrounded them. Crazy Horse pulled his own pony up and it skidded on its haunches and turned. Buffalo Rabbit glanced at the top of the rise. Legs was baring his teeth and snapping and snarling with excitement. Beside him were the Lakota women. They were waving blankets, jumping up and down and shouting insults.

'Come up here!' they goaded the Crow warriors. 'Come see a real woman!'

By now, bowstrings were pinging and arrows were whistling past Buffalo Rabbit's ears. She caught a glimpse of elk-rib breastplate, its chevrons gleaming in the sunshine. Above it was a high black pompadour. There was no mistaking its distinctive style. The rolled up fringe and padded hair was a trademark of the Crow.

'Coup! Coup!' she tried to warn her master as the Crow bore down. But Crazy Horse had already spotted the threat. His pony spun and reared, and the Crow's coup stick touched nothing but empty air.

'Yip, yip yip!' Buffalo Rabbit squealed with glee. 'Hoppo! Wahi!'

Suddenly, Young Man Afraid appeared at Crazy Horse's side. His arm was thrust forward and he was screaming above the noise.

'Little Big Man!'

Crazy Horse wheeled his pony round. Sure enough, Little Big Man had managed to get himself hemmed in by Crow. They hadn't noticed him yet, they were too busy chasing after their captured ponies, but if just one of them were to do so, then Little Big Man would be in real trouble.

'Round the back!' Crazy Horse screamed in reply.

Young Man Afraid veered away, his lance speeding through the melee. Meanwhile, Crazy Horse continued forward in galloping circles, timing himself, not wanting to reach Little Big Man too soon, or too late.

Little Big Man *was* in real trouble, now. Two of the Crow had spotted him and were trying to drag him from his pony. He was doing his best to fend them off, and his pony was spinning, kicking and biting, but it was still two against one. If the Crow could get Little Big Man to the ground, then they'd whip out their scalping knives, grab the top of his hair, make a neat slice - and tug.

Crazy Horse swapped his lance to his other hand, crashed his heels against his pony's sides, and charged.

Young Man Afraid had reappeared and was charging, too. Coming flat out from the opposite direction. The two friends were heading straight towards one another, lances parallel to the ground. They were all set to meet in the middle, just where Little Big Man was tussling with the Crow. Someone was going to have to give way, and it wouldn't be Crazy Horse. Buffalo Rabbit was certain of that. She ducked deeper into her fighting pouch and braced herself. If Crazy Horse got his timing wrong, the impact would be like hitting a mountain.

She saw Young Man Afraid let go of his reins and raise his club. Still riding, he drove his pony between the Crow and Little Big Man, and whacked a Crow with his club. There was a thud and a scream, and the Crow crashed to the ground. Crazy Horse moved forward on his pony. He galloped alongside Little Big Man, swung sideways and reached out a hand. Little Big Man grasped it, sprang from his pony, and leapt up behind Crazy Horse.

Buffalo Rabbit glanced back. Young Man Afraid had been joined by American Horse. They'd dragged the second Crow from his pony and pinned him down. He was screaming, the top of his head was an open wound, and his face was pouring with cherry-red blood. His proud hairstyle was spiked onto Young Man Afraid's lance.

'Yuk.'

Buffalo Rabbit had never seen a scalping firsthand because Crazy Horse didn't take scalps. It was another of his peculiarities, and one for which she was grateful. She'd been close *enough*, though. She'd seen the grimace on a warrior's face as his hair was grabbed tightly from behind, bunched up and twisted. She'd seen the flash of the razor-sharp blade and the lightning-quick cuts. She'd heard the final, popping rip. She'd seen how scalps were carried home and passed around the campfire. The ugly ones were laughed at, derided and tossed to the flames. Some were tossed to the dogs. The beautiful ones, those with long, thick, glossy black hair, were treated with care. The women washed them carefully, stretched and cured the skin, and decorated it with beads. They then hung the scalps at their husband's place, the proudest place, in their tipi, sewed them into his war shirt, or tied them onto his shield or lance.

CHAPTER THIRTEEN
The Powder River Country, Wyoming Territory.
Ten days later

A warrior's shields and lances were his proudest possessions. They protected him from harm and reminded him, and others, of the honours he'd won. When a warrior was at home, his shields and lances were displayed outside his tipi on a special stand.

Buffalo Rabbit and Legs were lying in the shade of one of these stands when Buffalo Rabbit suddenly sneezed.

'Ha...ha...choo! Ooh, shove over, Legs,' she said. 'The scalps on that lance keep tickling me on the nose.'

'No need,' Legs replied. 'It's time to turn it.'

A woman approached the stand, leant over it, and gently shuffled it. All over the village, other women were doing the same thing. They did this several times a day, always following the sun, so the shields and lances could soak up its life-giving powers.

'That's better,' said Buffalo Rabbit, 'no more tickles. Whose stand is it, anyway? Not No Water's, I hope.'

'No. Why would it be his? This isn't his village. And anyway, he's not home at the moment. I hear he's gone hunting.'

'Well, there are other things of his here,' Buffalo

Rabbit tipped her head. 'Like them, for example.'

Sitting in the shade of a cottonwood tree was a young woman. She had a baby strapped to her back, and a toddler on her knee. Another child, a boy, was standing beside her. His arms were wrapped around Crazy Horse's legs, and he was laughing and reaching up to grab the ends of Crazy Horse's hair.

The woman's name was Black Buffalo, and Crazy Horse was in love with her. He'd been in love with her for years. As a boy, he'd followed her around; as a young man, he'd queued up with other young men and waited his turn to talk to her. Everyone had known he was besotted with her, but Crazy Horse had not been a great warrior then, and Black Buffalo's family had thought him too poor and too ordinary to marry their girl. So her uncle had taken charge. He'd found Black Buffalo a more suitable husband and married her off, swiftly and in secret.

The husband was No Water, a fiery-tempered but well-connected member of the Bad Face band of the Lakota. The uncle was Red Cloud.

Crazy Horse had been devastated at losing Black Buffalo, but they'd kept in touch through friends, and been able to see each other whenever their villages camped close. Almost ten years had passed. She'd had three children, and he'd become a great warrior. They'd moved on with their lives, or so everyone thought. Recently though, there'd been rumours that Crazy Horse might be seeing a little too much of his old flame.

'Look,' said Legs. 'They're whispering to each other.

I think they're planning something.'

'Like what?'

'Like running away, is what.'

'Nonsense,' Buffalo Rabbit scoffed. 'They don't need to run away. If Black Buffalo wanted to be with Crazy Horse, she could throw No Water out. All Lakota wives can do that. They own the tipis, so they get to choose who lives in them.'

'Not this wife. Black Buffalo is married to No Water because Red Cloud says so. He chose No Water because he's rich, because he's a Bad Face, and because he has an influential brother. Black Buffalo has power in the tracks of her moccasins, power that Red Cloud doesn't want to lose. She can't throw No Water out.'

'Well, Red Cloud can keep his power. Crazy Horse doesn't want it. He isn't interested in power. That's Red Cloud's thing. Bad Face? He's two-faced! He sides with the Indians one day and the whites the next. He's in Washington even as we speak. Gone off on an iron horse to see The President. Again.'

'Be fair,' said Legs. 'He's gone to complain about the agency and try to get it moved. That's a good thing, isn't it? But you're right. When Red Cloud touched the pen he divided the Lakota. Even some of the Bad Faces think he made a big mistake. Those that don't see Crazy Horse as a threat. He may not be interested in power, but he has the respect of all the best warriors, including many Bad Faces. If he takes Black Buffalo from No Water, then the Bad Faces will be further divided. The *Lakota* will be further divided. We don't want that. We should be pulling together, not fighting amongst ourselves.'

'Crazy Horse knows that,' said Buffalo Rabbit. 'He knows that better than anyone. He's promised Worm he won't do anything about Black Buffalo. He takes his responsibilities very seriously. They are far more important to him than any woman.'

'Well, maybe he's a bit bored of his responsibilities. I would be. Maybe Crazy Horse wants to do something a bit crazy, for once.'

'No,' Buffalo Rabbit shook her head. 'You're wrong. And anyway, Black Buffalo wouldn't leave No Water for Crazy Horse. Crazy Horse is too poor and No Water's too rich. He has many, many ponies but Crazy Horse has only what he needs. At the moment that means two for hunting, one for fighting, and one for riding from place to place.'

'He's good at catching elk, though,' Legs teased.

'Grgggh,' Buffalo Rabbit snarled. 'Don't I know it.'

Crazy Horse had been whispering to Black Buffalo all along. Now he was handing her two huge, highly-prized, elk's teeth.

'And he saves them for her!' Buffalo Rabbit spat. 'Not me, you notice. Not his loyal companion. Have you seen her elk-tooth dress? It's *groaning* with teeth. She has thousands of the things. I've got about five.'

'Well, let's not exaggerate. She has maybe a hundred and you have at least a dozen. But, tell me. Do you know anything about Crazy Horse's plans to raid the Crow?'

'Again? We've only just got back'

'Quite,' said Legs. 'We've only just got back. So how come I overheard him talking about going again?'

'Perhaps you misunderstood,' suggested Buffalo

Rabbit. 'Perhaps we're just going on one of his trips.'

'Hm. Perhaps.'

Crazy Horse often went off alone with Buffalo Rabbit. He'd hunt on the way, then find somewhere safe and quiet, and take out his strike-a-light bag and rub the little flints together to make *peta* and cook his catch. Then he and Buffalo Rabbit would eat their supper and fall asleep under the stars. Buffalo Rabbit savoured these special times with her master. She loved her life in the Lakota village, but she liked her privacy, too. Crazy Horse was the same. His people didn't understand that. They called him strange. But Buffalo Rabbit understood. She and her master were very alike.

Legs got to his feet and had a long stretch.

'Are you going somewhere?' Buffalo Rabbit asked him.

'Just to catch us some supper,' the wolf replied. 'Long day, tomorrow.'

'Really? Why's that?

'You'll see.'

CHAPTER FOURTEEN
The following day

Buffalo Rabbit and Legs were chewing things over.

The wolf had been hunting again, and had caught a ground squirrel. Now he was sharing it with Buffalo Rabbit and Maka Mani.

'Thanks, Legs,' said Buffalo Rabbit as she tugged at the meat. 'Get your beak off my food, Maka Mani. Here, have this.'

She tore off a strip of fat and tossed it aside, and the raven swept it up in his talons and went to sit on top of a nearby tipi.

'I caught this squirrel on the high ground,' said Legs. 'Near the moose skull. Do you know the one I mean?'

'Yes, I know,' replied Buffalo Rabbit. 'You pointed it out the other day. There's an arrowhead in its eye socket. What about it?'

'If you stand beside that skull and look down on the Bad Face camp, you get a very good view of Black Buffalo's tipi.'

'You know her tipi?' asked Buffalo Rabbit. 'How's that?'

'Because I've been there with He Dog.'

'Oh yes, of course. Poor He Dog.'

Crazy Horse's best friend was also a cousin of No

Water.

'I was looking at the tipi...' Legs continued.

'Looking? Don't you mean spying?'

'All right, spying,' the wolf grinned. 'I was spying on the tipi and I saw Black Buffalo.'

'So? It's her tipi.'

'Yes, but she was leading her children away from it. I didn't think anything of it at the time, but now I realise they should have been having their afternoon nap. Everyone else was. What's more, No Water and Red Cloud are away from camp, as are your master's best friends.'

'He Dog's visiting relatives in the north,' Buffalo Rabbit confirmed, 'and American Horse and Young Man Afraid have gone hunting. So?'

'Will you stop saying "so"? Can't you see what's happening? Black Buffalo has moved her children. Her husband is away. Uncle Red Cloud is away. He Dog is away. American Horse and Young Man Afraid are away. And all of a sudden Crazy Horse is making up some story about raiding the Crow? Crazy Horse and Black Buffalo are going to elope!'

'No,' Buffalo Rabbit said. 'I've told you already. Crazy Horse has promised Worm he'll stay clear of that woman.'

'Trust me,' Legs insisted. 'Your master is going to run away with her, whether you like it or not. And when he does, there'll be heap big trouble.'

Legs fell silent, his pale blue eyes gazing into the distance.

'What are you thinking?' Buffalo Rabbit asked.

'That if I'm right, our biggest problem is No Water. I made some enquiries. It seems he went out alone and didn't take much with him. He won't be gone long. He'll get home to an empty tipi, realise his wife has run off with Crazy Horse…'

'…and go nuts,' Buffalo Rabbit finished the sentence. 'We're going to need a plan, Legs.'

Legs lay down with his head on his paws. His ears twitched and his tail swished.

'Come on, come on,' urged Buffalo Rabbit.

She was feeling anxious, now. Unlikely though it seemed, it was beginning to look as if Crazy Horse was about to do something crazy. Crazy because the Lakota needed to stay together, crazier still because No Water was a possessive man with a terrible temper.

'Come on, Legs,' Buffalo Rabbit said again.

'All right, all right,' Legs replied. 'Leave me in peace. I'm thinking.'

Finally, he sat up.

'Here's the plan,' he said. 'I go to the moose skull and keep an eye on Black Buffalo's lodge. You go with Crazy Horse. You wait until you're out of camp, then howl. Keep howling every so often to give me your bearings. Not too much. We don't want to raise suspicion. I'll howl back so Crazy Horse thinks we're just talking. We'll have to stop when No Water gets home, but I'll let you know when that is. No Water is bound to follow Crazy Horse, but so will I. Difference being that I'll have a head start. I'll have a good idea where you've gone, and should be able to get to you before No Water can. We can warn your master that No Water's on his way. The only thing is, that if Crazy Horse camps in a village, you must stay close to him. Don't leave his side, but don't let him carry you either. The quickest way for me to find him amongst other people is to find you first. For that, I'll need your scent on the ground.'

'Good plan,' Buffalo Rabbit sighed. 'But I think we need another…'

'Why?'

'Because I'm not sure Crazy Horse will want me with him. I haven't been very friendly to Black Buffalo. Whenever she's tried to stroke me, I've snapped at her. I can't help it, Legs. I just don't *like* her.'

'Don't look so miserable, Rabbit. I'm sure your master will take you along.'

'But what if he doesn't?'

'Then we'll go to Plan B…'

Buffalo Rabbit went *straight* to Plan B.

She wanted Crazy Horse to take her with him. She even thought he might, despite her treatment of Black Buffalo. But she also wanted to help him, and Plan B seemed like a better way of doing it.

As Legs set off for the moose skull, Buffalo Rabbit slipped into Crazy Horse's tipi and sniffed through his belongings.

'I need something of his,' she muttered to herself. 'Something he uses often, but wouldn't be too sad to lose. He's taken a few things already, so he's obviously going *somewhere*. Ah. This'll do. *Everyone* knows what this is!'

She picked up a scrap of red blanket and held it in her

teeth. The blanket had been a favourite of Crazy Horse's. He'd worn it everywhere, had even been wearing it when he and Buffalo Rabbit had first met. Over the years, though, the blanket had fallen apart. Now there were just a few scraps left, and Crazy Horse's mother had promised that, come winter, she would sew them into his moccasins for luck.

'Sorry, mother,' Buffalo Rabbit mumbled. 'Luck's been brought forward.'

She turned to leave the lodge, but then noticed that both of her beaded pouches, the one for hunting and the one for fighting, were still there. She felt a rush of disappointment and sadness, but quickly dismissed it.

'So what if my master hasn't taken them?' she asked herself. 'It doesn't mean he doesn't intend to take *me*. If Legs is right, then Crazy Horse isn't *really* going to raid the Crow. That's just a cover story, and I don't need a pouch to ride a pony. But...'

She flipped the pouches over and prodded them with her paws.

'Come on, come on. Ahah! That's what I was looking for!'

She dropped the scrap of blanket, picked up her fighting pouch and shook it furiously. When her pebble necklace finally fell out, she grabbed it by its cord, recovered the blanket, and raced for the pony herd.

Near to the herd were several piles of herbs. The women had collected them earlier in the week and spread them out to dry in the sun. Buffalo Rabbit chose a mound of wild sage, stamped her paws as hard as she could to frighten any snakes, then crawled under the sage and pushed through it with her nose.

She could see the herd very clearly, now. She could also see several warriors, and Maka Mani, who'd landed on a nearby tree. Amongst the warriors was Little Big Man, whom Crazy Horse and Young Man Afraid had rescued from the Crow. He and the other warriors were dressed to ride, with leggings and shirts, but they also had their battle gear.

'Does that mean Legs is wrong?' Buffalo Rabbit wondered. 'Are they really going to raid the Crow? No. They're not. They're only catching a pony each, and they are riding ponies, not fighters.'

'Pte Masteencala! Where are you?'

It was her master's voice.

She shoved her nose further through the sage.

Crazy Horse was all dressed up in his best white buckskin shirt, best breechcloth, and best, dark blue leggings. He had his pebbles, too, one around his neck and the other behind his left ear. Standing proudly beside him, and showing off her elk-tooth dress, was Black Buffalo.

Crazy Horse called Buffalo Rabbit's name again, but she didn't respond.

'I decided to follow Plan B,' she told herself. 'And that's what I'm going to do. I need to help my master.'

'Masteencala! Where are you?'

'I'm here,' Buffalo Rabbit whispered. 'I'm right here, master. I'll be right behind you.'

The warriors rode out of the village from its southern side. Crazy Horse and Black Buffalo were in their centre, and Maka Mani was swooping and darting above their heads.

Buffalo Rabbit followed at a safe distance. The scrap of blanket and her pebble necklace were still dangling from her teeth, and she could still hear her master muttering her name and wondering aloud where she'd gone. When she was certain she had his trail firmly in her mind, she turned away from him and bounded back to camp.

She knew the dogs would be ready for her. She'd heard Legs calling to them, giving them instructions. They hadn't answered him because they couldn't. Barking in camp was strictly forbidden. Legs got away with it because he was a wolf, and a wolf's bark was wild and very different from a dog's.

Buffalo Rabbit circled the pony herd, stopped on its far side and stood on her hind legs.

Three of the camp dogs did the same thing.

Good, they'd seen her.

She dropped to her feet, broke into a trot, and headed east. When she heard the hooves of seven ponies coming up behind her, she quickened her pace to a canter. The ponies followed. When she was well away from the village, she stopped again. Six of the ponies went past her, the seventh slowed to a walk.

A small, poodle-sized dog was sitting on this pony's back, and a much larger, wolf-sized one, was padding along beside it.

'Thanks,' said Buffalo Rabbit as the small dog slipped to the ground.

'Our pleasure,' the dogs replied.

'You have something of your master's?' asked the large dog.

'Yes. This scrap of blanket.'

'Perfect,' the large dog grinned. '*Everyone* knows whose this is!'

He took the blanket from Buffalo Rabbit's mouth.

'Don't worry, Rabbit,' he said. 'Legs has told us what to do. We must drop the blanket for all to see, drive the ponies through some water to mix up their scent, then bring them safely home.'

Buffalo Rabbit raised a paw.

'Thanks again,' she said.

She stood for a moment as the two dogs, one with small paw-prints, one with large, caught up with the ponies and herded them further away from the village.

'I'm surprised Crazy Horse didn't take you,' said Legs when Buffalo Rabbit joined him by the moose skull.

'I think he would have done,' Buffalo Rabbit replied. 'He was calling my name. I *could* have gone with him. I *could* have gone with the first plan, but I thought I'd be more use to him here. So I followed Plan B. Was that right?'

'Yes. Apart from anything else, you can tell me who *did* go with him.'

'No need to rub it in, Legs. You were right. It was Black Buffalo.'

'I didn't mean her. I meant whom of any *purpose*.'

'Oh. Five warriors, including Little Big Man. And Maka Mani.'

'Hmm. Well, I hope Little Big Man's on his best

behaviour. You know how rash he can be. All right. Let's just wait now, shall we? We'll take it in turns to stake out Black Buffalo's tipi and keep a lookout for No Water.'

'Can you help me with this, first?' Buffalo Rabbit asked.

'Of course I can,' Legs replied.

He took the pebble necklace from Buffalo Rabbit's mouth and dropped it gently over her head.

Buffalo Rabbit was on watch when No Water appeared.

'Quick, quick! Wake up!' she jabbed at Legs who was snoring beside her. 'He's back! No Water's back!'

'Where? What's he done?'

'Gone into the tipi. Oh-oh. Come out of the tipi. Talk about Bad Face. His is like thunder.'

Legs tipped his head.

'He's not the only one. Look at them.'

Buffalo Rabbit stared at the gathering Bad Face warriors. They were all friends of No Water, and they all looked absolutely furious.

'Let's go,' she said hoarsely.

CHAPTER FIFTEEN
Moments later

The wolf and the poodle had given themselves a head start. They already knew which way Crazy Horse had gone, whereas No Water and his warriors had two trails from which to choose, one that went south, the other east.

These warriors were excellent trackers and, although the scrap of red blanket caused some confusion, they soon realised that the eastbound trail featured riderless ponies, a large dog that could have been Legs but wasn't, and two small dogs, one of which had returned to the village.

Even so, they were delayed enough to give Legs some extra time. He was confident he could find Crazy Horse before No Water did. He knew the territory as well as anyone and, despite being one leg short, was very capable at travelling long distances. Buffalo Rabbit was *not* so capable and, when No Water and his warriors began to catch up, she hitched a ride on the wolf's back.

Soon after that, Legs left Crazy Horse's trail and carried Buffalo Rabbit to the top of a bluff.

'What are we doing here?' asked Buffalo Rabbit.

'Gaining an advantage, I hope,' said Legs. 'Keep your head down and watch.'

Sure enough, No Water and his warriors came tearing

into view.

'They're going to go straight past us,' said Buffalo Rabbit.

'No, they're not. They're following tracks, remember. They'll see that I veered away. They'll get down from their ponies to take a closer look. Then they'll dismiss us, and point to where Crazy Horse went. I hope. We're in open country, here. We can cut across the bluffs, and get ahead…'

'They're stopping,' Buffalo Rabbit interrupted.

Sure enough, No Water dismounted from his favourite mule, examined the soil, and then pointed, first at the bluff, then to the west.

'That way!' said Legs. 'But what's that?'

A raven was spiralling and diving in the sky.

'Oh. Wow!' Buffalo Rabbit yapped.

'Shush!'

'Sorry. Is that Maka Mani? Do you think he knows where my master is? Is that what he's trying to tell us?'

'Let's find out. Stay here.'

'What are you going to do?'

'Climb that tree.'

'On three legs? You're crazy. Even cats and bears need four legs to climb a tree. I'll do it.'

Buffalo Rabbit padded away.

'I can do this,' she told herself.

She took a deep breath, bounced on her paws, then ran at the tree, scrambled up its trunk and settled in its fork.

'Not bad for a beginner.'

'See anything?' Legs asked.

'Yes!' Buffalo Rabbit replied. 'There's a village. It's Oglala, for sure. I'm not sure which band, though. Maybe a mixture.'

'How far?'

'Not far at all. I can see the people, make out their faces. There he is! There he is!' she squealed. 'There's Crazy Horse!'

'Well, don't give him away *now*. Stop squealing and come back here. Quick. We need to move on.'

'Sorry?'

'Get down from the tree.'

'Um.'

'Backwards. You do it backwards.'

'Crazy horse has gone into a guest lodge. Its cover is painted with brown horses...'

'Good. Now stop changing the subject and *jump*. We're losing time. No Water's right behind us.'

Buffalo Rabbit didn't so much jump as flop, but she hit the ground running, and she and Legs raced towards the village and straight through the entrance to the guest lodge.

The guest lodge was filled with a large number of Indians. They'd formed a circle around the central fire, women and girls on one side, men and boys on the other. The youngsters' faces were flushed with heat and glowing with excitement. They'd been dancing to each other across the flames. Several large pots were bubbling at the edge of the fire and, though the air was heavy with steam, wood-smoke and pipe-smoke, the atmosphere was light with fun and laughter.

Buffalo Rabbit's eyes zoomed in on Crazy Horse.

He was sitting in the back row of men. Beside him was Little Big Man.

'No Water's coming!' she barked. 'With warriors!'

'No Water!' Legs repeated from over her shoulder.

Crazy Horse stood up.

'Toka he?' he asked. 'What is wrong?'

'They're here,' said Legs, his long ears twitching. 'No Water and his warriors have arrived.'

'Get down, get down!' Buffalo Rabbit yapped at her master.

'Toka he?' Crazy Horse asked again.

His arms were open, palms facing upward. He took a step forward.

'Masteencala? Toka he?'

Just then, the tent flap was hurled aside.

'I have come!' cried a voice.

Buffalo Rabbit spun round. No Water was poised at the tipi's entrance, revolver in hand.

'Ah,' said Crazy Horse. 'Now I see.'

He whipped a hand to his knife-belt, but Little Big Man grabbed his wrist and held him back.

No Water raised the revolver.

'No!' Buffalo Rabbit squealed.

'Put the gun down!' Legs snarled as Crazy Horse struggled to free himself.

The wolf leapt for No Water's arm. Too late. No Water aimed the revolver and fired. There was a crack and a flash and the wolf was thrown backwards. Suddenly Crazy Horse was swaying. He thrust out an arm to save himself, but then staggered and fell, face down.

For a moment nobody moved. Then one of the girls let out a piercing scream. That broke the spell. The whole place erupted. There were shrieks and cries and people tripping over each other; young women fleeing in panic or walking in a daze, older women rushing to shift the bubbling cooking pots, douse the fire and stamp out its red-hot embers. Meanwhile, braves were slipping under the lodge's covers, and old men were giving quiet, sombre commands from behind their eagle-feather fans.

Buffalo Rabbit saw it all, but she didn't feel a part of it. She could see things spinning round her, but she herself was silent and still. It was as if she was in the very eye of this mad tornado. She caught a glimpse of silver fur and realised it was Legs, but she didn't see where he went. She thought she saw Maka Mani, but she couldn't be sure. The gunshot had left her ears ringing, her eyes seeing spots, and her paws rooted to the ground.

The chaos subsided into an eerie quiet, and Buffalo Rabbit found herself standing alone by the wall of the lodge. It was sprayed with blood and punctured with a tiny, blackened hole.

Outside, No Water was on the run. He'd torn through the camp to search for his warriors but when he'd found them, and told them he'd killed Crazy Horse and must get away, they'd backed off and shaken their heads. This was not what they'd come for. A fist fight was one thing. Murder was something else. The Lakota did not tolerate murder amongst their own. Murderers were driven out of the tribe and sentenced to a life of loneliness and wandering. So, no. They wouldn't help him. Not now.

No Water had taken the nearest pony and galloped out of the village. Maka Mani and Legs had chased him for a while, but they weren't really interested. They wanted to get back to the village and find out how Crazy Horse was. When they did get back, word had spread that Crazy Horse was dead. Women were wailing, nicking their flesh and chopping their hair, and wise men were fretting about the dreadful death, and what it would mean for the Lakota.

Back in the lodge, Buffalo Rabbit was still staring at the hole in the wall and its surrounding pattern of blood. The spots of light had cleared from her eyes, but her ears were still ringing, and her body was racked with a terrible trembling.

'Look at me,' said Legs. 'You're in shock, Rabbit. *Look at me*!'

He swiped her cheek. Her head jerked sideways, hit the soft, blood-spattered wall, and rebounded.

'Wha…?'

'Sorry,' he apologised. 'But you need to pull yourself together. The medicine man is here. He's been calling for you. He wants you to come and see your master.'

'Medicine man? Master?' Buffalo Rabbit stammered.

'Yes. Do you remember what happened?'

'Master?'

'Turn around, Rabbit. You master's over there.'

Buffalo Rabbit glanced over her shoulder. Someone had rolled up the lodge's sides. Light and air were flooding in from outside and she could see three or four figures. They were crouched over something. It was lying near where the fire had been, but there were no flames, now, just steam and soggy grey embers.

'Come, Rabbit. Come see your master.'

Crazy Horse had been lifted onto a buffalo robe. His body was glistening with sweat, and his face was deathly pale. The bullet had torn through his upper lip and come out at the base of his skull. His jaw was streaming with blood, and more blood was dripping from the pebble in his hair. The blood had already turned the pebble a scarlet red. Now it was soaking into the buffalo robe.

'He's bleeding,' said Buffalo Rabbit dully. 'Crazy Horse is bleeding.'

'He's been shot,' said Legs. 'No Water shot him.'

Buffalo Rabbit batted her ears with her paws.

'Of course!' she said as the sparkle returned to her eyes. 'I remember, now! We have to find No Water!'

'No, we do *not* have to find No Water. We need to stay here with your master. He needs you, Rabbit. He needs your medicine.'

'He's alive?' Buffalo Rabbit asked.

'Yes. He's alive.'

'Black Buffalo? Where's Black Buffalo?'

'Gone. Forget about her. Sit beside the medicine man, now. Concentrate on Crazy Horse.'

The medicine man chanted softly in Lakota and pressed a pad of mule-skin over Crazy Horse's face. The skin had been taken from No Water's mule. The animal was dead, hacked to death by angry warriors, but its flesh was still warm. It was still oozing pin-head-sized droplets of life. The medicine man reached out a hand and hovered it over Buffalo Rabbit's head. He chanted some more, then deftly removed her pebble necklace. He swung the necklace backwards and forwards until the pebble was turning in circles, then lowered it gently and laid it next to Crazy Horse's own pebble necklace. He delved into his medicine bag and withdrew the foot of an eagle, the paw of a bear and the feather of an owl. He leant forward and snapped a sprig of sweet sage from a basket by the fire. He unravelled a ribbon of weasel fur from one of his braids and used it to bind everything together. Finally, he blessed this bundle of magic medicine and placed it on Crazy Horse's chest.

'Wa ma kan,' he said. 'Wa ma kan. What I do is ancient. It is sacred.'

A few days later, American Horse, Young Man Afraid and He Dog arrived to visit Crazy Horse. By then, he was sucking soup through a goose quill. A few days more, and he was eating mashed-up fruit. Buffalo Rabbit barely left his side. When she did, it was only because Legs threatened her with terrible consequences if she didn't take a break. So she'd go for a walk with her wolf friend, try to eat what he'd caught for her, and try to show interest in something other than her master. When Crazy Horse was strong enough, he was transferred to a travois and hitched to a pony. He Dog rode this pony, carefully towing the travois behind him. American Horse and Young Man Afraid trotted alongside with Buffalo Rabbit and Legs, and Maka Mani swooped and darted in the skies above. They were taking Crazy Horse home.

CHAPTER SIXTEEN
A few weeks later

When Crazy Horse was able to speak, He Dog and Worm gave him a talking-to.

They told him that his recovery had shown his strength, his determination, and the power of his pebbles. These gifts from the spirits must be handled with care. Strength, determination and power could make a great leader, but they could also divide a nation.

They reminded him of his childhood vision. It had warned him never to allow one of his own people to take him by the arm and hold him back. Yet, on that fateful day in the guest lodge, Crazy Horse had done exactly that. Little Big Man had held him back.

'He was only trying to prevent a fight,' Crazy Horse protested though his wounded lip. 'He didn't think No Water would fire that gun.'

'Not the point,' Worm told his son. 'You did not heed your vision. That almost cost you your life. Do not allow it to happen again. Meanwhile, No Water has apologised. He has sent you good ponies.'

'I accept his apology, father,' Crazy Horse replied, 'but I do not want his ponies. I will give them to you. What of Black Buffalo? Is she well?'

'She is well,' said He Dog. 'She has returned to her

husband and children. They are living with Red Cloud. He is home from Washington. He had many talks with The Great Father and now the agency will be moved. It will be given a new place, near to Fort Laramie, and also a new name. It will be called The Red Cloud Agency.'

'Hah! OUCH!' Crazy Horse tried to laugh. 'Red Cloud will be pleased at such a thing.'

'I do not think so,' Worm shook his head. 'They say that Red Cloud is changed. They say that Washington, and the place they call New York, have changed him. They say he saw many, many white men and many tall buildings. Many traders and many posts. They say that Red Cloud has seen a power in the white man that we cannot beat. They say that his spirit is broken. He has come home to the agency and hung up his lance.'

'Well, my spirit is not broken,' Crazy Horse slurred through the side of his mouth. 'I am not moving to any agency. I will still fight. I will always fight for the Lakota.'

'Then He Dog and I will bring you some help.'

'I don't need help. I just need to get better.'

'We mean help at home,' He Dog explained. 'Someone to take care of you, look after you. Someone who will love you and Buffalo Rabbit.'

'Not a wife!' Crazy Horse protested. 'Please. Do not bring me a wife!'

'Yes, a wife. A wife is what you need,' said Worm. 'He Dog and I will bring you a wife.'

CHAPTER SEVENTEEN
The Rosebud Country, Montana Territory.
Two years later
July, The Moon of Cherries Ripening, 1872

He Dog and Worm had been true to their word. They'd found the perfect wife for Crazy Horse. Her name was Black Shawl, and she was sweet and kind, especially to Buffalo Rabbit. Better still, she and Crazy Horse had quickly had an adorable daughter, They Are Afraid Of Her.

It was a glorious summer's day, and the Crazy Horse family was lounging by the river at the camp of their friends, the Hunkpapa tribe of the Lakota. Old men were sitting under the trees, smoking pipes and fanning themselves with eagles' wings, women and children were bathing, washing their hair or splashing each other. Girls were picking flowers, warriors were skimming pebbles, and boys were racing ponies.

Crazy Horse was tickling They Are Afraid Of Her. He had a rabbit tail on a string and was bouncing it on her nose. They were both laughing, They Are Afraid in bird-like giggles, Crazy Horse with the faintest of snarls, thanks to the scar on his lip. It was the one, permanent reminder of No Water's bullet.

Buffalo Rabbit was lying next to Black Shawl, who was putting the finishing touches to her daughter's latest toy, a tiny pony made from doeskin. But Buffalo Rabbit wasn't watching Black Shawl. She was pretending to help He Dog, American Horse and Young Man Afraid. They had gathered a pile of feathers, and were picking out the best and trimming them into fletchings. Buffalo Rabbit was pretending to help them, but other things were on her mind.

Sitting within a coup stick's touch of her were two of the fiercest and finest warriors in the entire Sioux Nation. They were war leaders of the Hunkpapa, and their names were Sitting Bull and Gall. The Hunkpapa were much wilder than Crazy Horse's Oglala, some were so wild they'd never even seen a white man.

Gall was about the same age as Crazy Horse, and was huge, very powerful, and built like a buffalo. Compared to Gall, Crazy Horse seemed like a girl. Six years previously, Gall had been bayoneted by white soldiers and left for dead. He'd survived, thanks to his incredible strength, but he'd hated the white man ever since. Legs had said that Gall only ever fought with a hatchet. He roared up to his enemies at full gallop and split open their heads. Buffalo Rabbit could well imagine it. She'd never seen Gall in fighting mode, and thought she'd rather not.

Next to Gall was Tatanka Iyotanka, or Sitting Bull. He had a large head, heavy features, and skin that was mottled with smallpox scars, just as Spotty's, the captain of the Irvine's wagon train, had been. His body was squat, lumbering and slightly plump, and he walked with a limp, courtesy of a Crow who'd shot him in the foot.

Sitting Bull was a little older than Crazy Horse and Gall, and was considered extremely wise. He was a holy man, a medicine man and a brilliant horse-stealer with an amazing fighting history. He'd counted his first coup when he was fourteen-years-old, and had notched up over sixty since then. He'd also killed many whites, including, some said, women and children. Buffalo Rabbit preferred not to think about that. To her, Sitting Bull was just like a cuddly bear.

She craned her neck and licked his hand. Then she stood up, skirted the pile of feathers and jumped into Gall's massive lap. She was thinking of having a snooze. One of the most feared men in America was fondling her ears when something caught her eye. American Horse had tipped his chin towards the bluff that overlooked the river. He was about to say something.

Buffalo Rabbit sat up sharply and watched him sweep his right hand over his legs, raise it to the side of his head and make a V shape with his first two fingers. Then he tucked his second finger away and moved his index finger backwards and forwards in front of his face. He was 'talking' in Plains Indian, and what he was saying was 'legs' 'scout' and 'now'.

Buffalo Rabbit quickly picked out Legs and the scout. She could see them at the top of the bluff. The scout was saying something, too. He was using the language of long-distance signals. These signals could be made by flashing mirrors, waving blankets, firing arrows, lighting fires or wafting smoke. Or simply by running. The scout was running from west to east. He and Legs had found a buffalo herd.

Back at camp, the scout smoked a pipe to show that he would not lie, then began to describe the herd in more detail. Buffalo Rabbit sat with Legs and listened intently. The more the hunters could learn, the more successful their hunt would be.

They needed to know the lie of the land, whether there were places for them to hide, whether there was water to be crossed. How easily could they stay downwind of the buffalo? How many head were there, and what sort of mood they were in? If they were skittish, the hunters would have to be extra careful. A skittish herd was difficult to manage and dangerous to hunt. It might also mean there were Crow about, a pack of wolves or coyote, or maybe even a grizzly bear.

When the hunters' questions had been asked and answered, a plan was formed. There *would* be a hunt, it would begin early next morning, and Crazy Horse would lead it.

It was still dark when Buffalo Rabbit, Legs and Crazy Horse crept from their tipi and walked to the pony herd. Their friends, including Gall, Sitting Bull, and a Northern Cheyenne named Two Moons, were already there, catching their ponies. They would take two each; an easy-going riding pony to get them to the buffalo, and a hunting pony for the chase itself. Hunting ponies were as specialist as fighting ponies. They were highly trained, fearless, nippy and fast, and the trust between them and their riders was absolute. It needed to be.

Buffalo Rabbit's heart was in her mouth as Crazy Horse led his ponies out of the herd. Hunting was a perilous business, and the build-up was always nerve-racking. She knew she'd feel fine once the party set off. She caught sight of Legs and felt better already.

'Oh, my,' she giggled. 'Don't *you* look gorgeous.'

'Very funny,' the wolf replied.

He was wearing a waistcoat. It was brown and woolly, with holes for his forelegs and rawhide laces that pulled together over his chest to make everything fit snugly. It had also been smeared with a generous helping of fresh buffalo dung.

Legs was excellent at detecting buffalo, but buffalo were equally excellent at detecting wolves. The merest whiff of wolf could cause a stampede. So, though Legs had always gone scouting and found the herds, he'd never been able to join the hunt.

Then, on a day when the hunting party had left him at home, Legs had gone for a wander. He'd known where the buffalo were, and had been careful to avoid them, but all of a sudden, he'd seen them. The warriors were with them, but they'd travelled a long way from the start of the hunt.

'Something must have spooked the herd,' Legs had observed. 'Still, they've settled now, and I shall settle down too, and watch from here. The wind is strong today. I can feel it in my fur, but it's coming towards me. The buffalo can't detect me.'

Just then, though, his nostrils had flared and tickled.

'Smoke,' he'd said. 'I can smell smoke.'

He'd climbed onto a boulder and scanned the plain. Sure enough, there was a whisper of smoke and a flicker of flame. It was close to where he and the scout had spotted the buffalo. Close to where the hunt would have started, and where the warriors would have hobbled their riding ponies. Legs had leapt from the boulder, raced past the buffalo and reached the ponies just in time. The prairie fire had almost surrounded them. A few had managed to break their fetters and escape, but most were still hobbled and screaming and spinning in panic. The wolf had chewed through the fetters, then he and the ponies had joined the thousands of other creatures that were darting out of the grass and careering away from the path of the fire.

Two days later, Legs had been made an honorary member of the hunt, and presented with the waistcoat. It had been specially made from the skin of a buffalo calf, so Legs was now The Wolf In Buffalo Clothing, and The Guardian Of The Ponies. He could join the hunt at any time, so long as he wore his waistcoat, and plenty of dung to disguise his scent.

Buffalo Rabbit took her place on Crazy Horse's riding pony, and the hunting party quit the village and rode towards the bluff. When they reached its top, Buffalo Rabbit looked down and gasped. Below her was the biggest herd of buffalo she'd ever seen. From where she was sitting, it looked as though someone had taken a huge sack of coffee beans and tipped it all over the plain.

'My grand-mother used to talk about herds like this,'

whispered Legs. 'They were commonplace in her day. All over the plains, they were. But they're getting rarer by the minute. They don't like the white man's roads, you see. And they *hate* the iron roads. Those iron horses frighten them, what with their huffing and puffing and noise and steam. It's different up here. That's why the buffalo come. No roads means plenty of buffalo. Your master's about to sign, Rabbit. I think we're ready to go.'

Crazy Horse turned to face his friends. As leader of the hunt, he had to give them directions, and he had to do it in absolute silence. The slightest noise could alert the buffalo. Crazy Horse held his hands ahead of him, palms facing and slightly apart, left hand ahead, then moved them forward in a snaking motion.

'Follow.'

He returned his hands to their starting position and moved them forward again, this time in short jerks.

'Slow.'

The hunters nodded and fell into line behind him as he zigzagged his ponies down the slope, towards the buffalo. He chose the route with care, finding cover in the occasional bush or boulder, and checking constantly for anything that might make a pony slip or shy.

As the ground began to level out, he reached the spot he'd been headed for, a stream surrounded by cottonwood and willow trees. The air was still, and the buffalo were grazing calmly. Buffalo Rabbit could hear them grunting contentedly as they tore at the grass and swished their tails or stamped their hooves to brush away the flies.

The buffalo nearest her was a large bull. Its head

was massive, and it had small, mean eyes, a moist black nose and short, stumpy horns. Its fur was dense, tightly curled on its head, but longer elsewhere. It ran down its chest and forelegs and across its shoulders. Then, except for a ridge along its spine, it stopped. It was as though someone had taken a cut-throat razor and shaved the last two-thirds of the beast all the way back to its charcoal skin.

The Indians slipped silently from their riding ponies and hobbled them in the shade of the trees. Legs took up his guarding post beside them, and Buffalo Rabbit was transferred to Crazy Horse's hunting pony, where she slid into her beaded pouch with its likeness of a leaping poodle. The warriors kept their hunting ponies between themselves and the buffalo, and tiptoed softly apart. Each was heading for a predetermined position. They couldn't just charge at the herd. That would scare it away. They had to work as a team, surround the buffalo, and then come at them from several angles to split them up.

Crazy Horse slid his hands quietly onto his pony's withers and grasped its mane. When the other hunters made various animal noises to signal that they were ready, he gave his own signal, the cry of a hawk. Then he sprang onto his pony and galloped towards the buffalo.

The bulls were first to spot the danger. They threw up their tails and snorted, then charged away. Heifers and calves followed, and soon the whole herd was on the move. The noise was incredible. Bellowing, snorting, grunting, bleating, the thunder of thousands of hooves.

The warriors let the bulk of the herd escape, then

moved in to cut off the rest. They had to be quick, now. The commotion was grinding up the dry earth and pounding it to dust. They must do something whilst they could see. A buffalo could turn in a flash. Riding into one could be death. Hit it straight on, and you'd be dead before you knew it. Hit it sideways, and you'd be knocked from your pony and minced to pieces.

Crazy Horse and He Dog picked out a young bull and steered it away from its friends. The bull's tongue was lolling at the side of its mouth, and its eyes were wide with fear and effort. Crazy Horse whisked a fistful of arrows from his quiver and held them in his teeth. Then he leant across his pony's neck, slipped an arrow into his bow, pulled back slowly, and fired. The bull was struck clean between the ribs, but it didn't seem to notice. It just lowered its head and spurted forward. Crazy Horse fired again. This time there was a roar, and the buffalo stumbled and crashed to the ground, shoulder first.

Buffalo Rabbit heard a squeal and a whinny, and Two Moons and Gall came careering through the dust.

Between them was a heifer. The warriors had run her out of the main herd and shot her twice. She was still on her feet and galloping strongly, but then they fired again. The heifer spun, collapsed to her knees and rolled onto her side. She appeared to be dead, but then her hooves scrabbled and she tried to get up. She raised her head and bellowed for help, but the rest of the herd was well away by now. The heifer sighed and trembled, then lay down and died.

With the buffalo gone, the dust began to clear. Five kills

were lying on the plain. They were still and dark, like giant molehills.

The warriors regrouped and handed their exhausted ponies to American Horse and Gall, who took them and Buffalo Rabbit back to the stream by the cottonwood trees.

Whilst the hunting ponies cooled off in the water, the riding ponies were unhobbled and roped together. They were needed again, this time to carry the meat back to camp. American Horse led them away, and Gall stayed behind with Legs and Buffalo Rabbit. Extra vigilance was vital now. The hunting ponies were hot and exhausted and the air was heavy with the scent of blood. Hidden eyes were watching, and it wouldn't be long before the wolves, coyotes and mountain cats began to circle. They would be after scraps of buffalo, but they'd happily take a tired-out pony whilst they waited.

Buffalo Rabbit watched from afar as the warriors carved up the kill. This was a skilled job, but the Indians did it deftly and swiftly, almost instinctively. First, they chopped off the buffaloes' heads. Next, they removed the skins. That done, they cut out their favourite fillets of meat, which they ate, warm and raw, right there on the plain. They then hacked the carcasses into manageable pieces, loaded everything onto the riding ponies and lashed it all together. Finally, they gently turned the buffaloes' heads to the east, where the sun would always rise on them and their spirits would be forever honoured.

Buffalo Rabbit yawned in the sunshine.

'A perfect hunt,' she mumbled. 'One of the ponies

has gashed a leg, but the wound isn't serious. Worm will wrap it with a poultice of sage and it will soon mend. Five whole buffalo! There'll be a feast tonight.'

She wriggled against the cool grass and put her head on her paws. The warriors were returning to the cottonwood trees. She could see them jostling each other and laughing. She stood up, shook herself, and ran to the edge of the trees to meet them. She should have known better. She *did* know better. Crazy Horse and Legs had both taught her never to rush. Rushing was not the Lakota way, and for good reason.

She heard the snake before she saw it.

'Tch.Tikkichee-tch-tikkichee-tch-tikkichee-tch.'

She froze, and the viper repeated its hideous rattle.

'Tch.Tikkichee-tch-tikkichee-tch-tikkichee-tch.'

She could see it now. It was right in front of her, caught between her shadow and a large boulder. She'd inadvertently cornered it, threatened it. Its short, stumpy body was lying in the shape of the letter S.

'S is for sun,' Buffalo Rabbit recited. 'Why sun? Why not snake? And why am I thinking of reading lessons?'

The snake's oval eyes were hypnotising, studying her through slit-like pupils. Its forked tongue was flickering to taste the air. Its flat, triangular head was raised, as was its tail. It was flagging its intention to strike.

'Concentrate, concentrate,' Buffalo Rabbit told herself. 'Remember your training. If alone, move very slowly backwards. If help is close by, you may bark an alarm, but you must stay absolutely still. Rattlesnakes are deaf as rock but can sense the slightest movement.'

She opened her mouth as far as she dared. She wanted

to bark for Gall and Legs, but barking and staying still at the same time proved easier said than done. She managed a timid 'woof'. The snake didn't stir, but then neither did her rescuers. She turned her head very, very slowly. She slackened her jaw, took a deep breath, and prepared to bark properly. It was then that she saw Gall. He was crouched to one side of the boulder.

'Oyuhlagan sni,' he said. 'Stay where you are.'

He reached out slowly and snapped a long, slender stick from a willow tree.

'Oyuhlagan sni,' he repeated.

Still crouched, he inched his hatchet from his belt and crept around the back of the snake. Buffalo Rabbit followed him with her eyes. The snake seemed to have calmed down. It was no longer rattling. Gall tapped the ground with his willow stick. *Now* the snake was rattling.

'Tch.Tikkichee-tch-tikkichee-tch-tikkichee-tch.'

It whipped towards the stick and snapped its jaws around it.

'Go!' screamed Gall.

Buffalo Rabbit veered sideways just as Gall's hatchet whistled forward in an arc and landed with a thud. She turned. The hatchet's blade was buried in the ground, its handle still vibrating from the force of impact. On either side of it were two perfect rattlesnake halves.

'Heavens above,' said Legs as he appeared around the boulder. 'What happened here?'

'Gall did a hatchet job,' Buffalo Rabbit replied.

CHAPTER EIGHTEEN

*Where The Yellowstone and Powder Rivers meet,
Montana Territory.
One year later, August, The Moon of Ripe Plums, 1873*

The cloud rushed closer. It broke into a haze of scattered dots. Closer still, and the dots became a wave of sound. It buzzed towards the raven's air space. The buzz became a drumming, the drumming became a scraping. It flew beneath the raven, continued on its mission and faded to a distant hiss. As quickly as they'd arrived, the hoppers were gone.

'Off to munch through another few hundred acres,' Maka Mani chattered to himself.

The grasshoppers had been swarming for weeks. They'd landed in columns one-hundred-and-fifty miles wide and two feet deep. They'd munched through farms in Kansas, Nebraska and the Dakotas, and they were still munching. The plains were alive with the rubbing of their legs, the rustling of their wings and the snap of their collective jaws. They were devouring anything that stood still, including curtains, clothes and furniture. They were devouring the white man's crops. Maka Mani wasn't particularly sorry about this. As far as he was concerned, most white men got what they deserved. But he wasn't completely cold-hearted.

'I hope they don't settle on Mr Joseph's farm, or Mr Parker's. They are good people. They work hard and keep themselves to themselves. They were both snowed-in last winter, and then poor Mr Parker only just missed being hit by a spring tornado. It passed within a whisker of his land.'

Maka Mani had seen the consequences of these hopper attacks. He'd flown over vast swathes of sad, dried-up plants that would never recover from the insects' voracious gorging.

He'd flown over other things, too.

Way back when, the eagles had spoken about an iron road in California. It had been headed east, towards the ones the raven had been watching. The birds had wondered then if the two roads might meet up with each other. Well, they'd been right to wonder. The roads *had* met up. Their tracks had been linked, and so had the Atlantic and Pacific Oceans. Now, the iron horses huffed and puffed and belched their way from one side of America to the other and back again. The American states were truly united, and the white men were so pleased with themselves they were calling the railroad The Eighth Wonder of the World.

That wasn't all.

Last September, the tracks of the iron road in Kansas had reached a place called Dodge City. Dodge City had been nothing but a couple of tents and a box car, then. It had been so quiet that a vast buffalo herd had been grazing on its outskirts. The herd had been a sitting target. The white men had propped their guns on three-legged sticks and fired at the buffalo, point-blank. They'd driven stakes through the animals' noses, roped them to horses, and torn away their skins. That done, they'd dumped them onto iron horses and chuffed them down the brand new road to the tanners and meat packers in the east. In just three months, more than forty-thousand buffalo had gone that way, and Dodge City had grown into a bustling, thriving butchery.

'That's just the half of it,' the raven spat. 'At least those buffalo were killed for meat. Now the white men are pushing guns through their iron horse windows. They shoot hundreds of buffalo in a matter of minutes and call it sport. They don't take the skin or the meat, or any of the good things. They just leave the bodies to rot where they fall. If this goes on, the southern plains will have buffalo no more. And here in the north? Here in the north, we have this...'

Maka Mani wheeled in the sky.

He was four-hundred miles north of the nearest railroad. He was so far north he could see into Canada. He could also see other things.

Beneath him were scores of parked up wagons and hundreds of horses, mules, and beef and dairy cattle. The animals were grazing beside a huge encampment, an encampment of soldiers and surveyors. Another iron road was about to be laid. It would follow the course of The Yellowstone River, cut through The Rosebud Country and run straight across the Lakota hunting grounds. So far, the tracks themselves were a long way short of The Yellowstone, but the railroad men were not. The surveyors and their measuring sticks were right here, deep into Lakota country. Which was why they needed fifteen-hundred soldiers to guard them.

Maka Mani did a quick count of the cavalry horses.

'Mmmm,' he mused. 'There's a company missing. And I'd bet a bald eagle to run away from a mouse if I don't know whose it is.'

He flew west, along The Yellowstone and over tall grass that was studded with flowers and teeming with every type of animal, from buffalo, elk and antelope, to cats and coyotes, bears and wolves.

'Though there's rather less of each since Custer arrived,' the raven mused. 'He's been hunting his heart out, as usual. He keeps *some* things alive. He has a pet porcupine, and a wildcat. As for the rest, well, he drags his stove and his very own cook behind him, and he and his officers have a daily roast, thank you very much. What doesn't get eaten gets stuffed. Custer's brought along his own, personal taxidermist. Now he has lessons on how to stuff things and hang them on his wall.'

Maka Mani shook his head bemusedly.

'Custer,' he thought, 'is a very strange man. He's been away from the plains for two years. You'd think he'd behave himself, now he's back. You'd think he'd do what he's supposed to do, which is to protect this new iron road from the Indians. Instead of which, he's been off on a round of fun and games. The other week, he and his 7th Cavalry were sent to the back of the line as punishment. They had to ride behind the foot soldiers. They were eating dust for days, but it didn't have much effect. Custer doesn't exactly *disobey* orders, he just doesn't seem to get around to hearing them. Not that I care. I couldn't care less. Let him go galavanting in his

bright red flannel shirt in the middle of Indian country...
Well, now, what d'you know? Here's the man himself!
He's taken eighty men and gone even *further* into Indian
country. Looking for the next campsite for the soldiers
and surveyors, I've no doubt. He's closer to the Lakota
than ever. They're bound to spot him, if they haven't
already. This should be interesting. This should be *very*
interesting.'

Not far from where Maka Mani was deliberating, there
was another, very different campsite. A campsite on
which there were many hundreds of tipis. These tipis
were arranged in circles according to tribe. A few were
Cheyenne, but most were Lakota Sioux. Of these, some
belonged to Crazy Horse's Oglala, but the majority were
from the wilder, northern tribes; the Minneconjou, Sans
Arc, Blackfoot and Hunkpapa.

Crazy Horse was sitting in his tipi with his pets, some
of his friends, and his daughter, They Are Afraid of Her,
who was snuggled in the well of her father's crossed
legs. She was wearing American Horse's grizzly bear
necklace, and kept pulling the collection of teeth and
claws over her head and shrieking with laughter. Lying
next to her were Buffalo Rabbit and Legs, who'd spent
the morning picking berries with the little girl. They Are
Afraid had her own little basket for this, but only one in
four of the fruits ever reached it. The others went straight
to her mouth. Now she had a purple tongue and purple
stains all over her face. They Are Afraid was nuts about
berries. They'd been the first thing she'd ever tasted.

The Sioux believed that a mother's milk was tainted for the first few days of a baby's life, and should only be drunk by an adult. So, Sioux women didn't suckle their new-borns, they suckled a grown-up female friend instead, and the baby was fed with berry juice until the milk was considered clean.

They Are Afraid laughed again, and Crazy Horse's friends laughed with her. They were being entertained, but Crazy Horse was looking anxious. He glanced across the fire, to where Sitting Bull was packing a pipe. Crazy Horse was very superstitious about pipes. He would only smoke them if the mixture of tobacco and herbs had been squashed into the bowl with a thumb rather than the usual tampering stick. If Sitting Bull so much as *looked* at a tampering stick, Crazy Horse would refuse to smoke.

'Thank the Crows!' said Legs at last. 'Sitting Bull has done well. The pipe is properly filled and lit. It has been shown to the four corners, raised to the heavens and lowered to the earth. Now it can be passed around. The conversation begins.'

'The scouts have seen horse soldiers?' Sitting Bull asked.

'Yes,' replied Crazy Horse. 'Eight tens of them. Coming this way.'

'They are alone?' Gall puffed on the pipe.

'For the moment,' Crazy Horse nodded. 'We think they are searching for a new campsite. If that is the case, then they will be followed by their foot soldiers and measuring men.'

'Then we should do something quickly,' suggested

Gall, 'before we are outnumbered.'

'We are already outnumbered,' said a young Minneconjou. 'The horse soldiers are eight tens, but well-armed. Our three hundreds of warriors have few guns, and most of those are short on powder.'

Crazy Horse laughed.

'You are learning fast, my friend,' he said. 'Perhaps we will not have a repeat of last year.'

Legs and Buffalo Rabbit gave each other a sideways glance.

They knew what Crazy Horse was talking about.

Almost a year ago to the day, Sitting Bull and Crazy Horse had attacked the very same survey party. It had been the first time these two great warriors had fought together, and it should have been a glorious combination, but they'd forgotten something. Unlike them, the youngsters of the northern Lakota had had no experience of fighting white soldiers. These youngsters, the Minneconjou included, had treated the attack like a raid on the Crow. They'd rushed in to drive off the soldiers' horses and cattle, and the Indians' cover had been blown.

'The soldiers went away,' said the Minneconjou defensively. 'We scared them away. They took their measuring men and went home after that.'

'I think that was a coincidence,' said Sitting Bull kindly. 'I think they had finished their work for the year. They had to leave before the snows came. But now they have returned. They are further west than ever before. They are deep into Lakota country.'

'They are building their iron road on land that they gave to us,' said a Sans Arc.

'*Gave* to us?' Gall was furious. 'They did not *give* it to us. It was *already ours*! The only thing they *gave* to us was a promise that it would remain so.'

'Yes. But only if we agreed to move to their agency and eat their biscuits,' added He Dog.

'They made that arrangement with Red Cloud,' Crazy Horse spat. 'I did not agree to that. I did not touch the pen. Red Cloud can live in their agency. I will not.'

'Nor I,' chorused the others.

'They made promises to our southern tribes, also,' said Two Moons. 'They promised us our hunting grounds, but then they laid down their iron roads and slaughtered our buffalo. There *are* no hunting grounds in the south, now. There is nothing left to hunt.'

'There is still hunting here, by The Yellowstone,' Crazy Horse sighed. 'But if we allow the white man to build this new road, then they will bring their iron horses. They will kill the buffalo, just like they did in the south. They will kill the buffalo, and we will have nothing to eat. We want no iron horses here.'

He stroked his daughter's mop of shiny black hair.

'We must stop this road,' he said. 'We must stop these iron horses.'

CHAPTER NINETEEN
The Tongue River, Montana Territory.
The following morning

Maka Mani was perched in a tree.

He tipped his head and peered at the nearby river. Eighty 7th Cavalry horses were grazing on its banks. Their riders were lazing close to them, playing cards and cracking jokes. Most had removed their jackets but, further along the riverbank, one man had taken off his entire uniform, bundled his red flannel shirt into a makeshift pillow, and tipped his hat over his face. Now he was dozing in his long-johns and vest.

'Look up! Look up!' Maka Mani cawed at him. 'Oh, all right. Don't then. See if I care.'

Had Custer heeded the raven's advice, had he removed his hat, pushed away his pillow and sat up in his underwear, he might have caught sight of an eagle feather bonnet, or seen sunlight reflecting on coal-black hair. He might have had a clue that over three-hundred-and-fifty Indian warriors were watching him from an overlooking bluff. He might even have spotted the small black poodle that was huddled amongst them. But Custer didn't heed the raven's advice. He didn't even stir.

Above him, on the bluff, Buffalo Rabbit was crouched between Crazy Horse and Sitting Bull.

The two war leaders were sharing a pair of long-seeing glasses, passing them backwards and forwards over Buffalo Rabbit's head, and whispering about what they could see and what they might do about it.

Crazy Horse trained the binoculars on the horse soldiers. The scout had been right. They were well-armed. They were relaxed now, but they had lookouts all around, and many of their horses were fully tacked. It would take them only seconds to mount up. Well, perhaps not all of them.

'That one is sleeping,' Crazy Horse observed. 'He has taken off his first clothes and is sleeping in his second clothes. Why do these white men wear *so* many clothes?'

Sitting Bull snatched the binoculars and focussed them on Custer.

'As you say. He is fast asleep. Still, the others are awake. I do not like our chances on open ground. Our only hope is a decoy. What do you think? You are the expert at decoys.'

'I would stampede the loose horses and steer them towards that copse,' Crazy Horse suggested, 'the soldiers should chase after them. If we can draw them into the woodland...the trees will make it hard for them to aim their guns...'

'...and easy for us to aim our arrows,' Sitting Bull nodded. 'Who do you want for the decoy?'

'Two Moons, He Dog and American Horse,' Crazy Horse replied.

'Ooh, goody. All my friends,' Buffalo Rabbit wagged her tail.

'Then I will take the rest,' said Sitting Bull. 'We will go around the back, sneak into the copse and wait.'

'Done.'

Sitting Bull and Crazy Horse signalled to their warriors, and everyone reversed down the bluff and silently mounted their ponies.

Sitting Bull led his men away and Buffalo Rabbit slipped into her fighting pouch. Then she and Crazy Horse waited with their three friends for the signal that Sitting Bull was in place.

When Sitting Bull cried like an eagle, Crazy Horse raised an arm. When Sitting Bull cried again, Crazy Horse whipped the arm forward, and he and the decoys galloped their ponies over the bluff, down the other side and straight towards the cavalry horses.

The soldiers' lookouts were quick off the mark. They met the decoys with a hail of bullets.

Buffalo Rabbit crouched low in her pouch. This was her first ever soldier fight. She hadn't been there the previous year, when the youngsters had got things so wrong, she'd been left at home with a thorn in her paw. She could see now what made soldier fighting so very different from raiding the Crow. Soldiers meant business. There would be no counting coup for them.

They meant to kill.

The decoys realised they'd never get the horses into the woods whilst the lookouts kept firing. So they concentrated on making them waste their ammunition. They did this by riding close enough to warrant a shot, yet not so close that they could actually be hit. This was one of Crazy Horse's favourite tricks, but getting it right took courage, supreme horsemanship and split-second timing.

'Well, if I must be here,' Buffalo Rabbit mumbled, 'I'm in the best possible hands. Pouch. I'm in the best possible pouch.'

She touched her paw to her pebble necklace.

'I have my pebble to protect me. And my master, of course. He's the expert when it comes to soldier fights.'

Maka Mani was still in his tree, still watching Custer.

Custer was up on his feet at last, pulling on his red flannel shirt. Trousers. Jacket. Boots. Reaching for his rifle. Ordering his men to mount up.

He selected twenty men to follow him and then trotted towards Crazy Horse and the decoys. This gave Crazy Horse a new idea. If he couldn't drive the loose horses into the woods, then maybe he could tempt these soldiers there instead. He signalled to his decoys to ride closer to the woods.

The soldiers followed.

The decoys circled their ponies.

Buffalo Rabbit peeked over the top of her pouch.

She could see the soldiers very clearly, now. One of them stood out from the rest. His clothes were different from the others' and he had piercing blue eyes, curly blonde hair and a matching moustache. His hair was so long it was flying out from beneath his hat.

Buffalo Rabbit was watching this man when he suddenly halted his horse.

The decoys halted their ponies.

The man looked about, the decoys looked about.

The man held up his hand and waved away all but two of his men. He walked his horse forward.

Crazy Horse and the decoys walked their ponies backward. When the man stopped, the decoys stopped. When the man moved, the decoys moved. The distance to Sitting Bull's ambush was closing fast.

Maka Mani held his breath.

Sitting Bull's warriors were more than ready. They'd crept through the copse and taken up position. Now they were waiting silently, ready to pounce. Just a few more steps, and Custer would ride straight into them. The trap was set. The tension was almost more than Maka Mani could bear. Suddenly, the silence was broken by a bloodthirsty scream. The raven jumped with fright and a group of warriors hurtled out of the woods and headed straight for Custer.

'What the..?'

Sitting Bull and Crazy Horse looked on in bemusement. They had no idea why these few warriors had broken rank and spoiled the plan. But Maka Mani knew.

'They've recognised him!' he squawked. 'Those warriors have recognised Custer!'

They had indeed.

Three weeks after Red Cloud had touched the pen at Fort Laramie, Custer had attacked a Cheyenne village at The Washita, Kansas. The attack had taken place early one snowy winter morning when the people were asleep. Ninety-two women, children and old folk, including the village chief, Black Kettle, had been killed. Custer and his men had then slaughtered the Cheyenne's eight-hundred ponies and looted the village for treasures. Custer had kept a particularly beautiful, almost white tipi. What the soldiers hadn't stolen, they'd burned.

Black Kettle's people had been through this once before, at a place called Sand Creek. That time, the soldiers had scalped their victims, then taken the scalps to the theatre in Denver and strung them across the stage. Some of the warriors now charging towards Custer had been at Sand Creek. *All* of them had been at The Washita. They hated white soldiers, but they particularly hated Custer. They called him Long Hair, and they'd gone completely wild at the sight of him.

Sitting Bull and Crazy Horse had heard stories about Custer, but they'd never come across him in the flesh. They hadn't realised that the man they'd been trying to ambush was the infamous Long Hair of The Washita. They knew now, but it was too late. Custer's entire force was mounted up and coming to his rescue. They were too well-armed to be fought head-on. Crazy Horse and Sitting Bull had no option but to call off their men and ride away.

Keeping out of range was one of Crazy Horse's talents, but by the time the bullet struck, he wasn't even thinking about range. He'd left the soldiers far behind him. The bullet was a rogue. A stray. Buffalo Rabbit felt it blast through her fighting pouch at chest level. For a moment, she was stunned. Then she looked down. Blood, her

128

blood, was pouring over her pouch. She shook her head and the blood sprayed left and right. She screamed and, somewhere over her head, Maka Mani screamed, too.

Rather than stopping his pony, Crazy Horse urged it on. American Horse was galloping alongside, now. He was lying across his pony's neck and signing to Crazy Horse. He pointed with the middle finger of his left hand, then flipped the palm open and beat it with his right fist.

'Over there,' he was saying. 'Rock.'

Crazy Horse was off his pony before it even reached the rock. He whipped Buffalo Rabbit from her pouch, dived to the ground and rolled with her until the rock was behind them and covering them from any more bullets. American Horse and Maka Mani followed.

'What happened?' American Horse asked.

'She was hit by rogue bullet,' Maka Mani squawked.

'I think she was hit by a rogue bullet,' said Crazy Horse. 'Can you hold her? I want to look at something.'

'Of course,' American Horse replied. 'Throw me my blanket. I will keep her warm.'

Buffalo Rabbit wasn't cold, but she *was* trembling. The sight of her own blood had given her the shivers.

Crazy Horse handed her to American Horse, fetched the blanket, and returned to his pony.

'Toniktuka hwo?' American Horse whispered as he wrapped Buffalo Rabbit up and cradled her gently. 'How are you?'

'Nahan rei ni wayon heon,' Buffalo Rabbit whimpered. 'I am still alive.'

'Look at this,' said Crazy Horse.

Buffalo Rabbit thought she'd rather not look. Crazy

Horse had collected her fighting pouch. It was covered in blood. He snatched a handful of grass and wiped it clean.

'See?' he said as he pointed to a hole in the pouch's centre. 'See how the beadwork has been pushed inwards? This is the bullet's entry hole. It would have been level with Rabbit's heart.'

He parted Buffalo Rabbit's blanket and ran his hands over her chest.

'There is not a mark on her. Not one. Except for this...'

The pebble in Buffalo Rabbit's necklace had a small but unmistakable dent.

He pointed to another hole in the pouch.

'Here the beadwork is splayed outwards. This is the bullet's exit hole. It went in, bounced off the pebble, and went out again! It caught Rabbit on the chin. There is much blood but the wound is very shallow.'

'It looks worse than it is,' American Horse nodded. 'Flesh wounds often do. Do not worry, Rabbit,' he added kindly. 'We will get you home to Worm. You will be on the mend by tomorrow.'

'What about my pouch?' Buffalo Rabbit wondered. 'Can it be mended, too?'

'My mother will clean this properly,' said Crazy Horse as he slipped the pouch into his knife-belt. 'She will clean it and tie in the beads. But she will not repair the holes. The holes must stay.'

American Horse ruffled the top of Buffalo Rabbit's head.

'Shot by a soldier, eh? You are a true Lakota, now,'

he laughed. 'From this day forward, you may mark your chin with red war paint.'

Buffalo Rabbit wagged her tail.

'No,' Crazy Horse replied. 'No paint.'

'Ah!' American Horse sighed. 'But your master is right. He must stay true to his vision. He cannot paint his pony, so he must not paint you, either. Perhaps, then, he will let me give you a gift?'

He glanced at Crazy Horse, who nodded and smiled.

American Horse then took a knife from his belt and cut away one of the claws from his grizzly bear necklace.

'This is for you,' he said. 'It is for Buffalo Rabbit, who is brave and strong like a bear.'

'It's beautiful,' said Buffalo Rabbit. 'Pilamaya ye. Thank you.'

CHAPTER TWENTY
Bo's House.
The 21st Century

'Did you ever hear of someone called Long Hair?' Bo asked Cavendish.

'Long Hair, Hard Ass, Iron Butt and Ringlets. He had many nicknames. His real name was George Armstrong Custer, but his wife called him Bo.'

'Bo?' said Bo. 'No. You're making that up.'

'I am not. His wife called him Bo. She adored him. Quite right, too. Every Bo should be adored. Why d'you ask?'

'Because Buffalo Rabbit got shot by one of Long Hair's soldiers. They were in Lakota country, looking to build a railway. Crazy Horse and Sitting Bull were afraid they'd scare the buffalo, so they tried to lead Custer into an ambush, but then some of the Cheyenne went a bit mad and spoilt it all. They told us later that Custer had attacked their village at a place called The Washita. They *hated* him.'

'They weren't the only ones,' Cavendish chuckled. 'Custer was one of those people who you either worshipped or abhorred. There was no middle ground with him. It all depended which side of him you saw, brave and brilliant or reckless and vain. He could be horribly cruel one moment and extraordinarily kind the next. He'd mete out terrible punishment to his men, then turn around and nurse an injured animal.'

'He sounds a bit confused,' said Bo.

'Confused and confus*ing*. Eccentric, for sure. The day that Buffalo Rabbit was shot, Crazy Horse and Sitting Bull caught Custer napping. He was fast asleep, flat out in his underwear.'

Bo giggled.

'How do you know that?' she asked.

Cavendish wavered.

'Didn't you just tell me that Buffalo Rabbit saw him?'

'No,' Bo answered. 'I said she was shot by one of his soldiers. She *did* see Custer. She saw him quite close-up, but he wasn't in his underwear. She didn't see *that*.'

'Oh? How odd,' said Cavendish quickly. 'I could have sworn...well, never mind. Now then, where were we?'

'The railway,' Bo replied. 'I'm worried about the railway.'

'No need,' said Cavendish. 'Custer and his soldiers soon packed up and left. The railwaymen went with them.'

'They'd done that the previous year,' said Bo, 'but only because they'd finished their work and winter was coming. They came back the following spring.'

'Not this time. This time they didn't come back in the spring. They didn't come back at all. The Indians thought they'd frightened them off, but they hadn't. What frightened them off was money. They went bankrupt.

The railway went bankrupt. The whole country went bankrupt. Banks collapsed, stock markets crashed, factories closed, businesses folded, farmers starved, workers begged on the streets.'

'I don't understand,' Bo batted her ears. 'I thought America was rich. I saw it, remember? Buffalo Rabbit saw it. She saw the new towns, the railways and the telegraph wires. America was rich. She was booming.'

'Well, the boom turned to bust. America went bust. She'd grown too fast. She was over-spent, over-stretched and over-budget.'

CHAPTER TWENTY-ONE
The Rosebud Country, Montana Territory.
Winter 1873

When the men who'd come to measure the iron road had gone, the Indians in The Rosebud Country picked up their lives and made ready for winter. They hunted for buffalo, elk and antelope, squirrels, weasels and birds.

Meat was dried, hides and skins were stretched, csarped tanned and dressed, firewood and herbs were collected, tipis were cleaned, and furs and buffalo robes were aired. The Crazy Horse tipi was made cosy and snow-proof. Black Shawl laid down sweet-grass and cherry bark to scent its fire, stored meat and dried berries within its walls, and made-up its beds to be deep and warm.

The first snowfall brought joy and excitement.

It freshened the village and made things seem clean. It covered the muddy tracks, buried the leftover bones and hid the fallen scraps of feather, rawhide and willow. Children threw snowballs and slid across the frozen streams, ponies and dogs frolicked and rolled, and They Are Afraid Of Her was introduced to her brand new miniature sledge.

The sledge had taken weeks of work. Crazy Horse had

rubbed down a set of buffalo ribs. He'd smoothed them away so they'd shone like glass. He'd used two of these ribs as runners, then lashed the others crossways to make a seat. He'd painted this seat with brightly coloured stripes and spots, and decorated it with bunches of ribbon. Meanwhile, Black Shawl had woven a hood of willow stems, lined it with squirrel fur and made her daughter a matching, squirrel-fur travelling bag.

They Are Afraid Of Her climbed onto the sledge happily enough. She wriggled into her travelling bag happily enough. But when Crazy Horse tugged at the pulling rope and the sledge began to move, she burst into tears.

Crazy Horse stopped pulling and knelt down beside her.

'Wa,' he said gently. 'Lila washteh.'

They Are Afraid stopped crying and rubbed her eyes, and Crazy Horse tried pulling again. Again, the little girl cried.

'Snow *not* very good, apparently,' said Legs.

'It's not the snow she doesn't like,' Buffalo Rabbit replied. 'It's the sledge. I think she's afraid of the sledge. She's only ridden on adult sledges, and always on Black Shawl's knee.'

They Are Afraid was screaming, now. She was screaming so loudly that Crazy Horse couldn't make himself heard above the din. He had to resort to sign language. When he'd managed to catch his daughter's eye, he quickly moved his hands out in front of him, palms up, index fingers curled. They Are Afraid was intrigued. She stopped screaming and smiled wanly.

Snot and tears were streaming down her face.

'That is enough for today,' said Black Shawl. 'We will try again tomorrow.'

'No. Wait a minute,' Buffalo Rabbit pranced in the snow. 'I have an idea. She'll love it, you'll see.'

'What idea?' asked Legs.

'*You* pull the sledge,' Buffalo Rabbit replied. 'Don't look at me like that. Take hold of the rope. Quick.'

The wolf picked the rope up in his teeth, and They Are Afraid hiccupped and began to giggle.

'Now what?' Legs asked.

'Walk backwards,' Buffalo Rabbit ordered.

'What?'

'You need to walk backwards.'

'Why?'

'Because it's funnier that way.'

Legs did as he was told. They Are Afraid was now in such a fit of the giggles that she didn't notice that the sledge was on the move.

'How long do I have to do this?' the wolf asked through a mouthful of rope.

'What? I can't understand what you're saying,' Buffalo Rabbit teased.

'I said, how long? Oh, never mind.'

In the end, Legs did an entire circuit of the village. Children and dogs were running beside him, Maka Mani was darting and diving over his head, and people were stopping to watch and cheer him on.

Before she'd set out, Black Shawl had filled a buffalo bladder with water, hot stones and meat. By the time the family got home to their tipi, the meat had cooked and the bladder was full of warm soup. Crazy Horse took the still giggling They Are Afraid from the sledge and everyone sat outside, Legs and Buffalo Rabbit included, and sipped, or lapped, their soup.

'That was *funny*,' said Buffalo Rabbit. 'I can't wait for the next time.'

'I'm hoping there won't be a next time,' Legs replied. 'They Are Afraid likes her sledge now. Crazy Horse can pull it in future. He'll *want* to pull it.'

'Dogs pulled sledges in the old days,' said Buffalo Rabbit. 'Before the Lakota had ponies. You told me that yourself.'

'Yes, but they didn't have to walk backwards because it was "funny" and anyway, I'm not a dog.'

'Why are you in such a bad mood? We've had a lovely morning, all of us.'

'Sorry. I know we have. I'm just not very keen on winter, that's all. I don't like being cooped up for months on end.'

'Well, maybe you won't be. Maybe the snows won't be too bad. You'll be able to hunt and stuff.'

'Maybe,' said Legs.

When winter arrived with a vengeance, so did more snow. Sometimes it came in soft flurries that floated gently to the ground. Sometimes it came as icy shards that stung the villagers' faces and drummed against their tipis. Sometimes it was slush, sometimes sleet, sometimes a blizzard of flakes on a howling wind. Whatever its form, the snow kept coming.

This was the time to renew and repair. The warriors restrung their bows, repainted their shields and redecorated their lances. The women mended and sewed and made buffalo robes. They sewed until their fingers were raw. Black Shawl and Crazy Horse rattled through these chores. They wanted to finish them quickly, so they could concentrate on making things for their daughter.

Black Shawl was beading They Are Afraid's squirrel-fur travelling bag. The pattern included her daughter's favourite colours and shapes; blue stars and yellow ponies, white eagles and red stripes. She'd also had an idea for a white buckskin dress, and a miniature cradleboard so that They Are Afraid could carry her dolls. Crazy Horse had made plans, too. He was going to carve a wooden pony. A pack pony. It would have a tiny travois on tiny lodge poles. He'd even thought about pinching a piece of fur and some doeskin from his wife's sewing bag, and making a teeny tiny buffalo robe and a teeny tiny tipi cover. They Are Afraid could roll and fold them and lash them onto the travois with teeny tiny strips of rawhide.

The snow piled into drifts as high and solid as a buffalo bull. Several times, Crazy Horse tore himself away from his pack pony project, strapped a pair of snow shoes onto his fur-lined moccasins, and tramped off with Legs and a rifle to see if he could find any snowbound animals. He often came back with nothing, but on one occasion he found some elk. The beasts had been trapped by the snow, and Crazy Horse shot them dead. So much fresh meat was a rare treat in the middle of winter. Everyone ate well that night, and then the carcasses were left to freeze and be carved up over the following days. Better still, Buffalo Rabbit and They Are Afraid were each given a set of the elks' highly prized front teeth.

When the thaw came, the streams flooded and rushed with sparkling water, and the Crazy Horse people dismantled their tipis and moved them to patches of fresh, untrodden ground. The blankets, buffalo robes and bearskins that stank of humans, animals, stale food and smoke were hung out to air. New grass shoots appeared, and the ponies, whose thick winter coats could no longer hide their protruding hip bones and hollow ribs, began to eat again.

The ponies built up their strength, and Crazy Horse and Gall decided to check on the Crow. The buffalo would be arriving soon, so the Lakota wanted to drive the Crow west and give themselves first pick of the hunting.

A good hunt seemed more important then ever, now.

News had come from the The Red Cloud Agency. The Indians who'd moved there had barely survived the winter. The white men had promised them supplies, but the clothes and blankets they'd received had been thin and riddled with lice, and the food had been rancid and heaving with worms. Beef cattle had been let loose so the Indians could shoot them. It was the white men's idea of a hunt, but the cattle had been driven up from Texas and were so exhausted and scrawny that even the wolves and coyotes had turned their noses up at them.

The Indians at the agency had been forced to extreme

measures. They'd eaten some of their dogs and ponies.

Crazy Horse and Gall were more determined than ever to make sure that their people ate well.

On the morning they were due to leave, Buffalo Rabbit was lying inside her tipi. She was curled up between Black Shawl and They Are Afraid, who were dozing by the fire. Legs and Maka Mani slipped beneath the tipi's rolled up sides.

'Come on,' said Legs. 'It's time to go.'

'I'm not going,' Buffalo Rabbit replied. 'I want to stay here.'

'But why? It's springtime and you haven't been out for months.'

'I have *so*. I've gone with you to scrabble for lichen and dig poor, sleeping mammals from their cosy beds.'

'So we could eat something fresh.'

'Yes. Sorry. I just don't feel like going anywhere right now. I'm worried.'

'About what?'

'I don't know, but I have a bad feeling. I don't think I should leave home.'

'Then I'll make a deal with you,' the wolf suggested. 'If you go with your master, I won't. I'll stay here. I'll stay with Black Shawl and They Are Afraid.'

'Promise?'

'Promise.'

'Thanks,' Buffalo Rabbit sighed. 'Stay with us, by all means, but I'm still not going.'

'Then tell that to him,' said Legs.

The flap of the tipi had been drawn aside, and the

vast figure of Gall was looming over Buffalo Rabbit.

'I have come for Buffalo Rabbit,' he told Black Shawl. 'Crazy Horse is ready to leave. He said to take care of yourself. Go to Worm if there is anything you need. We will not be long.'

Black Shawl hesitated, then held a consenting hand towards Buffalo Rabbit.

'Please, take,' she said.

'No.' Buffalo Rabbit whimpered as Gall swept her into his massive arms. 'You don't understand. I need to stay here.'

'Bye,' said Legs as he lay beside the fire. 'Don't worry. Enjoy yourself. Maka Mani's going with you.'

Despite her misgivings, Buffalo Rabbit did enjoy herself. It was good to clear her smoke-befuddled head, good to be on a pony again, and good to have Maka Mani flying alongside. It was also good to spend time with Crazy Horse. Buffalo Rabbit loved Black Shawl and They Are Afraid, but she'd got to know Crazy Horse when he was a bachelor and, on trips like these, he was a bachelor again; living on his wits and jesting and joking with Gall.

When the two friends were satisfied that the Crow wouldn't get to the buffalo before the Lakota could, they turned and headed for home. Maka Mani also turned but, rather than staying with Buffalo Rabbit and the warriors, he suddenly let out a screech, tore into the sky and flew off in a terrible hurry.

'Heavens,' Buffalo Rabbit mumbled. 'What's got into

him? He doesn't usually tear away like that. He must have spotted some carrion.'

As Buffalo Rabbit and the warriors got closer to their campsite, they realised they could see no fires. Closer still, and they saw that the place was deserted. The tipis had gone. All that remained were doused fires, discarded lodge poles and some rusty cooking pots.

The people had moved.

'Very sensible,' thought Buffalo Rabbit. 'They've gone to find fresh grass for the ponies. They may even have found a buffalo herd.'

Crazy Horse and Gall followed the travois tracks and the guiding sticks that had been laid on the trail. Soon, they saw plumes of smoke in the distance. They trotted on towards the site of the new camp. When a black shadow passed over their heads, Buffalo Rabbit glanced up and saw Maka Mani circling in the sky.

'Oh, *that's* nice,' she muttered. 'Look, master, Maka Mani's come to guide us home.'

Then she heard the howl of a wolf.

Legs.

Buffalo Rabbit trembled as she listened to her friend's words.

'I must have misheard,' she muttered to herself.

But then Legs howled again, and Buffalo Rabbit knew that she hadn't misheard.

At the outskirts of the village, she leapt from her pony and raced to find her tipi. She was still searching for it when she saw Worm. He was walking slowly towards Crazy Horse. She spun round and heard him tell Crazy

Horse to be strong. She saw Crazy Horse's body slump, saw Gall reach out and lay a comforting hand on his shoulder. Buffalo Rabbit found her tipi and wriggled beneath its covers.

A collection of small objects was lying beside Crazy Horse's bed. Buffalo Rabbit recognised them all. Worm's most precious medicine necklace was there. So, too, were several scraps of Crazy Horse's famous red blanket and a lock of her own fur. She saw bears' paws and eagles' feet and all of They Are Afraid's favourite toys and clothes. Her first rattle, her first, ever-so-tiny pair of moccasins, her doeskin pony, the white dress that her mother had spent all winter cutting and sewing. The rabbit's tail on a string, the painted sledge with its beaded squirrel-fur blanket, the wooden pony with its miniature travois and tipi.

Buffalo Rabbit shook her head as if to clear it, then stepped towards Black Shawl. She was lying beside the fire, under a heap of blankets and buffalo robes. Buffalo Rabbit reached out a paw and touched her mistress's cheek. It was damp with tears. She lay down and began to lick them away. She heard her master's footsteps running fast towards the tipi. He flung aside the opening and stared at the collection of toys. Then he stepped inside and sank to his knees.

'No!' he groaned. 'No, no, NO!'

His head was in his hands, and his body was crouched, curled in on itself. His long hair streamed around him like a protective curtain. Buffalo Rabbit shuffled up to him and parted the curtain with her nose. Hot tears were teeming down his cheeks.

He sat up, pushed his hair from his face, and gave Buffalo Rabbit a brief, crestfallen smile. Then he threw back his head and let out a terrible, harrowing howl.

'Please, master,' Buffalo Rabbit pleaded. 'Please. Cante chante sica yaun sai ye.'

'He *will* have a sad heart,' whispered a familiar voice. 'He will have a very sad heart for a very long time.'

Legs laid a paw on Buffalo Rabbit's shoulder.

'I knew something was wrong,' Buffalo Rabbit mumbled. 'I knew it, and yet I still went away. I should have stayed here. If I'd stayed here, They Are Afraid would still be alive.'

'No,' said Legs. 'She would not be alive. There was nothing to be done. Worm tried. Everyone tried.'

'I know,' Buffalo Rabbit replied. 'I know you tried.'

She looked across the fire at her mistress, so miserable in her grief. She glanced at her master, the bravest warrior in the world, now huddled in a heap and sobbing like a baby. She stared at the tiny things that The Are Afraid had owned and loved, and the other things, the things that friends had brought to try to cure a little girl and bring her alive again. Buffalo Rabbit stared at these things for a long time, then she, too, threw back her head and howled.

CHAPTER TWENTY-TWO
Moments later

Crazy Horse left the village immediately. He took Legs and Buffalo Rabbit and retraced his steps to the old campsite. That was where They Are Afraid of Her had died, and that was where she'd been laid to rest.

She was lying on a platform at the top of a high scaffold. Her body had been wrapped up warm in a buffalo robe and enclosed in a willow basket. Gifts for the afterlife, toys and trinkets, had been tied to the scaffold, and there was a constant tapping as they swung in the breeze and knocked against the scaffold's frame.

Crazy Horse had brought more toys. The rattle, the rabbit's tail, the doeskin pony, the painted sledge with its squirrel-skin blanket, the wooden pony with its travois and tipi. He carried these things, one by one, to the top of the scaffold, and placed them on the platform.

Then he lay beside his daughter and wept.

After two days, Legs began to worry.

'Do you think I should catch him some food?' he asked.

'No,' Buffalo Rabbit replied. 'He won't eat it.'

'What about water? He hasn't had a sip since we got here.'

'There's water on his pony. He doesn't want to

drink.'

'How long can he stay like this?' Legs asked.

'As long as it takes,' said Buffalo Rabbit.

CHAPTER TWENTY-THREE
Bo's House.
The 21st Century

Bo's head was resting on her paws. Her tail was tucked beneath her, and her ears were flat to her head.

'Cante chante sica yaun sai ye,' said Cavendish kindly.

'I *do* have a sad heart,' Bo replied. 'My heart is very sad. I can't help that. It's sad because Crazy Horse's daughter has died. Why? Why did she die?'

'She probably had a tummy bug,' said the spaniel. 'Small children often died of things like that in those days. Not just Indian children. These were Victorian times, remember. The medicines weren't as good as today's.'

'Indian medicines were,' Bo retorted. 'Indian medicines were made from natural things like herbs and roots. Crazy Horse was shot in the mouth, remember. He was shot in the mouth and the bullet came out through the back of his skull, but *he* survived.'

'Yes, but Crazy Horse wasn't a child. He was immensely strong. He rode every day, had loads of fresh air and a fantastic diet. He also had a will of iron. That is why Crazy Horse survived.'

'And his pebbles. Don't forget his pebbles.'

'Those, and maybe the Indian medicine. Something certainly worked. Crazy Horse's injuries were bad, but he wasn't alone. Other warriors got shot by Crow, gored by buffalo, attacked by bears, bayoneted by soldiers, bitten by snakes. All sorts of things happened. Painful things. Things that would have killed most people. And yet they recovered. Without so much as an aspirin. Remarkable, really.'

'But not They Are Afraid?'

'No,' Cavendish replied. 'They Are Afraid was too little. She wasn't as strong as the warriors were.'

'What did Crazy Horse do? His heart must have broken.'

'Yes,' said Cavendish. 'But Crazy Horse had a big heart. A strong heart. You know that. He believed in the afterlife. He knew that the spirits would take care of his daughter. He knew she was safe. Her death made him focus. Now, more than ever, he wanted to fight for life. The old way of life. He began to teach, to pass down his knowledge. He wanted every child to grow up with that knowledge, just as he had done.'

'I remember that,' said Bo. 'Now you say it, I remember watching him. He'd teach the boys how to make fletchings and arrows, how to string a bow, how to notch it differently for fighting or hunting. He'd give them lessons on their ponies. He'd show them how to train a riding pony, a fighter, a hunter. He'd even show them how to steal meat from the drying lines. He'd find the best old ladies in the village, and get them to teach the girls about curing and stretching the animal skins, and how to bead a buffalo robe. The children loved him.

They loved learning how to live wild.'

'He believed it would keep them free.'

'Yes,' said Bo. 'He did. He wouldn't have bothered, otherwise.'

CHAPTER TWENTY-FOUR
North of Paha Sapa, Dakota Territory.
July, The Moon of Making Fat, 1874

A ribbon of dust was puffing across the sun-scorched plains. The dust had been kicked up by hundreds of wagons and thousands of men, most of them soldiers. They were headed straight for Paha Sapa, the sacred Black Hills, and their leader was George Armstrong Custer.

Custer and his men made camp in a beautiful, flower-filled valley. Maka Mani knew the valley well. It was where he'd been hatched and fallen from his nest. It was where he'd lain, half-dead and with both wings broken, until Worm had found and rescued him. Now the raven was back, and watching closely as the men who weren't soldiers began their work. Some collected wild flowers, laid them on blotting paper and pressed them flat. Others dug up the bones of the giant beasts who'd lived many, many moons ago. Still others found the imprints of ancient ferns and creatures embedded in the rocks. The men made drawings and wrote things down in notebooks. They were strange men, and what they were doing was strange, but the raven could see no harm in it all.

Far more worrying were the other men, the men who

crouched by Paha Sapa's streams, who sifted the water and peered at its contents. These men were searching for something, and the raven knew what it was. This something had been found in Paha Sapa before, but it had never been allowed to leave. It had never reached the outside world because its finders had always been murdered. These finders hadn't all been white men. Some had been Indian. Indians did not murder their own. Not unless that murder could save a whole people. Not unless it could save a dark secret. The secret of Paha Sapa was dark. It was dark as her mountain pines. It was sparkling as her rushing streams. Paha Sapa's secret was gold.

Later, Maka Mani would say that he could have stopped the letter. He could have dive-bombed the soldier who carried it, knocked him from his horse, even killed him, if necessary. The other birds had told the raven not to blame himself. Custer was always writing letters. There'd been no way of knowing that one of them had contained the secret. And so, the letter had not been intercepted. It had arrived at Fort Laramie, where its message had been converted to code and tapped out by telegraph. Soon, the wires had jumped, the newspaper presses had rolled, and the bankrupt, penniless cities of the east had been cock-a-hoop with joy.

Paha Sapa's secret was out.

Custer had found her gold.

Custer had saved America.

CHAPTER TWENTY-FIVE
The Powder River Country, Wyoming Territory.
The following Summer, 1875

Buffalo Rabbit was cooling off in a stream. She'd waded to a spit of pebbles and was lying prone. Her hind legs were spread out behind her, and her chin was resting at the water's edge. She was relaxing, almost asleep, when two ponies plunged in beside her and splashed her all over.

'Crows!'

She scrambled to her feet and shook herself furiously.

'Good day to you, too, Rabbit!' said one of the ponies' riders.

'Young Man Afraid? Is that you? It is! It is!' Buffalo Rabbit tried not to bark. 'And American Horse!'

She hadn't seen Young Man Afraid and American Horse since they'd moved their people out of the wild and into The Red Cloud Agency. That had been nearly two years ago. Crazy Horse hadn't agreed with this decision, but he'd supported it. He loved these two old friends of his. More importantly, they were Lakota. They'd been free to do whatever they believed was best for their people. And they'd believed that agency life would be easier for the young, the old and the sick.

Buffalo Rabbit leapt onto American Horse's pony.

'Stop, stop!' he laughed as she licked his face. 'Where is your master? Will you take us to him?'

'Yes!' Buffalo Rabbit wagged her tail.

She hitched a ride across the river, then proudly escorted the friends to Crazy Horse's tipi.

'How long are you staying?' Crazy Horse asked them excitedly. 'Long enough to hunt with us, I hope. We will take He Dog. It will be just like the old days.'

'We will certainly stay a night or two, if we may,' American Horse replied. 'We also have a message for you. But first, here are some gifts.'

He handed Crazy Horse a package.

'It is not much. Some beads and ribbon for Black Shawl, and a box of American bullets for you. We heard about They Are Afraid Of Her. We are so sorry.'

'Thank you,' said Crazy Horse as he unravelled the package's yellowing paper. 'And thank you for the gifts. It was not needed. It is good to see you. Come. Let us go for a walk. You can give me your message.'

'The message can wait for this evening,' Young Man Afraid replied. 'Do you know where Sitting Bull is? He should also hear our message.'

'Sitting Bull?' Crazy Horse frowned and narrowed his eyes. 'Yes, of course. He is camped nearby. We can send someone to fetch him. Should they fetch Two Moons as well? How important is this message of yours?'

'Very important,' said Young Man Afraid. 'It is very important.'

When Crazy Horse and his visitors had left for their

walk, Buffalo Rabbit wandered over to the package.

'Pretty ribbons,' she mumbled. 'Black Shawl will be pleased with those. And a box of proper, American bullets. But what's this?'

She placed her paws on the package's paper and gently smoothed it flat. In its centre was a picture of a man. The picture was in black and white but, even without any colour, the man's long hair and matching moustache were unmistakable.

Buffalo Rabbit grabbed the paper in her teeth and ran to find Legs.

'Young Man Afraid and American Horse have come to visit!' she told the wolf. 'They brought presents! And you'll never guess what they were wrapped in. Look,' she spread the paper on the ground. 'It's a picture of Long Hair Custer. In a newspaper!'

'So this is what he looks like,' Legs growled as he examined the photograph. 'My, my. The famous Custer. He puts me in mind of a hawk, what with his long nose and sharp eyes. I wonder what he's done to get himself in the paper.'

'It must be something important. It's on the front page! See the size of the letters? They're *huge*. That's what you call a *headline*.'

'And what does this *headline* say, Rabbit? You can read, can't you?'

'I *used* to be able to. A *bit*. A long time ago...'

'Well, then. See what you can remember.'

Buffalo Rabbit stared at the paper.

'I'm not sure. I...'

She racked her brains and tried to recall McGuffey's

Reader, how Effie had pronounced its letters, and what they had stood for.

'This first one's a G,' she finally said. 'G is for girl.'

'Good. Go on.'

'**G** is for girl. **O** is for ox, **L** is for lark, **D** is for dog. Girl, ox, lark, dog.'

'Girl, ox, lark dog?'

'I know. It doesn't make sense. But that's what it says.'

'What are the next two letters?'

'**I** for ink, **N** for nut.'

'Then?'

'**B** for box, **L** for lark, **A** for ax, **C** for cat, **K** for kid.'

'The last five. What are they?'

'**H** for hen, **I** for ink, **L** for lark, another **L** for lark, **S** for sun.'

'I'm none the wiser.'

'Me neither,' Buffalo Rabbit agreed. 'But I *can* tell you one thing.'

'What's that?'

'This paper isn't recent. See how yellow it is? When Mr Irvine knew he was going to Oregon, he started keeping his papers for the packing up. The older they got, the more yellow they got. This one's six months old, at least.'

'Then so is its news,' said Legs. 'We might not be able to read it, but we already know what it says. The Indians will have heard this news when it was still fresh. They probably heard it before this paper was even printed. Nothing gets past the Indians.'

Black Shawl had been cooking all afternoon, and now everyone had gathered inside her tipi.

Sitting Bull and Two Moons had arrived, and so had He Dog. They would *all* listen to Young Man Afraid and American Horse's message.

Crazy Horse filled the barrel of his pipe and tampered it down with his thumb. He held the pipe to the four corners of the earth, to the ground beneath and the skies above, then lit it and handed it to Young Man Afraid.

'Tell us,' he said. 'Tell us your message.'

Young Man Afraid sighed a long sigh.

'Smoke,' Crazy Horse urged him. 'Smoke the pipe and speak the truth.'

'The truth,' Young Man Afraid replied, 'is that The Great Father in Washington is sending his people to talk with us.'

'Talk about what?' He Dog asked.

'The Black Hills.'

'Paha Sapa?'

'Yes,' said Young Man Afraid. 'The white men want to buy Paha Sapa.'

'Now they ask us,' said Crazy Horse quietly. 'It is many moons since Long Hair found the yellow powder. The white men have already built their mines in Paha Sapa. They have built their places for the sleeping and the whiskey drinking and the meeting with bad women. They have done all of this without asking us.'

'They have done all of this,' American Horse nodded, 'and now we who live at the agency have no berries, no hunting and no trees from which to take our lodge poles. These things are not given to us at the agency.

We had them from the hills, but since Long Hair found the yellow powder we cannot enter the hills. We cannot collect its berries and meat and we cannot reach its trees. We at the agency have a new name for Long Hair. We call him Wamanuncha.'

'Wamanuncha?' Buffalo Rabbit repeated.

'Thief,' Legs translated. 'Wamanuncha is Lakota for thief.'

'The hills are still ours,' said Crazy Horse. 'They are ours and we will not sell them. One does not sell the earth upon which the people walk.'

'We have no interest in the yellow powder,' Sitting Bull added. 'We just want the hills. They are a sacred. The hills are not for sale.'

'That is what we hoped you would say,' said Young Man Afraid. 'We say the same. We should not sell the hills.'

'You will fight for them?' Sitting Bull asked.

'We *will* fight,' Young Man Afraid replied, 'but not with the gun. We must learn to live in peace with the white man. If we do not, then he will wipe us out. He will wipe us out, just as he is wiping out the buffalo. He will wipe out our customs, our language and our ways. He will do all of this if we cannot learn to live with him.'

'Why must it always be us?' Sitting Bull wondered aloud. 'Cannot the white man also learn?'

'I agree,' Two Moons nodded. 'The white man is new to this land. We could teach him many things.'

Crazy Horse shook his head.

'Have you forgotten our brothers?' he said. 'Have you forgotten the tribes who welcomed the white man? They welcomed him and gave him their knowledge and the white man drove them away. Or killed them. We were many, many nations before the white man arrived. Now we are few.'

'That is true,' Two Moons said sadly.

'And what of Red Cloud?' He Dog asked. 'Red Cloud has the ear of the white man. What is Red Cloud's opinion on the hills?'

'He thinks we should sell,' said American Horse. 'He says we should talk whilst we still have the chance. We should fix a good price. The yellow powder makes many dollars. We should take many dollars for the hills, and then we should touch the pen. Red Cloud believes that if we do not sell the hills, then the white man will take them anyway.'

'He could be right about that,' offered He Dog. 'This talk, is the place and time arranged?'

'Yes,' Young Man Afraid nodded. 'It will be on The White River in the Moon of the Black Calf.'

'I will not go,' said Crazy Horse. 'Tell the agency I will not go. I will send someone to hear what is said, but I do not wish to sell Paha Sapa.'

'I will not go, either,' Sitting Bull added. 'I will not sell Paha Sapa.'

He brushed his hand over the floor of the tipi and gathered a pinch of earth.

'Not even as much as this.'

He open his fingers, and the earth flew into the fire.

CHAPTER TWENTY-SIX
Bo's House.
The 21st Century

'To sell, or not to sell?' Cavendish asked. 'That was the question.'

'I would have sold,' Bo replied. 'I'd have held out for as much money as I could get, and then I'd have touched the pen. Red Cloud knew the white man. He knew how they operated. He thought they would take the hills, no matter what the Indians did, and I think he was right.'

'And what would Buffalo Rabbit have done?'

'She would have said Paha Sapa could not be sold. No land could be sold. Land was where the spirits lived. It reached to the sky and deep under ground. How can you sell that? How can you sell the streams and wild berries? Why are you laughing?'

'Because you've put your paw right on the button,' chuckled the spaniel. 'The Indians and the white man could not have been more different. One wanted the old ways, the other wanted the new. The white men were *inventors,* never more so than in Crazy Horse's time. The sewing machine, the typewriter, the can opener, safety pins, bicycles, barbed wire, plastic, dynamite, lifts, traffic lights, mail order catalogues, the beginning of the car, all sorts of newfangled gadgets...'

'But the Indians didn't need those things,' Bo protested. 'They didn't need machines to sew. They sewed by hand, with buffalo needles and buffalo twine. They didn't need can openers. There was fresh food on their doorstep. They didn't need to type when they couldn't read or write. And why would you want a bicycle when you have a pony?'

'You wouldn't,' agreed Cavendish. 'The Indians had everything they needed, and more. The only things they ever invented were the tipi and the travois.'

'Both were thousands of years old,' said Bo. 'And yet they were perfect. The tipi was warm in winter, cool in summer and easy to look after. There wasn't any housework. When things got dirty, you moved the whole house. You bundled everything up, loaded it onto a travois and went elsewhere. What's not to like? What could be easier? It gave the Indians time. They always had time. Time to swim and play with their children. Time to chat and sit in the sun. The Irvines didn't have time. Mr Irvine was always chasing his tail. He milked cows at dawn, ploughed or sowed or harvested all day, milked the cows again, then collapsed into bed after supper, only to fret about the cost of horse shoes.'

'He was one of the lucky ones...'

'*Lucky*! Why lucky?'

'You think that life on a farm was hard? Life in a city could be hell. You wouldn't believe how some people lived. They were crushed together in small rooms with no windows, no water, no nothing. When they got up at dawn, they didn't go out to milk cows, they went to terrible, dangerous factories, and they took their children with them.'

'Red Cloud had been to the white man's cities.'

'Yes,' the spaniel nodded his silky head. 'He had. The white man's power and wealth had been a big shock to him. Goodness knows what he'd have thought of how that wealth was made, the factories and the eight-year-old children who worked in them. He never saw those, but he saw the broken promises. He didn't trust the white man. He was certain they were trying to cheat him. He told them Paha Sapa was not for sale.'

CHAPTER TWENTY-SEVEN

The Powder River Country, Wyoming Territory.
December, The Moon of Popping Trees, 1875

Three months after the Indians refused to sell Paha Sapa, a messenger arrived in The Powder River Country. It was the middle of winter, a blizzard was raging, and yet this messenger had ridden all the way from The Red Cloud Agency. No one could quite believe what they were seeing.

'You rode through this snow?' Crazy Horse was incredulous.

'Yes,' the messenger shivered. 'I barely stopped for rest, and it *still* took me three times longer than usual.'

'You could not have waited for spring?'

'No,' said the messenger. 'And neither can you.'

He took a deep breath.

'I have been sent here to tell you that you must move your people to The Red Cloud Agency. Not just your people. Every Indian on the plains must go there. You have until the end of January.'

'January? What is January?'

'The next moon,' the messenger replied. 'The Moon of Frost in the Lodge.'

'We cannot do that!' Crazy Horse exclaimed. 'How can we move our people in this weather? It is impossible out there. You know that. Your journey has taken you three times longer than usual, and you are just one man and a pony. You have no old people, no one young or sick. You have no ponies to herd or travois to haul. Look. Look at this!'

He knelt down, gathered a fistful of snow and scrunched it into a ball. Then he stood up and hurled it out of the village, where it disappeared into the drifts.

'That is how far we would get!' he spat. 'And what are we supposed to do at night? We are sheltered here, and still the wind blows around the tipis. Out there on the plains? We would not stand a chance.'

'It is ridiculous,' the messenger agreed, 'but that is what they want you to do.'

'Who are *they*?'

'The government.'

'Is this because of Paha Sapa?' asked Crazy Horse. 'Are they doing this because we will not sell the hills?'

'I do not know. All I know is that they want you in the agency. They say that if you do not meet their deadline they will consider you hostile. They will send their soldiers against you.'

'They might,' said Crazy Horse. 'But not yet. If *we* cannot move in this weather, then neither can they.'

CHAPTER TWENTY-EIGHT

The Powder River Country, Wyoming Territory.
Six weeks later
February, The Moon of the Dark Red Calves, 1876

The snow had continued to fall. It had fallen so heavily that even the messenger had been trapped in camp.

The government's deadline had come and gone.

Now, in an unexpected thaw, He Dog came to Crazy Horse's tipi and tapped on its walls. Legs and Buffalo Rabbit wagged their tails, but He Dog refused to enter the tipi, even when Black Shawl called to him.

'Please,' she said. 'Come in. Take a seat.'

He Dog pushed the entrance flap aside, then stayed where he was, head bowed.

'What is the matter?' Crazy Horse asked.

'The messenger is going to use the thaw to get back to the agency,' He Dog said quietly. 'I will go, too. I will take my people to the agency. I do not expect you to agree with me, I just wanted to... '

'Come in,' Crazy Horse coaxed. 'Sit. We will make you some coffee. I think we have a few grains left.'

'Thank you,' He Dog sighed. 'You are a good friend. I do not expect you to agree with me,' he repeated as he crouched by the fire. 'But I believe we must *all* go to the agency, sooner or later. I do not want to be chased there by soldiers. I do not want my children to be chased there by soldiers. I would rather take them there myself.'

Crazy Horse drew Buffalo Rabbit onto his lap.

'I understand,' he said. 'But we do not know how long this thaw will last. If the snows return...'

'We will travel as swiftly as we can.'

'Are your ponies good for the journey? The ground will be heavy going. What will you do if something goes wrong?'

'My ponies are good enough.'

Crazy Horse glanced at Black Shawl who handed He Dog a horn of hot coffee, then quietly left the tipi.

'Go to the camp of Two Moons,' Crazy Horse suggested. 'He and his Cheyenne are south of here, just two sleeps away. They will welcome you. You can stop overnight. If the thaw holds, you can move on. If not, you can stay. You will be safe there.'

'Thank you,' He Dog replied. 'I will do that.'

He sipped his coffee.

'Don't go, He Dog,' Buffalo Rabbit whimpered. 'Stay here. *Please* stay here. It'll be spring, soon. There'll be new grass and new buffalo to hunt. We've already lost Young Man Afraid and American Horse to the agency. We don't want to lose you, too.'

'We won't lose him, Rabbit,' said Legs. 'He'll come back to visit.'

'But supposing they don't let him come back. Supposing they keep him there.'

'They can't do that. They can't force people to stay at the agency. It isn't a prison...'

Legs tailed off, and Black Shawl re-entered the tipi.

'Drink up,' Crazy Horse told He Dog. 'Take your people south before the snows return. Take my hunting pony, too. He is strong and well and waiting outside.'

He Dog shook his head.

'No,' he said. 'I cannot do that.'

'Take him. I want you to take him,' Crazy Horse smiled. 'You know that I will need him for the spring hunting?'

'Thank you,' He Dog smiled back. 'I will return him in time for the hunting. We will hunt together.'

He stroked Buffalo Rabbit's ears and ruffled Legs' deep, silvery fur.

'I will be back soon,' he said. 'Keep your master and mistress safe, you two. Good-bye.'

He stood to go, and there was a rustle of wings. Maka Mani had left his perch at the top of the tipi. Now he was prancing at He Dog's feet.

'Maka Mani's going with him,' Buffalo Rabbit groaned. 'Everyone's leaving us. Everyone's going to the agency.'

'Maka Mani's not leaving us,' said Legs. 'He's just seeing He Dog on his way. That's all. Maka Mani will never leave us.'

CHAPTER TWENTY-NINE

The Powder River Country, Wyoming Territory.
March, The Moon of Snow Blindness, 1876

In the middle of March, the snows returned.

Then, early one morning, Crazy Horse's tipi began to shake. Something was pounding its outer walls.

Crazy Horse threw aside his buffalo robe and grabbed his rifle. He was unpinning the entrance to his tipi when the pounding stopped, there was a piercing squawk, and Maka Mani hurtled through the vent in the roof and dived, bill first, towards the floor.

'What's up?' Buffalo Rabbit asked as the raven glanced off the ground and threw himself against the tipi's sides.

'Snow-blindness,' said Legs. 'He must have snow-blindness. See how bedraggled he is? His feathers are all messed up.'

'It's no wonder. If he keeps flying into things like that he'll have no feathers left. We should get him to Worm. Worm will sprinkle his eyes with snow. That'll cure him.'

Crazy Horse had come to the same conclusion. He was holding out a finger and calling Maka Mani's name.

But the bird was having none of it.

He settled beside a buffalo robe and caught it in his beak. Then he beat his wings and tugged.

'What does he want with a robe?' Legs wondered aloud.

'And what does he want with wasna?' Buffalo Rabbit added.

The raven had dropped the robe and was now raking at Black Shawl's store of wasna.

Black Shawl went to help him.

'Are you hungry?' she asked. 'Here. Take it.'

Maka Mani took the dried meat in his beak but, rather then gulping it down as expected, he hopped towards the tipi's entrance.

'Follow him!' said Legs.

'Something is wrong,' Crazy Horse told Black Shawl. 'Fetch me a pony, No. Fetch me *two* ponies. Anybody's. Find the fittest you can. And get the village crier. Legs? Come here. You, too, Rabbit.'

Whilst Black Shawl hurried away, Crazy Horse began to gather every robe, fur and blanket in the tipi. He threw some onto Legs' back, some onto Buffalo Rabbit's, and carried the rest outside.

The wasna was still in the raven's beak, and his eyes were still darting, but he'd calmed down a little. He seemed pleased to be getting his message across, and when Black Shawl returned with the village crier and not two, but three ponies, he cawed in approval.

'What has happened?' the crier asked.

'I do not know,' Crazy Horse replied as he hurriedly lashed the robes and furs to the ponies. 'But I know it is something bad. I want you to wake the village. Tell everyone to feed their fires and heat any food they have.'

'Where are you going?'

'I do not know that, either. But he does,' Crazy Horse nodded in Maka Mani's direction. 'I hope.'

Maka Mani took the cue. He guided Crazy Horse, Legs and Buffalo Rabbit out of the village and onto a well-worn travois track. The snow was beginning to melt, but the track had frozen into sharp ridges and icy ruts. The rising sun was pale and milky, the earth was shrouded in fog, and every sound was amplified in the stillness; the frosty crunch of footsteps, the dripping of thaw water, the scampering of small animals.

They heard the pony before they saw it.

It was trotting fast on the iron-hard ground. Maka Mani flew towards the noise and, for a moment, both he and it were lost in a dip in the track. Then, suddenly, the pony emerged through the fog. It was Crazy Horse's hunting pony, the one he'd lent to He Dog, but the rider wasn't He Dog. It was a boy. Tears of relief were streaming down his face and his teeth were chattering with cold. He was one of Two Moons' Cheyenne.

'I was coming to fetch you,' he stammered.

He pointed behind him but Crazy Horse raised a hand.

He didn't need to be told.

He could see them, now.

There was something unearthly about them. They had no face or form as they rose out of the dip. Their features were lost in a swirl of fog. But, as they moved closer, the fog cleared, and they became terribly, horribly, desperately human.

They were women and children and old folk. Most were wearing nothing but a sodden blanket. All were walking. Some were barefoot, others had managed to bind their feet with strips of cloth. Their ankles were puffy and grey and swollen, and the cloth was wet and muddy, bloody in some cases. Babies and toddlers were clinging silently to their mothers' naked chests. Their flesh was blue. Youngsters were trying to stop the old and proud from stumbling. They were holding them up by their elbows and pushing away the strands of hair that plastered their faces.

'How long?' Crazy Horse asked.

'Four days,' the boy replied.

There were no swear words in the Lakota language.

'Ride to the village,' Crazy Horse urged the boy, 'tell them we are coming.'

The boy nodded, pressed his bare legs to the pony's sides and began to trot away.

'No. Wait!' Crazy Horse called after him.

'Yes?'

'He Dog?'

Buffalo Rabbit and Legs whipped their heads round. They'd completely forgotten about their old friend.

'He is well,' said the boy.

'Two Moons?'

'Him, too. They are both well. They are somewhere at the back.'

Legs and Buffalo Rabbit stood quietly as the people filed past and took the robes and furs from their and the ponies' backs. Crazy Horse handed a robe to an elderly couple. They'd been sharing a blanket that was so frozen it had stiffened to their shape. When they took it off, it stayed like that. Crazy Horse threw it aside in disgust, turned his head, wiped the tears from his eyes, and looked back towards the village. The crier had done as asked. Fresh smoke was billowing from the tipi tops and the outdoor campfires had burst into life. Hot food would soon be bubbling in the pots. Crazy Horse sighed and smiled at Legs and Buffalo Rabbit. They had seen his tears, but the people had not. He would not show his tears to them.

The refugees straggled into the village, and all were welcomed. Every tipi played host to eight or more guests, over three-hundred in all. Only a few were He Dog's Lakota. Most were Two Moons' Cheyenne.

That night, He Dog and Two Moons told their story.

'After we left you,' He Dog began, 'we headed for Two Moons' camp. The thaw held and we reached the camp easily. We stayed awhile, then, just as we were about to move on to the agency, the snows came again.'

'We were camped in a creek,' said Two Moons. 'We were sheltered there. We had not even posted guards. On the second day of snow, one of the boys went to check on the ponies. It was very early. Dark outside. We were all fast asleep.'

'The boy saw horse soldiers,' He Dog continued. 'There were hundreds of them, coming forward in a line. We had no time to get dressed. The men grabbed their weapons. The women and children ran. They hid in the undergrowth. We could not reach our ponies. The horse soldiers had cut them off from us. We were fighting on foot. Mostly with arrows. We were lucky to lose only one warrior.'

'The soldiers were four times our number,' Two Moons explained. 'Bullets were whistling all around, but the soldiers did not stay long. Before they left, they drove our ponies away and set fire to our village. They burned everything. We did not understand that. They were cold, yet they did not take our furs and robes. They must have been hungry, yet they did not take our meat. They burned it all. They burned our lodges. We had more than one hundred lodges. Now we have none.'

'We decided to come back here,' added He Dog. 'So the women, children and old folks set off, and Two Moons and I stayed behind to help find the ponies. Then we caught up.'

'How many ponies?' Crazy Horse asked.

'We had more than ten hundreds,' Two Moons replied. 'We got five hundreds back. It would have been more, but the warriors ran into more soldiers. One of them recognised the soldier chief.'

'Long Hair,' groaned Crazy Horse.

'No. It was not him,' said Two Moons. 'The way the soldiers came at dawn, in the snow, when everyone was sleeping? That is what Long Hair did at The Washita. But this was not Long Hair. This was another. We call him Three Stars. The white men call him Crook.'

'I do not understand these white men,' Crazy Horse shook his head. 'They ask us to go to the agency. They give us a deadline, but we cannot move because of the snow. Even their messenger cannot move. Then, at the first sign of thaw, He Dog heads for the agency. He stops to camp with you, Two Moons, but the snow comes again. And what do these white men do? They attack you both. They creep up like the wolf who digs the sleeping animal from its winter burrow. Well, I am not going to any agency. Not after this.'

'Me neither.' He Dog replied.

'I agree,' said Two Moons, 'but the soldiers will come again. The deadline of the government is past. They told us they would send soldiers if we did not go to the agency, and they have done so. Those soldiers will come again.'

'We will be ready,' Crazy Horse answered quietly.

CHAPTER THIRTY

The Tongue River, The Rosebud Country.
May, The Moon of the Strawberries, 1876

As soon as the He Dog and Two Moons people had recovered, Crazy Horse had moved everyone to Sitting Bull's village in The Rosebud Country.

The first thing Sitting Bull had done was to ask his Hunkpapa to help their friends who'd lost so much. The Hunkpapa had responded immediately. They'd donated tipis, robes, travois, ponies, packsaddles, food, clothes, pots, pans, blankets and cradle-boards. By the end of the second day, the He Dog and Two Moons camps had been given all they needed to hunt, cook, travel and stay warm.

Meanwhile, Crazy Horse and Sitting Bull had been making plans and sending signals. Mirrors had glinted on hilltops, blankets had fluttered on ridges, and puffs of smoke had risen from the earth.

'Come!' the signals had said. 'Come join us for the summer! Come join Sitting Bull and Crazy Horse! There will be hunting and feasting for all!'

The invitation had been irresistible. Indians had come from every direction, and so had the latest news.

The Santee Sioux had reported seeing a huge army camp on The Yellowstone River. They'd said that the camp had guns on wheels, many supply wagons, and a whole herd of beef cattle, just to feed its soldiers. There were hundreds and hundreds of soldiers. One of those soldiers was Long Hair Custer.

The agency Indians had reported seeing Three Stars Crook. He'd gone south to get more soldiers, then come north again. Now he and his soldiers had built a camp at Goose Creek in The Powder River Country.

'Goose Creek?' Buffalo Rabbit had said when she heard this news, 'but that's less than a hundred miles from here!'

She'd raised her head and gazed at the Big Horn Mountains.

'Mountains to the west of us,' she'd said quietly, 'cities to the east. Long Hair to the north and Three Stars to the south.'

'Indeed,' Legs had nodded, 'but look at what we have right here. This may be the largest gathering of Indians the world has ever seen, and they're still arriving.'

'We have something else, too,' Buffalo Rabbit had added. 'We have Crazy Horse. We have the finest *warrior* the world has ever seen.'

CHAPTER THIRTY-ONE

Ash Creek, The Rosebud Country, Montana Territory.
16th June, The Moon of Making Fat, 1876

The Sitting Bull and Crazy Horse village was now so vast that it had to keep moving just to feed its seven-thousand people and ten-thousand ponies. This amazing exercise was always carried out in the same way. The Cheyenne went first. They dismantled their tipis, packed their possessions, loaded their travois and set off. They were followed by the Lakota: Brulé and Oglala, Minneconjou, Blackfoot, Sans Arc, Two Kettle and Santee. Finally, bringing up and guarding the rear, came the Hunkpapa. By the time Hunkpapa reached a new camp ground, the Cheyenne would have pitched their circle of tipis and cooked and eaten their supper.

Yesterday, the village had moved to Ash Creek.

Buffalo Rabbit sat down on the warm grass and looked around her.

Women were gossiping, children were playing, teenagers were strutting and flirting. Boys were racing ponies and girls were playing with dolls. There was plenty of grass, plenty of wild fruit, and plenty of buffalo in the nearby herd. Nothing was urgent. No one was rushing. The weather was wonderful, the hunting sublime. The

Indians were trying not to think about the soldiers on The Yellowstone and down at Goose Creek. They were trying not to think about any of that. They were having the best summer of their lives.

Nobody was enjoying the summer more than the agency Indians. The young ones were desperate to meet their famous war-leaders. They'd heard stories about Gall, Sitting Bull and Crazy Horse, but they'd never seen them. Some had never seen a buffalo. Now they were learning how to hunt them.

'With guns,' Buffalo Rabbit noted sniffily. 'They all have guns. Why guns and not arrows?'

'Because the agency give them guns,' Legs explained. 'They have to, really. The agency supplies are erratic, to say the least. Those guns are old and cranky, but they're fine for shooting the odd bit of game. If the agency Indians couldn't do that, they'd probably starve. There was hardly any food at all this winter. People were eating their dogs and ponies.'

'Young Man Afraid and American Horse were wrong, then,' Buffalo Rabbit sighed. 'Life at the agencies isn't easier. It's harder.'

'Much harder,' Legs nodded.

'So do you think Young Man Afraid and American Horse will join us for the summer?'

'No,' Legs replied. 'I don't think they will. They don't believe in fighting the whites.'

'But there might not be a fight. The soldiers might not come.'

'They'll come,' said Legs. 'Listen,' he held up a paw,

'can you hear something?'

Buffalo Rabbit tipped her head.

'Yes,' she said. 'I can hear wolf cries. *Human* wolf cries. From Cheyenne, I think.'

'They must have spotted something. Quick, Rabbit. We need to get back to Crazy Horse.'

The Cheyenne had been on a hunting trip. Now they'd come racing home. They'd seen Three Stars Crook. He'd left his camp at Goose Creek and was marching towards the village.

Sitting Bull called a meeting in the council lodge. By then, the story was out, and the peaceful camp had boiled into a cauldron of speculation.

'The soldiers are many,' one of the Cheyenne told the meeting. 'Ten hundreds or more.'

'Ten *hundreds!*'

'Are they walking or riding?' asked Gall.

'Both.'

'Where are they?'

'Less than one sleep away.'

'Do they know we are here?'

'I do not think so,' the Cheyenne replied. 'But they have many scouts. Good, Crow scouts.'

'Then they will find us,' He Dog groaned.

'Yes,' Gall agreed. 'But not if we find them first. We must find them first and chase them away.'

'We cannot do that,' said a Sans Arc. 'We cannot leave the women and children. There are other soldiers, too. Supposing they come when our warriors are gone?'

'What is the news about these other soldiers?' Sitting

Bull asked a scout.

'They are still on The Yellowstone,' the scout replied. 'They have not moved.'

'Then they are four sleeps from here,' said Crazy Horse quietly. 'They cannot reach Three Stars before we do. We have plenty warriors. We could take ten hundreds for the fight against Three Stars and leave twice that many to guard the people.'

'That is true,' He Dog nodded. 'I will follow Crazy Horse!'

'I, also!'

'HOYE!'

'But how will we do this thing?' muttered a Minneconjou. 'We have never met with so many soldiers.'

'We will start by travelling in darkness,' said Crazy Horse.

'Travel in darkness?' whispered a man at the back. 'We never travel in darkness.'

'Exactly, my friend,' Crazy Horse smiled. 'The soldiers are many, but they do not know this land. They do not know the Lakota. They will look to the Crow for knowledge and the Crow will say that the Lakota do not travel in darkness. If we travel in darkness, we can arrive in early morning. That will take the soldiers by surprise!'

'As they do to us?'

'Just as they do to us. And we will do something else the soldiers do. We will ride in a line. A long and orderly line. Four abreast. No more.'

'We never ride in a line.'

'We will ride in a line,' said Crazy Horse firmly. 'That is the way to keep the warriors in check. They must not charge ahead. They must listen. I want akicita on both sides of our line and at the rear. He Dog will organise that. Let him start with them,' he added with a tip of his head.

Some of the younger warriors were already up on their ponies and careering round the council lodge.

'When we find Three Stars,' Crazy Horse continued, 'I want no counting of coup. I want no one to pause for the taking of scalps. The warriors must swear to that. Anyone who does not swear to it must stay behind. We will take ten hundreds and we will leave at the darkest hour. The Cheyenne will ride with me. They will take us to Three Stars. Hoppo!'

'HOYE!'

The air was sharp when the warriors left camp. Buffalo Rabbit was shivering with a mixture of cold, excitement and fear. She could have snuggled deeper into her fighting pouch, but riding through the night with one-thousand warriors was a new experience. She didn't want to miss a second of it, especially as Legs was trotting beside her.

'I don't think I've ever been up this late,' she told him.

'Early,' the wolf corrected her. 'I think you'll find it's early.'

'Everything's so still. The ponies' hooves are like thunder. I hope the soldiers don't hear us.'

'So do I,' the wolf replied. 'Now shush!'

Four hours of travel later, the Cheyenne guides raised their hands and halted their ponies. Three Stars and his soldiers were just ahead, stopped at Rosebud Creek and cooking themselves some breakfast.

The warriors rode a little closer to the creek, found a hidden spot and began their preparations. Out came the mirrors and pouches of pigment, the mixing tools, the feathers, the charms and the talismans. Out came the hatchets, the bows, the arrows and the guns. One young lad had a silver-mounted rifle and a magnificent war-bonnet.

'Who's he?' Buffalo Rabbit asked as the boy strutted about with the bonnet's feathers streaming out behind him. 'Surely he's too young for such a bonnet. A bonnet like that must be earned.'

'It was,' Legs told her. 'Though not by the boy. Red Cloud earned those feathers. The rifle's his, too. It was a present from the government. The boy is his son, Jack Red Cloud.'

'Then he shouldn't be wearing that bonnet,' said Buffalo Rabbit sternly.'

When the warriors were painted and preened, they began to relax. Some took out the food that their women had packed for them. Some went to pick berries and stretch their legs. Others slept.

Crazy Horse caught He Dog's eye, touched his right thumb to his chest, laid the first two fingers of his right hand on his left cheek, then lifted them and pointed towards a ridge.

'I am going to look over there,' he was saying.

He moved his hand back to his face, pushed it out in front of him, curled the index finger and drew it towards him. Finally, he made a two-fingered V followed by a thumbs down.

'Come with me. Bring five scouts.'

Looking down from the top of the ridge, the scouting party could see about a thousand soldiers, a mix of cavalry and infantry.

'Crows,' Buffalo Rabbit whimpered. 'That's plenty soldiers.'

'Yes,' Legs agreed. 'I'm afraid it is.'

'I don't want to go down there,' Buffalo Rabbit backed away. 'I don't want to fight those soldiers.'

'No,' Legs sympathised. 'I wouldn't want to, either.'

He Dog and Crazy Horse were discussing the lie of the land. The creek emerged from a narrow canyon and meandered through a valley. The valley was level but the ground was rough and dotted with boulders, scraggy trees and hundreds of rose bushes.

'That canyon would be good for a decoy,' He Dog suggested. 'If we can lead some of the soldiers into it…'

'Maybe,' Crazy Horse considered, 'but the soldiers are nicely scattered. We should scatter them some more. We should come at them from every side.'

'We have never done that before,' said one of the scouts.

'No,' Crazy Horse replied. 'We have not. Which is why we are going to do it now. These soldiers do not fight like us. They fight to kill or be killed. I think sometimes that they have no wives or children. No homes to go to. They do not fight like us, and we cannot fight like them. We can do something better. We can treat them as if they were buffalo. We can work as a team to split their herd. That is what we will do. He Dog? Will you tell the others? The rest of you? Ride a little further. Take a look beyond those trees. Make sure they do not hide something. I will wait here. Come, Rabbit,' he added, 'it is time to get into your fighting pouch. Be quick, now...'

'What should I do?' Buffalo Rabbit whispered to Legs. 'What should I do?'

'I think you should...'

The wolf was interrupted by a sudden shout of surprise. It came from the trees below the ridge, and was followed by several rounds of gunshot. The scouts had stumbled into some of Three Stars' Crow guides. Now the guides were tearing back to the soldiers and hollering at the top of their heads.

'LAKOTA! LAKOTA!'

The noise of the guns and the squealing of the guides had alerted Crazy Horse's warriors. They were already up on their ponies and haring towards the ridge.

'GET DOWN, Rabbit!' Crazy Horse screamed. 'Get down!'

'This way!' Legs barked. 'Come this way, Rabbit. MOVE!'

But Buffalo Rabbit couldn't move. She was mesmerised. She'd never seen warriors from this angle. She'd never seen them come straight at her. So *fast*, they were. So *noisy*. So *colourful*. So *frightening*. So *streaming* with their feathers and pelts, their black braids and their ponies' manes. So *gleaming* in the early morning sunshine. Gleaming skin, gleaming lances, gleaming guns, gleaming, open mouths.

'Oh, for heaven's sake...' the wolf sprang forward, clamped his jaws over Buffalo Rabbit's scruff and dragged her sideways, out of the path of the charging ponies.

'What were you doing?' he asked as the galloping hooves receded into the valley. 'You almost got killed.'

'I don't know,' Buffalo Rabbit replied shakily. 'I don't know *what* I was doing. I just couldn't take my eyes off them.'

'Well, let's hope the soldiers can't, either!' Legs laughed. 'That'll make things easy. Come on. We can watch from the edge of the ridge.'

CHAPTER THIRTY-TWO
Moments later

The Crows' warning had sent the soldiers scrambling into action. The cavalry leapt to their horses, the infantry reached for their guns. Indians were sweeping in from every side. The infantry lined up in blocks, front rows on one knee, back rows standing, then aimed their rifles and fired. Legs and Buffalo Rabbit jumped at the sound, then jumped again as the Indians with guns fired back. Another volley from the infantry, and the cavalry roared, raised their pistols and charged. The Indians nearest them retreated. They caught their breath, reloaded their guns and adjusted their quivers. Meanwhile, more Indians were haring past the soldiers, scattering them, then retreating.

'What's happening?' Buffalo Rabbit asked Legs. 'I can't see much. Except petals. There's an awful lot of petals.'

'You're right,' Legs replied. 'The roses are falling apart. There's a lot of smoke and dust, too. And noise. It's hard to make much out. I *can* see one thing, though.'

'What's that?'

'Red Cloud's war-bonnet.'

Buffalo Rabbit peered through the haze.

'Oh, yes,' she said. 'I can see that, too. It's streaming

out behind young Jack.'

'Well, if *we* can see it, then so can the...whoops! Oh, dear, they've spotted him. The Crow have spotted Jack Red Cloud...'

Jack didn't see the Crow until it was too late. Far too late for his pony. The animal was shot. It crumpled between Jack's legs and crashed to the ground. Jack stumbled out from under it just as one of the Crow swept past him. The Crow lunged, grasped the fabulous warbonnet and whipped it from Jack's head. Another Crow bore down. Jack was shaking by now. He grabbed his father's silver-mounted rifle by the barrel and offered the gun, stock first, to the Crow. The Crow barely paused. He whisked up the desperate offering and galloped away. Jack stood for a moment, then crouched low and zigzagged through the fight.

'Where's he going?' Buffalo Rabbit asked bemusedly.

'Back to daddy, I should think,' said Legs. 'Back to daddy and the agency.'

Whilst Legs and Buffalo Rabbit had been watching Jack Red Cloud's antics, Three Stars Crook had been up to his own. He'd sent three-hundred of his men to the canyon.

'Nuts,' Legs growled. 'The man's nuts. That's a third of his force.'

'So why's he done it?' Buffalo Rabbit asked.

'I don't know. I can't figure it out. Unless he's looking for the village. That could be it. The Crow will have told him the Lakota never travel at night. He probably thinks we've come from nearby.'

'Well, he's wrong. The village is miles away, but the canyon is narrow and dark. Its sides are steep and covered in trees. It's the perfect place for an ambush. Those soldiers are bound to be ambushed.'

'I don't think so,' Legs shook his head. 'Crazy Horse has a thousand warriors. Three Stars *had* a thousand soldiers. The odds were even until Three Stars sent those men to the canyon. Now, though, the odds have turned.'

He raised his head to where Maka Mani was twirling in the sky.

'The odds have turned, Rabbit,' the wolf smiled. 'The odds have turned.

His black gums were glistening in the sunshine.

CHAPTER THIRTY-THREE
Bo's House.
The 21st Century

'You didn't stay to see what happened?' asked Cavendish.

'No,' Bo replied as she snuggled up to her spaniel friend. 'I thought I'd hear that from you. You can tell me.'

'What, because you think I was there?' the spaniel licked a paw. 'You think I was Legs?'

'I *know* you were Legs,' said Bo.

'And *I* know what happened at The Rosebud,' Cavendish grinned, 'it doesn't prove I was there.'

'All right, all right,' Bo conceded. 'Just tell me. Were you correct? Sorry, I mean was *Legs* correct? Had the odds turned?'

'Yes, they had,' the spaniel replied. 'But what's more important is what Crazy Horse did about it. He realised that fighting soldiers was very different from raiding the Crow.'

'To raid the Crow,' Bo intervened, 'you study the village and work out where the ponies are. Then you swarm in and try to steal them. The Crow swarm back at you, everyone shows off...'

'And then you all go home for tea.'

'Well, no. It's a bit more dangerous than that. Very dangerous, actually.'

'I was teasing,' said Cavendish. 'My point is that raiding the Crow was all about honour. It was braver to touch someone than it was to kill them. Soldiers were different. They didn't count coup. They didn't swarm. They had drills. They formed orderly blocks. They stayed together. If they were cavalry, they charged together. If they were infantry, they fired together. They didn't let off one bullet at a time, they let off fifty.'

'A wall of fire,' said Bo. 'You can't swarm into that!'

'Ah! So what do you do?'

'You do what Crazy Horse did,' Bo replied. 'You treat the wall like a buffalo herd. The herd is strong when it's running together. But if you *split* it, you weaken it. To do that, you must work as a team. Or a pack. It's just what a pack of wolves would do, but I'm sure you know that...'

Cavendish ignored the bait.

'Go on,' he said.

'You come in from every side. Some of the herd will escape, but that's all right. The rest won't like being separated from their friends. They'll panic. They'll bunch together in smaller groups. It's easier to deal with them, then.'

'My word. Lieutenant Bo!' Cavendish laughed. 'You've got it exactly. Treat soldiers like buffalo, *that's* what Crazy Horse had learned. Work as a team and you weaken the wall. It was a brilliant piece of thinking. More brilliant still, Crazy Horse managed to carry it through. He got his warriors to work together, just as if they were hunting.'

'Three Stars did him a favour when he sent those soldiers to the canyon,' said Bo. 'He split his own herd!'

'Yes,' said Cavendish. 'Crazy Horse took notice of that. He did his sums, saw an opportunity, and took it. He ignored the soldiers in the canyon and concentrated on the rest.'

'Did he kill them?'

'No. Well, he killed some, but he never wanted an all-out battle. The soldiers' guns were good, but his were old and downright dangerous. They were almost impossible to aim from a moving pony. The whole idea was to stay away from the guns but scatter the soldiers. Crazy Horse achieved that. He gave Three Stars a terrible fright.'

'What did Three Stars do?'

'He went back to Goose Creek.'

'So Three Stars is out of the picture,' said Bo. 'But what about the soldiers on The Yellowstone? What are they doing? What is Long Hair Custer doing?'

'Heading south,' Cavendish replied. 'He has six-hundred 7th Cavalry troopers, a string of supply mules and some of the best and most experienced Indian guides in the business. It's hot, but he's making his men ride hard. They ride all day in searing heat. Then they find a travois trail. They can hardly miss it. It's a mile wide. They change course and pick up speed to follow it.'

'Has the village moved?' Bo mumbled. 'It must have. It had to keep moving so its people could eat.'

'Yes, it's moved,' said Cavendish. 'It's gone north, to the valley of The Little Big Horn.'

'Custer south, village north,' Bo's voice was trembling. 'Custer will find our village. He'll find our women and children. I know what soldiers do to women and children. I don't want to watch that. I don't want to be there. Don't make me go back there, Cavendish. Please don't make me go back there!'

'Oh, but you must,' the spaniel said gently. 'You *must*! You can't miss this! I wouldn't miss it for the world!'

192

CHAPTER THIRTY-FOUR
The valley of The Little Big Horn River,
Montana Territory.
Dawn, 25th June, The Moon of Making Fat, 1876

Last night, Custer had marched *all* night. He and his 7th Cavalry had ridden through the dark with their mules braying and their canteens clanking on their saddles. Maka Mani had been able to hear them from the village, more than fifteen miles away.

Now, at dawn, Custer had stopped at last. His soldiers had lit campfires and were frying bacon and boiling kettles. Plumes of smoke and steam were rising into the sky. The raven flew towards these giveaway signs. He wasn't the only one. Lakota and Cheyenne scouts were already crouching in the landscape. They were watching the soldiers and smelling the coffee.

'Ah,' the raven cawed as he circled the soldiers. 'The usual rabble. Outlaws, farm boys and foreigners. Half of them can barely speak English. They look weary and dusty, and their clothes are grubby and creased. I see they have pistols and rifles but I can't see any sabres. Nor any of the guns on wheels. That's good. The Indians hate sabres. They call them long knives. They hate the big guns, too. Those poor horses! They're exhausted. Custer has driven them far too hard. Speak of the devil, there he is!'

Custer was lounging outside his tent, feet up, drinking coffee and eating bacon. His 'uniform' was a fringed buckskin jacket and matching trousers, tall boots, a red neckerchief and a pale, broad-brimmed hat.

'Standing out again,' the raven chuckled. 'Shame about the hair, though. He's chopped off his curls. Long Hair Custer is Long Hair no longer. He's Short Back and Sides!'

By noon, the mist in the valley had lifted, and the heat was beginning to build. Soon it would tip one-hundred degrees. All was quiet in the Sitting Bull and Crazy Horse village. The younger warriors were dozing in their tipis. They'd been stuffing themselves with buffalo meat since The Rosebud battle. Now they were sleeping it off. The older warriors were chatting in the shade, and a group of women were heading out to collect wild turnips. Beyond them, the ten-thousand-strong pony herd was calmly grazing. More ponies, mostly valuable fighting animals, were hobbled near their masters' lodges.

Maka Mani landed on a cottonwood tree and gazed into the clear waters of The Little Big Horn River. He picked out the pebbles near its shoreline, and the smooth flat rocks that lay at its deepest part. He chattered at the small children playing at its edge, and cocked his head to watch their siblings swim. Some of them had reached the river's far bank. Now they were scrambling up its steep, one-hundred foot sides, dodging its spiky cactus plants and exploring its rolling ravines.

The raven stretched his wings.

'I'd love to stay here,' he muttered as he tapped his beak against his beaded ankle bracelet. 'But no. I should go back to Custer. See what he's doing.'

Custer had moved closer to the village and was peering at it through a pair of field glasses. Maka Mani lined himself up with the glasses. He *knew* what lay ahead, yet he still couldn't see it. All he could see was the tail-end of the village and a portion of the pony herd. The remainder of the village and most of the ponies were hidden by a dip in the landscape. Custer was seeing only a fraction of what he was looking at.

His guides knew differently.

They knew that the trail that Custer had followed had been made by Indians from the east. There'd been hundreds of these Indians, but *only* hundreds. They'd come to join Sitting Bull and Crazy Horse, and their trail led straight to their seven-thousand friends.

'Otoe Lakota,' the guides said grimly. 'Too many Lakota. More Lakota than you have bullets on your mules.'

Custer wasn't perturbed.

'Too many Lakota?' he guffawed. 'There can never be too many Lakota for us! Don't you know who we are? Why, we are The United States 7th Cavalry! We could whip every Indian on this continent!'

'But they will know you are here,' the guides warned, 'their scouts will be watching you.'

'Well then!' Custer exclaimed. 'We had better get on with it. Take them by surprise whilst we can!'

He dropped his field glasses to his chest and bellowed

at one of his officers.

'Take your men south! Report sightings. Pitch in if you see any Indians!'

'No chance!' squawked Maka Mani as the officer trotted off. 'You've sent your man on a goose chase, Mr Custer! The Indians will never go south. They know that Three Stars Crook went...'

The raven paused mid-flow.

'Maggoty Crow!' he swore. 'Custer doesn't know about The Rosebud battle! He doesn't know that Three Stars had a run-in with a thousand warriors. He doesn't know he's not here anymore. I'd bet Custer and Three Stars were meant to join forces. That would make sense. But Custer doesn't care. He never does what he's meant to do. He only does what he wants.'

Nine miles outside the village, Custer split his men yet again. He gave one-hundred-and-seventy-five troopers to his second in command, Major Reno, and kept two-hundred-and-twenty for himself. A further one-hundred-and-seventy-five were told to stay with the mules and guard the spare ammunition. Custer and Reno stayed together, the mules and their ammunition plodded on behind.

Three miles outside the village, Custer peeled away from Reno and headed for the high ground above The Little Big Horn River. Reno headed for the river itself, forded it, and trotted towards the village.

A Hunkpapa boy was nearest Reno's oncoming soldiers. He was cutting willow when Maka Mani screeched a warning. The boy looked up at the bird, then glanced to the south. Billows of dust were rolling towards him. He dropped his willow and ran.

'SOLDIERS!' he screamed. 'SOLDIERS!'

Within moments, his screams and Maka Mani's screeches were echoing around the Hunkpapa circle.

'SOLDIERS! SOLDIERS!'

Dogs yelped, pots and pans went flying, and women tripped and stumbled as they scooped up their babies and squealed for their children. Children plunged from ravines, splashed across the river and clambered out on their hands and knees. Warriors who'd been dozing were quickly awake, those who'd been chatting in the shade were quicker still. They sprang to their weapons and raced to fetch their fighting ponies.

Some of Reno's Indian guides had already reached the pony herd. They tried to drive the ponies off, but the herd was impossible to control. It was just too big. The guides stole some ponies and streamed away. They'd warned Custer. They'd said there were 'otoe Lakota', but Custer hadn't listened. Now they were leaving. They had more sense than to hang around.

CHAPTER THIRTY-FIVE
Moments later

'BUGLER SOUND THE CHARGE!' ordered Reno.

'Too-ra! Too-ra! Tarrah! Tarrah!' the bugle rang out.

'CHARGE!'

Reno's horses leapt into a gallop and pounded towards the village. They couldn't see what lay ahead. Much of it was hidden by trees or bends in the river. The rest was shrouded in dust, kicked up by people and panicking ponies.

The soldiers waved their pistols. The horses galloped on. The haze cleared, the horses saw the warriors. Some reared in fright, others bolted. One of the warriors was Gall. His arms were striped with bands of white and he was spinning his hatchet above his head.

'FORM A SKIRMISH LINE!' Reno screamed.

The soldiers swore, pulled up their terrified horses and jumped to the ground. One man in four led the horses to the safety of some nearby trees, the rest went down on one knee and tried to load their rifles. Their faces were pale and their legs and hands were shaking, but they managed to fire, reload and fire again. The warriors hollered furiously and tore towards them. The soldiers scrambled to their feet and ran to the trees. The warriors followed. They circled the trees, whooping and yelling

198

and firing off bullets and arrows.

Maka Mani landed directly above Reno. Reno's face was grey and beaded with sweat. He'd lost his hat and replaced it with a red bandana. He looked appalled and slightly mad, and his horse was spinning and reversing into the one next to it.

'MOUNT!' he screeched.

Most of his men didn't hear this order. Those that did had just sat down in their saddles when he screeched again, 'DISMOUNT!'

The woods were in chaos, now. Soldiers were jumping on and off horses, horses were rearing and kicking in fright, and arrows and bullets were pinging through the trees. Suddenly, there was a crack and a whizz and a horrible pop. The man next to Reno had taken a direct hit. Reno glanced down. His jacket was splattered with blood and bone. He shuddered, then spurred his horse and galloped blindly out of the woods. Some of his men followed, others couldn't move because their horses were dead. Those that could headed for the river. They were looking for the ford, but the warriors chased them, knocked them from their horses with clubs, or shot them with arrows. When the survivors reached a sudden bend in the river, their horses had no choice but to plunge straight in. Many unseated their riders, bullets and arrows hissed in their wake, and the water turned pink with blood. The soldiers who made it to the other side clambered up the cliffs and sank into a wet and wounded heap. Maka Mani took a head-count. Reno had lost half his men. Those still alive were exhausted, shocked, frightened and injured. They wouldn't be able to do anything for a while, if ever.

Maka Mani left them to it and flew north.

Custer and his men had reached the high ground. They were standing at its edge and gazing down on the centre of the village.

'Good,' the raven murmured. 'Custer still has no idea how large this village is. He can't see more than half of it. The rest is hidden by trees and bends in the river. They're also hiding something else, I'm pleased to say. Even I can't make it out.'

He rose vertically in the sky and tipped his head.

'Ah, now I can, but only just.'

Far beneath him, walking through the cottonwoods and hugging the banks of the river, was a quiet old pony. Its rider was dressed in everyday clothes; leggings, moccasins and a buckskin shirt decorated with porcupine quills. He wore a single feather in his hair, and his braids were bound with otter skin. The rider was Sitting Bull, and he was surrounded by women, children, old folks and dogs. He was leading the people to safety.

The raven cawed in approval and turned to fly away. Just as he did so, he noticed a movement on the ground below him. Some Cheyenne scouts had swum the river and climbed to the high ground. Now they were hiding in a ravine and watching Custer.

Maka Mani held his breath.

The Cheyenne hated Custer. If these scouts were to recognise him, and word got out that Long Hair was here, then Crazy Horse could lose control of his warriors. They might forget everything he'd taught them. They might rush in and spoil the plan.

'The scouts haven't moved,' the raven exhaled at last. 'They don't know it's Custer. He's chopped off his hair and they don't know it's him. If they can't recognise him, then neither will anyone else. Good. The plan is safe.'

Crazy Horse had been told of the Reno attack, but he hadn't gone to help. There'd been no point in racing three miles to the other end of the village. Gall was there. He'd have things in hand. If he needed help, he'd send for it. Crazy Horse was more concerned about the soldiers on the high ground.

'We know what must be done,' he said as he mixed his war paints. 'Gall and Two Moons know what must be done. We have made our plans. We are ready for the hunt. Ho-ka Hey, Rabbit!' he added as he ruffled the poodle's fur. 'Ho-ka Hey, Legs! It is a good day to fight!'

'Ho-ka Hey,' replied a Cheyenne voice.

One of the scouts had re-crossed the river. His breechcloth and plaits were dripping with water.

'You have news of the soldiers on the high ground?' Crazy Horse asked him.

'Yes,' the Cheyenne nodded. 'They are still the same number. Two hundreds and two tens.'

'They are still without their long knives?'

'Yes.'

'There has been no sign of the big guns?'

'No.'

'Good,' Crazy Horse laughed. 'That *is* good! Even I fear the long knives and the big guns. And what of Long

201

Hair? Have you seen him?'

'No,' the Cheyenne shook his head.

'That is strange,' said Crazy Horse. 'I thought that only Long Hair would dare to come this close. But then again, Long Hair does not attack in daylight. So who is this soldier chief? Who leads his men under such a high sun? Who comes here so soon after The Rosebud?'

'I do not know,' replied the Cheyenne. 'But his horses are tired. Some are lying down and refusing to move. The soldiers look tired, too. Except for one. He does not look tired. He has removed his jacket, rolled his shirt sleeves to his elbows and pinned up the brim of his hat. He looks more like a hunter than a soldier.'

'He *is* a hunter,' said Crazy Horse. '*All* soldiers are hunters. They are hunting us. They think that our women and children are easy prey. They are wrong. They have not seen *us*. We are the wolf pack. They are the buffalo. We guard our cubs to the death, and we also watch the buffalo. Go back and watch them some more. We will be ready soon. Until then, thank you, my friend.'

The scout rose to leave, and Buffalo Rabbit got to her feet.

'Are you going somewhere?' Legs asked her.

'Yes,' she replied. 'I'm going to follow the scout.'

'Are you *made* of nuts?' the wolf guffawed. 'You'll have to cross the river. Have you seen how deep it is? You wouldn't get halfway.'

'I would. I've crossed it before.'

'Yes, but not here. You crossed it at the ford. On a pony, if I remember rightly.'

'You could carry me.'

'Then we'd *both* drown.'

'*Please*, Legs. *Please* take me across the river.'

Buffalo Rabbit was trembling.

'Why? Why do you want to cross the river?' asked Legs. 'Is it because you don't want Crazy Horse to take you to the fight?'

'No.'

'Yes, it is. You're shaking, Rabbit.'

'So what if I am? You were at The Rosebud. You saw the soldiers. You said you didn't want to go down there, but I've done it, don't forget. I've seen soldiers up close. Remember that time with Long Hair? I've never been so scared in my whole life. Those soldiers mean business, Legs.'

'I understand,' said Legs kindly, 'but you don't have to cross the river. Why don't you hide?'

'No, I couldn't do that,' Buffalo Rabbit wrinkled her nose. 'I want to help, I just don't want to fight.'

'You could join the other dogs,' Legs offered. 'You could help take care of the women and children. Or how about a post? I could make you a lookout. '

The wolf was well-up on the latest news. He'd been communicating with the camp dogs. He'd sent most of them with Sitting Bull to guard the people, but had also posted lookouts around the village and its outskirts. They had full permission to bark if they saw any soldiers.

'I'd rather help the scouts,' said Buffalo Rabbit meekly.

'And what will happen when the fight begins?' Legs asked. 'The scouts will join in, and you'll be left on your own. All alone in a dark ravine. Anyway, Crazy Horse might not take you. He might leave you with me and Black Shawl.'

Buffalo Rabbit glanced anxiously at her master.

He'd almost completed his battle preparations. He'd painted a zigzag down his face and spotted his chest and shoulders in white. He'd dusted himself and his pony with earth, put on his pebble necklace, and braided his other two pebbles into his hair and his pony's tail.

'He saved your life, Rabbit,' whispered Legs. 'Now he's trying to save thousands of other lives. If he wants to take you, you'll have to go.'

Just then, Black Shawl emerged from her tipi with Buffalo Rabbit's fighting pouch and pebble. She handed them to Crazy Horse, and he strapped the pouch to his pony and lowered the pebble over Buffalo Rabbit's head. Then he picked up Buffalo Rabbit and slipped her into the pouch.

'You'll be fine,' said Legs as he stood on his hind leg and wrapped his front paws around his friend. 'Crazy Horse will take care of you, and you have your magic pebble. It will take care of you, too. It stopped a bullet the last time.'

'And sent it through my chin,' Buffalo Rabbit whimpered.

'No. Not *through* your chin. *Past* your chin. It skimmed your chin, that's all. You were fully recovered by the next day. So stop thinking about yourself and think about your master. Don't you think he's scared, too?'

'No, I don't. Crazy Horse is never scared.'

'I don't mean scared of fighting. I mean scared of this day and what it might mean. The people are depending on him, Rabbit. This day is important, however it ends. Who ever lives to tell its tale, this day will go down in history.'

CHAPTER THIRTY-SIX
A little later

Maka Mani was hovering.

At either end of the village, north and south and three miles apart, was a whirlpool of mounted warriors. These warriors were painted, preened and armed to the teeth, and there were more than three-thousand of them.

Buffalo Rabbit was in the northern whirlpool.

She was feeling better. Her nerves had gone. They'd been swept away in a blur. She peeked over the top of her pouch and stared at the hurtling fighting ponies. Their eyes were circled with paint and their manes were studded with feathers. Their knotted tails were threaded with ribbons, and there were hand-prints, lightning streaks and spots and stripes on their shoulders and necks. Manes, tails, braids, feathers, ribbons, blankets and war-bonnets were flying out behind them, and their mouths were foaming with excitement.

Their riders were bare-armed, bare-chested and bare-legged. They wore only breechcloths and moccasins on this hot afternoon, but what they lacked in clothing they made up for in decoration. Some had painted their faces black, others had black lips or noses. There were zigzags of yellow, streaks of white, and patches of red. There were necklaces of teeth and claws, earrings of silver, and bangles of horn; strips of fur, locks of hair, beads and buttons and human scalps. There were many, many feathers. They streamed from fabulous, six-foot long war-bonnets, fluttered at the tops of lances, and spiked the backs of heads.

In all her days with the Lakota, Buffalo Rabbit had never seen anything quite like this.

No one had.

Buffalo Rabbit felt her pony lurch and skid sideways.

'HOPPO!' Crazy Horse screamed. 'LET'S GO!'

The pony lurched again, made a little buck, and galloped towards the river. Buffalo Rabbit saw its ears prick as it lowered its head and hesitated, just for a beat, before springing into the glittering water. She felt its hooves lift from the bottom, heard it snort as it began to swim. Water was pouring over the top of her fighting pouch. She was getting wet, but she hardly noticed. She was too busy watching the one-thousand other ponies that were swimming around her, plunging down the river's banks or unfurling from the whirlpool. Crazy Horse's pony touched the riverbed, found its feet and scrambled onto the edge of a ravine. Buffalo Rabbit looked back. Fighting ponies were streaking up behind her, fit, feisty, and fat on new grass. Crazy Horse led them around the high ground, over to its farthest side and into another ravine. Then he signalled to his warriors to spread out, duck down and stay out of sight.

The southern whirlpool was led by Gall and Two Moons.

Maka Mani could see Gall's hatchet glinting in the sunshine. Gall screamed an order, peeled away from his whirlpool and rode for the river. Two Moons followed, and the whirlpool unravelled as its warriors streamed forward and urged their ponies into the water. The ponies swam, then scrambled for footing and divided, Gall's to the right, Two Moons' to the left. Towards the top of the one-hundred foot cliffs, the ponies slowed and the warriors slipped silently into position. Gall's men hid in the shadows of a ravine. Two Moons' gathered on a natural shelf in the cliffs. Custer was right in front of them. The 7th Cavalry was almost surrounded.

Almost, but not quite.

Eighty of Custer's men were very distinctive. Their horses were a pure, sparkling white. Maka Mani could see these horses very clearly. Custer had sent them to the northern edge of the high ground. Now they were looking down on a clump of cottonwood trees. The trees were dense, but not dense enough. They couldn't conceal the women, children and old folk.

'The people!' Maka Mani squawked. 'The white horse soldiers can see the people!'

He wheeled in the sky and searched for help.

Two Moons' Cheyenne were closest.

'Stop those soldiers!' he screeched at them. 'Stop them! They've found the people! Blast! They don't recognise me!'

It was true. Many of the warriors were young visitors. They hadn't noticed Maka Mani's telltale ankle bracelet, and even if they had, they probably wouldn't have known what it meant. Some even aimed their bows at the flapping, swirling, screaming bird.

He rose out of range and scanned the ground. When he spotted Two Moons, he swooped, landed on the Cheyenne's pony and pranced up and down on its withers. Then he tipped a wing and pointed north.

'Something is wrong,' Two Moons told the warrior next to him. 'Something is wrong to the north. Go there. Quick!'

Two Moons' warriors careered towards the white horse soldiers. The soldiers got down from their horses, knelt on one knee and fired a volley of shot. Crack, crack, crack. Indians fell from their ponies, and ponies squealed and crashed to the ground. Meanwhile, some of Two Moons' men had left their ponies and were side-winding on their bellies. They slithered and wriggled through the knee-high grass, then silently loaded their bows. Whoosh, whoosh, whoosh. Hundreds of arrows rained down. The soldiers huddled together, then broke up and scattered. Some dropped their rifles and ran to a gully. Others scrambled for their horses. Those in the gully were bludgeoned to death. Those on horses were shot.

Two Moons turned his attention to Custer.

This time, his warriors didn't charge the soldiers, they irritated them. They popped up from gullies and whistled, jumped out of bushes and whooped. They waved their blankets, twirled their weapons and lobbed off an arrow or two. The soldiers did their best. They remembered their drill and formed their blocks. They dismounted, knelt down and loaded their rifles. The Indians skirted around them. Arrows whistled and hailed, horses reared and swerved, soldiers were toppled and shot. Indians were popping up all over the place. They popped up, but then they popped back down again. The soldiers were frightened and frustrated. They were shooting at shadows. They must have wished they could see the colour of their enemies' eyes. Maka Mani could have told them it was brown. No matter. They were about to see that for themselves. The Indian cavalry was on its way.

When Gall waved his hatchet and screamed, his pony and a thousand others tore up the side of the ravine and thundered over the high ground. Their hooves pounded the earth and their riders roared a bloodcurdling cry. They came at Custer from every side, and so did the rising dust. The warriors were used to dust. They were used to riding through it, but the soldiers could barely see. Their tidy blocks had long since crumbled. It was every man for himself, now. The soldiers cracked off pistol fire, but they were shooting blind. Painted ponies and hollering warriors were closing in and running them off. Some were struck with hatchets, clubs or rifle butts. Some avoided the inevitable. They laid their pistols to their heads and pulled the trigger. Those on horses were luckier. They had a *chance* to escape, if they could avoid being dragged from their saddles or shot in the back. They decided to make a run for it.

Crazy Horse was waiting patiently.

So, amazingly, were his warriors. They were still spread out along the ravine, still hiding in its shadows. They hadn't rushed in to join the fight. They'd listened to Crazy Horse and He Dog's akicitas. Even Little Big Man was behaving himself. Above the warriors, lying flat on their bellies and peering onto the high ground, were several scouts. These scouts had been watching everything. Now they swung their arms forward and leapt for their ponies.

'HO-KA HEY!' screamed Crazy Horse. 'HOPPO!'

Buffalo Rabbit ducked as her pony jumped fast and high, out of the ravine and onto the high ground. For one brief moment, the pony was flying. Its hooves were silent. The hooves of its one-thousand friends were silent. And yet Buffalo Rabbit could hear hooves. She could hear them very clearly. They were wearing shoes. They belonged, not to Indian ponies, but to soldier horses, and they were galloping straight towards her.

'In front of you!' squawked Maka Mani. 'They're right in front of you!'

The raven was one-hundred feet above Buffalo Rabbit. Even in the blue Montana sky, there was dust. Down there, it was thick as molasses. But the raven's sharp eyes could pick out the soldiers. These were the men who'd made a run for it. There were about forty of them, Custer included. They'd been galloping fast when Crazy Horse's scouts had spotted them. Since then, they'd found a small hill, scrambled up its sides and pulled their horses around them.

Buffalo Rabbit curled into a ball and buried herself in her fighting pouch.

She could feel Crazy Horse's knee as he steered his pony this way and that. She could feel him lean to shoot, hear him shouting instructions. Other than that, she couldn't hear much but a deafening blare. Gunfire, whinnies, shouts, hoof-beats and screams had all blended into one. Then, all of a sudden, the gunfire stopped. The whinnies stopped. The hoof-beats slowed and the screams were occasional, strangled and gasping.

Buffalo Rabbit peeked over the top of her pouch.

In front of her was a small hill. Its sides were shrouded in dust and draped in dead horses. Soldiers were lying across these horses. Most of them were also dead. Those that weren't were fumbling with pistols and trying to fire them. Some managed, but their aim was tired and their shots were wild.

Buffalo Rabbit thought one of the soldiers seemed familiar, though she couldn't think why. The soldier was on his hands and knees. He had a wound in his side and was coughing up blood. The blood was soaking into his red neckerchief and dribbling over his buckskin jacket. Between his broad-brimmed hat and his blonde moustache were his piercing blue eyes. They were staring at her. She turned her head and looked away. She couldn't block the sound of the man's wheezing breaths but she didn't need to watch him die. She didn't need to see the Indians, *her* Indians, swarm over him and finish him off with their clubs and hatchets.

She closed her eyes and held her breath. When she breathed again, the man with the piercing blue eyes was dead. Every last soldier was dead.

Buffalo Rabbit glanced at the warriors nearest her. Their war paint was smeared, and their faces were grimy. They had dust in their hair, dust up their noses and dust in their mouths. Their braids had unravelled, their feathers had tangled. Some had scrapes and grazes, bullet wounds or arrow wounds. Some had no wounds at all.

They turned their weary ponies and headed for home. As they straggled back to the village, they paused to give lifts to those who'd lost ponies or were too badly injured to ride. There were many dead bodies. Buffalo Rabbit saw bodies spiked with arrows, bodies missing arms or legs, and bodies peppered with shot. They weren't all soldiers. When the warriors found an Indian's body, they marked the spot with a lance. When they found a soldier's, they ignored it. Enemy bodies were women's work.

Black Shawl welcomed Crazy Horse and Buffalo Rabbit with tears of relief. She removed Buffalo Rabbit from the fighting pouch and handed her over to Legs. She took Crazy Horse's pony to the river, splashed the dust from its hot and heaving body, and left it alone to drink and recover. Then she returned to her husband. She bathed his hands and feet, combed out his hair and fed him with hot, freshly made buffalo stew.

All across the village, wives, mothers, sisters and daughters were doing the same thing. They were tending to their men.

Legs was tending to Buffalo Rabbit.

He was licking her coat and cleaning the dust from her nostrils, ears and eyes. Sitting on the ground beside him was Maka Mani. The raven was dusty, bedraggled and clearly exhausted.

'What's he been up to?' Legs wondered aloud. 'He's so tired he's not even preening himself. He looks like he took on the entire U.S. Army.'

'Close,' Maka Mani cawed.

'He was up on the high ground,' said Buffalo Rabbit. 'I saw him. I also saw Long Hair.'

'Long Hair?' the wolf repeated. 'No. You didn't see *him*. *He* wasn't there.'

'I think he was,' Buffalo Rabbit replied. 'I think he'd cut off his curls.'

'He had!' the raven squawked.

'I recognised his moustache,' Buffalo Rabbit continued. 'And his eyes. They were piercing blue and looking straight at me.'

'That was him!' the raven pranced. 'That was Custer, all right!'

'He was dying,' said Buffalo Rabbit.

'He was indeed!' said Maka Mani. 'He'll be very dead by now! He and the rest of his men. There must be more than two-hundred dead soldiers, what with his and Major Reno's lot.'

'What else did you see?' Legs asked. 'Hold still a moment.'

The wolf bared his teeth and gently removed something from Buffalo Rabbit's fur.

'What is it?' she asked.

'A piece of blue cloth,' Legs replied.

214

He spat out the fragment of uniform.

'Go on,' he said.

'I saw Long Hair,' Buffalo Rabbit continued, 'but I didn't see much else. There was so much *dust*. You wouldn't believe the dust. It was pandemonium up there. Also, Crazy Horse was only in the last part. The soldiers didn't get to his side of the high ground until the very end. It was very quick, after that.'

'How quick?'

'Quicker than Gall takes to eat his dinner. When he's really starving hungry.'

'Heavens!' the wolf exclaimed. 'That *is* quick!'

'I saw dead bodies,' said Buffalo Rabbit. 'Most belonged to soldiers, but there were warriors, too. I don't know how many.'

'We'll never know,' Legs replied softly, 'the village is too large for that.' He tipped his head towards a group of women with ponies and travois. 'Look, they're heading out already.'

The women would cross the river at its ford and climb to the high ground to look for the dead and injured. Warriors would be stretchered home to their tipis, soldiers would be mutilated. Being dead was not enough. Their arms and legs would be slashed, just to make sure they could never return.

CHAPTER THIRTY-SEVEN
Bo's House.
The 21st Century

'How many Indians died at The Battle of The Little Big Horn?' Bo asked Cavendish.

'Nobody knows,' the spaniel replied. 'The best guess is between forty and one-hundred.'

'And the soldiers?'

'About two-hundred-and-sixty, but even that's a guess. Some were never found.'

'They probably fell down ravines,' said Bo.

'Probably,' Cavendish nodded. 'It's also possible a few escaped. If they did, they disappeared.'

'Why would they disappear?'

'Because it was either that or be lynched for cowardice. America was in an uproar. The newspapers had a field day. They talked about their brave soldiers and how they'd been massacred by savages. People couldn't believe that Custer had been beaten. They had to find *someone* to blame. It was even suggested that Crazy Horse had been helped by a U.S. Army commander. Not such a mad idea. Custer had many enemies.'

'Well, there was no Army commander,' Bo replied. 'It was all Crazy Horse. He got the warriors to listen and work as a pack.'

'And use their local knowledge,' Cavendish added. 'The Indians knew that high ground like the back of their hands.'

'It was perfect fighting country for them,' agreed Bo. 'Plenty of gullies and tall grass to hide in. It was also the perfect time of year. The warriors and their ponies had eaten well. They were as fit as butcher's dogs and used to the heat, and the dust that came with it.'

'All good news,' said Cavendish. 'Good news for them and bad news for Custer. Added to which, Custer made some big mistakes. He could have had many more men. He was offered the 2nd Cavalry. He turned it down. He was offered heavy guns. He turned *them* down. He also packed away his sabres.'

'Thank goodness,' Bo remarked. 'Even Crazy Horse hated the big guns and the long knives.'

'Custer set off with more than six-hundred men and horses, drove them hard through blistering heat and didn't give them enough sleep or food. He split his troops three *times*, left his ammo behind, and didn't go where he'd been told to go, or when. He was supposed to wait for the following morning, that was the plan. Instead of which, he went rushing in at the hottest part of the day. His commanding officer said that if Custer hadn't died, he'd have been court martialled for disobedience.'

'So why did he do those things?'

'I think it was deliberate,' the spaniel mused. 'Custer wanted to take the Indians on, and he thought he could do it alone. If he'd won that battle, his reputation would have sky rocketed. Just in time for elections.'

'Custer wanted to be President of The United

States?'

'So they say,' Cavendish nodded. 'But President or not, Custer wanted those Indians and he wanted them quick. He had no clue how many there were. His guides tried to tell him, but he wouldn't listen. He couldn't see half the village through those field glasses.'

'When was this?' Bo asked.

'Um. Sometime that morning.'

'How do you know about it?'

'It's all written down, Bo,' the spaniel replied. 'Custer wasn't alone. Other people looked through those glasses. They couldn't see the village, either. So if you're thinking I know because I was Legs, then you're wrong.'

'I wasn't thinking that at all,' said Bo. 'Legs and Buffalo Rabbit were together that morning. Legs didn't even know that Custer was around. He didn't know *that* until after the battle. It still doesn't prove...'

'That I wasn't Three Legs Running?' Cavendish asked. 'No. It doesn't. I'll tell you the truth, one day. For now, though, you should go back to being Buffalo Rabbit.'

218

CHAPTER THIRTY-EIGHT

The valley of The Little Big Horn, Montana Territory.
July, The Moon of Cherries Ripening, 1876

A few days after The Battle of The Little Big Horn, the vast Crazy Horse and Sitting Bull village was dismantled for the final time. The tipi covers were slipped from their lodge poles, rolled up and folded. The lodge poles were slung with hide and made into travois. The travois were lashed onto ponies and loaded with possessions. The people said their good byes and went their separate ways.

Buffalo Rabbit was in two minds about this.

On the one hand, she was looking forward to having her master more to herself, and being able to share Black Shawl's suppers in quiet. Buffalo Rabbit had never been one to socialise. Her master had never danced around campfires, beaten the drums or shared in the gossip, and neither had she. But Crazy Horse was the finest warrior the world had ever seen, and in that great village, all the world had wanted to see him. There'd been a constant trail of visitors to his tipi. Buffalo Rabbit had welcomed some of these visitors. She'd wagged her tail for Sitting Bull, Gall, He Dog and Two Moons. They were old friends. It wasn't they who'd irritated her. It was the long-lost relatives, the wide-eyed, giggling women and the overeager, fawning young warriors.

On the other hand, Buffalo Rabbit had enjoyed the camaraderie of such a big village. She'd liked being able to wander through it and watch its goings-on. She'd also felt safe in its numbers. As the village broke up, she started to fret.

'Shouldn't we all stay together?' she asked Legs.

'No,' Legs replied. 'Winter is coming. If we stay together, we'll starve.'

Buffalo Rabbit glanced at Crazy Horse, Sitting Bull and Gall. They were crouched on a grassy mound, sharing a herb-filled pipe and talking in low, sombre voices.

'I'm not stupid,' she told the wolf. 'I've heard what those three are saying. They're saying the whites will be furious that we won the battle. They think they'll be out for revenge.'

'They're right,' Legs nodded. 'Little do they know how right they are! They don't yet know that they've killed Long Hair Custer. The white men won't like that. Custer was their golden boy.'

'The newspapers are spinning tornadoes out there!' Maka Mani cawed as he landed beside the wolf and the poodle. 'All about the battle, precious Custer and the savages who murdered him. The whites are falling over themselves to take some redskin scalps. The army's never had so many volunteers! It's happening everywhere. From Texas to Nevada, Arkansas to Illinois. Where Custer was born, in Ohio, some boys took an oath at school. They laid one hand on their McGuffey's Readers, raised the other, and swore to kill Sitting Bull on sight!'

'We should stay together,' Buffalo Rabbit trembled. 'If we stay together, we'll be stronger. We'll have thousands of warriors to look after us.'

'Warriors can't fight when their stomachs are empty,' said Legs. 'Ponies can't fight when their stomachs are empty. This village is too large, Rabbit. It has to move every other day, just to feed us all. There's never any leftovers, nothing we can dry and store for winter. We have no choice, Rabbit. We must live in smaller villages.'

'But where? Where will we live?'

'The plains, I should think. Just for the summer. It's harder for soldiers to find us there. We'll probably travel with He Dog's people and go to Bear Butte. You like Bear Butte. It's where Crazy Horse was born.'

Buffalo Rabbit wrinkled her nose.

'I suppose,' she said.

'We'll set fire to the grass as we go,' Legs added reassuringly. 'Everybody will.'

'Good,' Buffalo Rabbit nodded. 'Our travois tracks will be covered that way. You can't follow tracks when the ground is charred.'

CHAPTER THIRTY-NINE
Bear Butte, just north of Paha Sapa, Dakota Territory.
August, The Moon of Ripe Plums, 1876

As Legs had predicted, the Crazy Horse and He Dog people travelled together and headed for Bear Butte, a bear-shaped, sacred hill just north of Paha Sapa.

Soon, Crazy Horse and He Dog began to make visits to Paha Sapa's gold mining towns. These visits were fleeting. Crazy Horse and He Dog whipped in, pinched what they could and galloped home with their loot.

One day, they came haring back to the village with two sacks. Crazy Horse slit one of the sacks with his knife and scooped out a fistful of raisins. Then he threw back his head and jammed the dried fruit to his mouth.

'Mmm,' he grinned with delight. 'Cunwiyapehe!'

'How can he eat those things?' Legs puzzled. 'They look like rat droppings.'

'Wrinkly and black,' Buffalo Rabbit agreed. 'But Crazy Horse loves them. They remind him of his childhood, when he lived down south near The Oregon Trail. The whites were more friendly then. Crazy Horse and his pals would go right up to the wagons and the people would give them raisins. I don't recall the Irvines having raisins. Maybe they did, but I wouldn't have eaten them. Raisins are poisonous to dogs. Anything grape is poisonous to dogs.'

'How do you know that?'

'I can't remember.'

On another day, He Dog and Crazy Horse stole some bolts of coloured cloth, and a handle with a curved end, a grooved side, and a black cotton cover.

'What *is* that?' Legs asked. 'A sleeping bat?'

'Sleeping for now,' Buffalo Rabbit replied, 'but if anyone…'

Crazy Horse had found a button on the handle. Now he was sliding it along the groove.

'Whoops!'

The bat woke with a start and stretched out its wings.

'An umbrella!' Buffalo Rabbit exclaimed.

The umbrella was given to an old man who'd once been attacked by a bear. The bear had left terrible scars that burned in the sun. Now the old man had permanent shade.

Sometimes, Crazy Horse ventured into Paha Sapa alone. He didn't even take Buffalo Rabbit. She found out why this was when He Dog lost his temper and shouted.

'This is foolish!' he hollered at Crazy Horse. 'You can no longer do as you used to do. You must think of the people. They need you. What will happen if you are caught? You must not go to Paha Sapa again. It is dangerous. You *must* stop killing these miners!'

'Paha Sapa belongs to us,' Crazy Horse answered quietly. 'Those hills belong to us.'

He said nothing else, but he did cease his secret visits to the hills.

One pouring wet morning in August, Crazy Horse, Legs and Buffalo Rabbit climbed the slopes of Bear Butte.

The Indian war-leaders had predicted that the whites would seek revenge for the battle at The Little Big Horn. They'd been right. Just as normal life had returned to the plains, so had Three Stars Crook.

Crook and his two-thousand soldiers had spent weeks crossing backwards and forwards, looking for Indians. Now they were dangerously close to the Crazy Horse village. Crazy Horse wanted to keep an eye on them, and the perfect place from which to do this was Bear Butte. The only problem was the rain. It had been raining for days and days.

'We should have brought the umbrella,' said Buffalo Rabbit. 'I'm soaked.'

The fur on her head had parted in the middle, her ears were plastered to her face, and a stream of water was cascading from her chin.

'I think you look very fetching,' Legs replied. 'And if you think it's wet up here, have a look down there.'

He tipped his head towards the plains. The soil had turned to mud, and the dry summer grass was drowning in marshland.

Buffalo Rabbit raised a paw.

'I can see them,' she whispered. 'I can see the Three Stars soldiers.'

'Where? Oh, yes...'

The soldiers straggled into view. They, too, were

soaking wet. Their shirts were splattered with mud, their trousers were drenched right through, and their horses were splashing through knee-high water.

'That is him,' Crazy muttered as he reached for his long-seeing glasses. 'That is Three Stars. He is stopping. Some of his men are searching for fuel.'

'Fuel?' Buffalo Rabbit guffawed. 'No chance. Nothing will burn in this weather. Not even buffalo chips.'

'There are no chips,' said Legs. 'There are no buffalo. Anyway, chips would dissolve in this mess. Still, the soldiers obviously think they'll find something to burn. They're about to kill that horse. They're so without food, they're killing a horse.'

'Poor horse,' Buffalo Rabbit murmured. 'It's not *his* fault the soldiers are starving.'

'Three Stars will go to any length to find us,' Legs agreed. 'But surely there's a limit. Look at the state of his men! They're covered in mud *and* sunburnt. How is that possible?'

'They have looked for us these many days,' said Crazy Horse. 'They have searched through sun and rain. But now it is enough. Now Three Stars will go home. He will go home, and then he will come back again.'

CHAPTER FORTY
Fort Robinson, Nebraska.
Three months later
November, The Moon of Falling Leaves, 1876

Maka Mani loved to fly. He loved to feel the wind in his wings, to spiral and hover and twist in the sky, to swoop and glide onto land, to prance and jump into take-off. Most of all, he loved the freedom of flight. He loved to go wherever he pleased, and the places he'd gone had pleased him.

But things had changed.

Fewer places pleased him now, and this was not one of them.

Fort Robinson was a mile or so west of The Red Cloud Agency. It was a soldier fort and, lately, a prison.

The raven landed on one of its snow-covered buildings.

'Brrrrh!' he shivered as he fluffed up his feathers. 'It's freezing!'

He tucked his head between his shoulders and remembered what had happened here.

Very soon after The Battle of The Little Big Horn, the government had told the Indians at the agency that they must give up Paha Sapa and The Powder River Country 'because you made war on us'.

The Indians had refused.

'It is not for us to give you Paha Sapa and The Powder River Country,' they'd said. 'Those lands belong to all of our people. We need agreement from three quarters of our men. That was your idea. You made that rule when we touched the pen at Fort Laramie. You told us you could not take anything from us unless our people agreed to it.'

'Ah, yes,' the government had replied. 'But that was many moons ago. Things are different now. We do not count the other people. We do not count those who live wild. We only count you. You must decide. Do you want us to give you food and supplies? Do you want to keep your ponies and your guns for the hunting? Then give us Paha Sapa and The Powder River Country. If you do not, we will stop your food. We will also take away your ponies and all of your weapons.'

The agency Indians had been given no choice. It was only September, and they were already hungry. What would they do when winter came? And so they had touched the pen. They had given Paha Sapa and The Powder River Country to the government.

A few days later, the government had taken the ponies and guns anyway. They'd also arrested every male Indian in the agency and locked them up in Fort Robinson.

The raven screeched his disgust, opened his wings and flew north. His destination was a second fort. This fort was on the edge of The Rosebud Country, and was so brand new it didn't have a name. It had been built after

227

The Little Big Horn battle for a soldier chief named Bear Coat Miles. Bear Coat's orders were to find Indians, and the Indians he most wanted to find were Crazy Horse and Sitting Bull.

Maka Mani didn't get as far as the fort. As he neared it, he noticed something snapping in the wind. He swooped into land, bounced on the snow, and folded his wings. Then he hopped towards a long stick that had been stuck in the ground. The top of the stick had been whittled to a point and pierced through a letter:

I want to know what you are doing travelling this road. You scare the buffalo away. I want to hunt in this place. I want you to turn back from here. If you do not, I will fight you. I want you to leave what you have got here and turn back from here.

I am your friend
Sitting Bull

P.S. I mean all of the rations you have got and all of your powder.

Sitting Bull spoke very little English and could not read or write. But Maka Mani was certain that these were his words. He'd dictated his thoughts to a trader, and the trader had translated them and written them down. They were directed at Bear Coat.

'Good for Sitting Bull,' the raven approved. 'And good for the trader, whoever he his. His translation is honest. I wish we had more like him.'

CHAPTER FORTY-ONE

The Rosebud Country, Montana Territory.
A few days later
25th November, The Moon of Falling Leaves, 1876

Sunrise, and the eastern sky turned pink and orange.

So, too did the western sky.

At the base of The Big Horn Mountains, two-hundred tipis were burning. Their covers were spitting and crackling, and their lodge poles were crashing to the ground. The fires were a long way off, but Maka Mani could see their flames. He pounded the walls of Crazy Horse's tipi, dived through its smoke vent and hurtled around inside it.

Crazy Horse understood. He knew that something was wrong. He wrapped up warm in a buffalo robe, lashed his snow shoes to his moccasins, and followed the raven out of the tipi and into the waist-high snow.

'What is it?' he shouted above the howling wind.

'Fires!' the raven screamed back. 'I saw them from the sky! A village is burning! It's south of here, somewhere south of The Big Horns! The people will come looking for you! They will search for help in this terrible snow!'

Even as he spoke, he was knocked sideways by an icy blast.

Crazy Horse picked him up and held him in the crook

of his arm.

'There is nothing we can do!' Crazy Horse shouted again as the wind buffeted his hair and sent it swirling. 'We are trapped by this weather! We cannot move!'

Crazy Horse ducked and ran for his tipi. Legs and Buffalo Rabbit had come outside to await instructions. They'd been there for only a few seconds, but already the fur on their windward side was covered with snow. Their eyes were half-closed against the wind and their jaws were open and snatching for breath.

Crazy Horse pushed at his tent flaps and ushered them back inside.

'What is the matter?' Black Shawl asked. 'Is it soldiers?'

'I think so,' her husband replied. 'They are not here but somewhere else. I think they have found a village.'

'You think there are people out there?' Black Shawl's mouth was wide with amazement and horror.

'Yes,' Crazy Horse replied. 'I think there are people out there.'

'There are! There are!' the raven pranced. 'I haven't seen them yet. I've only seen the fires. But I will try to find them, and if do, I will help them to find you!'

Maka Mani had to wait two days for a lull in the weather. When it came, he left the Crazy Horse village and flew south. He found the people more easily than he'd hoped. The drop in the wind had brought clear skies for him and silent land for them. Silent, endless, pure white land.

The people were Cheyenne. Their attacker was Three Stars Crook. He and his soldiers had arrived at dawn, when the village was fast asleep. The warriors had put up a good fight, but they'd known their task was hopeless. In the end, they'd driven off a handful of ponies, then fled with the women and children. Behind them, the mountains had echoed with whinnies and gunshot, and the sky had blazed with flames. The soldiers had slaughtered the pony herd and torched the people's possessions.

The first thing Maka Mani did was to show the Cheyenne his ankle bracelet. It let them know he was tame, gained him their trust and encouraged them to follow him. When one of the women said the bracelet's beadwork was Oglala Lakota, the Cheyenne faces lit up. Maka Mani was both pleased and distressed by this. The people were depending on him now. He had to lead them to Crazy Horse, and he had to do it through the hardest winter in living memory.

There were times when even he was grounded. Times when the blizzards blasted his feathers and forced him to close his eyes. He was lucky. He was a bird. He could always find something to peck at, somewhere to hide from the icy air. The Cheyenne had nothing to peck and nowhere to hide. They had no food and no shelter. Many had no clothes. Some were wounded. Daytime temperatures were freezing. At night they dropped to 30 below. Babies froze to death. Old people froze to death. Dogs froze to death.
The warriors had guns, but there wasn't much to shoot. The wildlife had hunkered down, disappeared into burrows or taken refuge in caves. One by one,

the rescued ponies were killed. The warriors scooped out their innards and coaxed the smallest children into the warm cavity. Older people warmed their hands on the ponies' dying flesh. The warriors cut around them, skinning and carving until they had shawl-sized pelts to give to the naked. They diced up the carcass before it could freeze, and handed the meat to the starving. The children crawled out from their shelter, the people withdrew their blood-covered hands. They wrapped their new shawls around them, sucked on their portion of meat and walked on. They walked for eleven days. And then, at last, they walked into the Crazy Horse village.

CHAPTER FORTY-TWO

The Rosebud Country, Montana Territory.
December, The Moon of Popping Trees, 1876

The Crazy Horse people did what they could. They shared their tipis and food, tended to the injured, and looked after the old and sick.

But things had changed.

Last March, when the He Dog and Two Moons camps had been attacked, Crazy Horse had taken everyone to Sitting Bull. His village had been both large and wealthy. His people had had plenty to spare and been generous with it. Now, though, Sitting Bull was being chased by Bear Coat. No one knew where he was, and even if they had, they couldn't have reached him.

Worse, the Crazy Horse people had spent their summer on the plains, where Indians were hard to find. So, too, was food. Crazy Horse had come home to The Rosebud Country with little in the way of winter stores. He'd hoped to make them up, but then he'd uncovered more bad news.

When the Indians had dismantled their vast village on The Little Big Horn, they'd headed off in different directions and set fire to the grass behind them. This was usual. Burning the ground covered their tracks so they couldn't be followed. But so *many* Indians and so *many* different directions had burned too much grass. The Rosebud Country had been reduced to a wasteland. Now, the Crazy Horse ponies were starving. The people were almost starving. They had hundreds of unexpected, sick and starving guests. Their camp was snowbound, they had no hope of finding Sitting Bull and, somewhere out there, were Three Stars Crook and Bear Coat Miles.

Two days after the arrival of the Cheyenne, Crazy Horse took Legs and Buffalo Rabbit and walked slowly out of his village. He found a path between the drifts and climbed through the snow to higher ground. Then he sat down and pulled the wolf and the poodle up close.

'My people are nervous,' he said out loud. 'They tremble at the slightest sound. The women are like ponies with new-born foals. Sometimes they raise their heads. It is as if they are smelling the air. As the mother pony smells for the lion that may eat her foal, so they are smelling for soldiers. What can I tell them? This snow may keep us safe for a while, but it cannot last forever. And then what? The soldiers will come. What should we do? What should *I* do?'

He gazed down on his village. It was late in the evening. There should have been a glow from every tipi. There should have been a warming fire in all of them, a bubbling pot and a cheerful plume of smoke. Yet half of them were lying in darkness. There wasn't enough fuel for them all. Heating was taken in turns, eating was taken in turns. There should have been a hum of conversation, giggles and laughs from the women, jests and jokes from the men. But the only sound was the moan of the wind.

Suddenly, Legs raised a paw and prodded Crazy Horse's arm.

'Something's happening,' growled the wolf. 'Do you see? Over there. Someone's dismantling a tipi.'

Crazy Horse and Buffalo Rabbit glanced to one side of the village. Sure enough, the covers of not one but several tipis had been removed and rolled up. Now their lodge poles were being lowered, laid on the ground and stretchered for travois.

'Are they leaving?' Buffalo Rabbit asked.

'I think so,' Legs narrowed his eyes. 'There are a couple of men at the pony herd. They've caught a few ponies. They're bringing them out.'

'They want to leave us,' Crazy Horse sighed as the men led the ponies to the waiting travois. 'They want to go to the agency.'

'They won't get far,' said Buffalo Rabbit.'

'They will not get far,' said Crazy Horse. 'They will die out there. If they do not, they will walk into soldiers. If they do not walk into soldiers, they will walk into the agency, and then they will lose their ponies and guns.'

'Serves them right,' snarled Legs.

'Should I let them to go?' Crazy Horse wondered aloud.

'No,' said Buffalo Rabbit. 'You are their leader. You must stop them.'

'AKICITA!' Crazy Horse screamed. 'AKICITA!'

He leapt through the snow and back to the village. Legs and Buffalo Rabbit bounded beside him. When they reached the village, they found the akicita ready and waiting with guns fully loaded.

Crazy Horse told the escapees that he could not let them go.

'The weather is too bad,' he said. 'Ask the Cheyenne. They will tell you how bad it is. If you survive the weather, you may run into soldiers. Ask the Cheyenne about that! Ask them why they have no tipis, no clothes and no ponies. They will say that the soldiers destroyed them. If you survive the soldiers you may reach the agency. Ask the Cheyenne about that! They left the agency because there was no food. It is worse there, now. If you go to the agency, you will have no food, but you won't be able to hunt. Your ponies and guns will be taken from you. Now ask the Cheyenne why they walked eleven sleeps to find us. They will say that they did it for friendship.'

He picked up a lodge pole, snapped it over his knee and flung the pieces aside.

'Have you forgotten our friendship?' he asked furiously. 'Have you forgotten how we take care of each other?'

He wrenched a bow from one of the men, crushed it, and threw it to the ground.

Then he turned away.

'Shoot their ponies,' he told the akicita. 'They would have lost them anyway. Tonight, we will eat. We will sit together and we will eat together. In friendship.'

CHAPTER FORTY-THREE
The Rosebud Country, Montana Territory.
The following days

Crazy Horse thought long and hard over the following days.

'I have ten hundreds of people here,' he muttered one night. 'All are tired. Tired of running, tired of fighting, tired of being hunted by soldiers. They are always afraid, always on the lookout, always waiting to be woken from their sleep.'

He pulled Buffalo Rabbit into the well of his crossed legs.

'My warriors would fight again,' he continued. 'I am sure of that. Yet our ponies are weak, our weapons are few, and we are low on ammunition. What little we have should be used for the hunt. We need meat. We also need hides. It will take many, many hides to make new tipis for our Cheyenne friends. Many, many hides mean many, many buffalo, but the buffalo will not come until the new grass moon.'

Buffalo Rabbit licked his hand.

'Then we'll wait, master,' she whispered. 'We'll wait for the new grass moon. This year's grass will be better than ever. We set it alight to cover our tracks and it always grows stronger after a fire. Our ponies will get fat as barrels! They'll get so fat, they won't be able to move!'

'The grass will come,' Crazy Horse mused. 'And when it does, so will the soldiers. I must do what is best for the people. They call me their leader, and their leader I must be.'

'What's best for them is *you*,' Buffalo Rabbit wagged her tail. '*You* are what your people need.'

'It is not about me,' her master sighed. 'It is not about what I want. If we go to the agency, we will be given food and warmth. We don't have to stay there forever.'

He stretched out a hand and ruffled Legs' ears.

'He's reached a decision,' said Legs. 'He always does that when he's reached a decision.'

'I have made up my mind,' Crazy Horse said finally. 'I will take my people to the agency.'

'No, master,' Buffalo Rabbit shook her head. 'Don't do that. You are Crazy Horse.'

'I will take my people in. They will be eat and be warm and be safe from the soldiers. That is what we are promised. We must wait until spring. Then we will go to The Red Cloud Agency.'

Soon after Crazy Horse made this decision, a messenger battled wind and snow to deliver a promise from Three Stars Crook. If Crazy Horse took his people to the agency, he would be given his own lands. He could return to The Powder River Country.

CHAPTER FORTY-FOUR

Porcupine Creek, Montana Territory.
February, The Moon of the Dark Red Calves, 1877

It took Maka Mani several weeks to find Sitting Bull.

The old war-leader's proud Hunkpapa, the fiercest and wildest of the Lakota tribes, had been scattered. Bear Coat had chased them all over the plains. Their once great village had been reduced to a few hundred people, many of whom were dressed in rags. They were exhausted, and so was Sitting Bull.

When Maka Mani crept through the vent in Sitting Bull's tipi, he found a lone figure hunched over the fire. The raven paused for a moment, then gripped the tipi's hides in his talons and walked backwards, like a parrot. When he reached the floor, he stretched his wings and jumped silently onto Sitting Bull's shoulder.

'Ah!' said the Hunkpapa. 'I knew you would come. You have come quietly. That is good. I do not want more bad news. How is your master? I have tried to find him. I have something to tell him. I could not send signals. I could not wave my blanket or tilt my mirror to the sun. We must all be silent now. Silent as the mouse when the raven is about. Eh?'

He chucked Maka Mani under the chin.

'Tell your master that I am leaving this place. Tell

him I can live here no longer. I cannot live beside this Great Father in Washington. I do not understand his ways. Tell Crazy Horse that I am going to the land they call Canada. It is the land of The Grandmother. Have you heard of The Grandmother, bird?'

'Yes,' Maka Mani stroked his beak along Sitting Bull's buffalo robe. 'The Grandmother is Queen Victoria.'

'Well, then,' Sitting Bull patted the raven's feet. 'I hear The Grandmother speaks with straight tongue. I hear her soldiers do not kill women and children. And so I am going to find her land. Canada...' He faltered and shivered. 'Long, long winters and wet summer nights. No matter. Tell your master when you see him. Tell him that Sitting Bull is gone to Canada.'

'I will,' Maka Mani replied.

CHAPTER FORTY-FIVE
The Laramie-Black Hills Road, Wyoming Territory.
May, The Moon of the Strawberries, 1877

The snow had stopped.

The time had come.

Crazy Horse was taking his people to The Red Cloud Agency.

The travois were light but the ponies were weak. Their tails were tucked, their ears were flat, and their ribs were sticking through their thick winter coats. They hauled as best they could, heads down, hooves stumbling on the frost-hard, rutted earth. The women, children and old folk rode alongside, legs hanging limp, moccasins dangling. They huddled in the buffalo robes that kept them warm and hid their ragged clothes, their dirty hair and matted braids. Their warriors rode or walked in front, behind, and to the side of them. They chivvied the ponies, encouraged the tired and helped the old. Dogs milled in and out, ducking under the ponies' necks, and young boys pushed at the travois to freed them from sticky ground.

It was a long, slow journey.

After ten days of travel, they heard the sound of braying mules. Then came the roll of wagon wheels, the bellow of cattle, the clop of well-shod hooves.

The sounds drew closer, and Buffalo Rabbit could make out shapes. The mules' long ears, the wagons' wooden sides, the cattle's pointed horns, the horses' riders. She thought the riders were all soldiers, until she realised that some were Indians in uniform. One of them was her old friend, American Horse.

'What's *he* doing here?' she asked Legs. 'And why is he dressed like a soldier?'

'He *is* a soldier, of sorts,' Legs told her. 'He's an Indian policeman at the Red Cloud Agency.'

'Policeman?' Buffalo Rabbit trembled. 'Have we done something wrong?'

'No, Rabbit,' Legs reached up to pat her. 'Nothing wrong.'

But there was a flicker in the wolf's eyes, a mixture of worry and surprise. Buffalo Rabbit whipped round. Crazy Horse had the same expression.

Just then, American Horse and eleven of his fellow policemen got down from their horses and sat cross-legged on the ground, arms folded, gazes fixed on Crazy Horse.

Crazy Horse hesitated, then nodded and sent two of his warriors down the line of travois to the pony herd. The warriors returned with twelve ponies and handed them over to American Horse.

'What? I don't understand,' said Buffalo Rabbit.

'It's...' Legs began. 'Crazy Horse is...'

'Crows!' Buffalo Rabbit interrupted. 'Who's *that*?'

Another Indian had ridden forward. This one didn't have a soldier's uniform, although he was wearing white man's trousers and a black Fedora hat. His shirt was of fringed buckskin, and his skin was dark and leathery. He had a very large nose, small eyes that glittered and darted, and deep lines on his forehead and down the sides of his wide, rather sombre mouth.

'That?' Legs responded. 'That is Red Cloud.'

'Red Cloud?' Buffalo Rabbit gasped. 'Well, I don't like him. He looks shifty to me. What the..?'

Crazy Horse was removing the blanket from his shoulders and laying it at Red Cloud's feet.

'...why's he doing that?'

'It's a sign,' the wolf explained. 'Your master gave his ponies to American Horse, then laid down his blanket for Red Cloud. These are both signs.'

'Signs of what?'

'Surrender, Rabbit. Your master has surrendered.'

'*Surrendered*? Who said anything about surrender? Did Crazy Horse know he'd have to do this?'

Buffalo Rabbit glanced at her wolf friend. His pale grey eyes were downcast and moist. He caught her gaze and turned away.

'No,' he said softly. 'I don't think he did.'

Buffalo Rabbit looked ahead.

Crazy Horse was standing with his back to her.

It was partly covered by his long, loose hair, but Buffalo Rabbit could see that the spine was straight and the shoulders square. She shuffled on her pony's withers, sat upright and squared her own shoulders.

She imagined her master's face. The crook in his scarred lip, the evenness of his light brown skin, the upward tilt of his chin, the steely pride in his almond eyes. She curled her own lip, raised her nose and narrowed her eyes.

'Grrrh,' she growled. 'We are the Crazy Horse people! We are Lakota! We are strong and proud!'

'Good for you, Rabbit!' said Legs. 'And quite right too!'

The wolf had recovered from his moment of sadness. Now his hackles were standing up like porcupine quills, his paws were threesquare to the ground, and his white-tipped tail was waving in defiance.

'I've just realised something,' Buffalo Rabbit whispered. 'Young Man Afraid's an agency policemen too, isn't he? Yet he's not here. I bet he chose not to come. He didn't want to see this. He didn't want to be a part of it. Unlike others I could mention.'

She stared at American Horse. She remembered the times they'd hunted together, the raids on the Crow, the days in the sun by sparkling streams. She recalled him with Young Man Afraid and He Dog, the three loyal friends who'd towed Crazy Horse home when No Water shot him. She had a flashback of They Are Afraid Of Her, wearing American Horse's grizzly bear necklace, pulling it over her head and giggling. That was the night before the day. The day of the Long Hair ambush. The day the stray bullet had caught her chin. She remembered how frightened she'd been. Blood pouring over her pouch. American Horse cradling her, whispering in her ear. He'd made her feel safe. He'd even cut her a claw from his grizzly bear necklace. And now here he was, wearing a soldier's uniform and gloating over her master's ponies.

The soldiers' mules and wagons had brought firewood,

tobacco and blankets, and food such as biscuits and bacon. There was also the cattle. That night, and for the next three nights, everybody camped together and the Crazy Horse people had their first proper meals in weeks. In winters past, they'd stolen cattle, mostly for the fun of it. They didn't like cow meat. Compared to buffalo, elk or antelope it seemed scrawny and tough. But for those three nights it tasted sweeter than honey and more succulent than spring grass. The people ate to their heart's content. They ate until they could barely move. The sparkle returned to their eyes. They began to laugh and talk. Some even began to dance.

Crazy Horse didn't dance, but he did smoke a pipe with American Horse, much to Buffalo Rabbit's chagrin. When He Dog came to join them, Buffalo Rabbit crept onto his knee. Legs was lying by the fire, Black Shawl was sewing, and Maka Mani was perched on Crazy Horse's shoulder. For a while it seemed like the old times.

Early on the morning of the fourth day, the people dug out their proudest clothes and washed and re-plaited their hair. The women put their finest saddles on the pack ponies, rolled up their tipis and loaded their travois. The warriors painted their faces, preened their lances and shields, and fluffed up their war-bonnets. The women and children dressed in their best.
The soldiers waited patiently. They didn't want to annoy Crazy Horse and have him change his mind about going to the agency. When he told them he was ready, they rounded up the remaining cattle and hitched the mules to

the wagons. Then they mounted their horses, took their places at front and behind, and began the final march to The Red Cloud Agency.

Maka Mani was first to spot them. He'd flown ahead and found a perch on top of an agency tipi. When he saw movement in the hills to his north, he flapped his wings and squawked. An Indian policeman glanced up and smiled at him.

'Can you see them?' the Indian asked.

'Yes, Young Man Afraid,' the raven replied. 'That is them. The Crazy Horse people are coming.'

By now, the Indians in The Red Cloud Agency had also seen the movement in the hills. As they shaded their eyes and looked towards the hill's dark pine trees, a posse of soldiers emerged. The people at the agency rose to their feet. Mothers took their children by the hand, warriors stood expectantly, old men leant on their walking sticks.

There was a pause.

More soldiers appeared.

Riding in their centre was Red Cloud.

The people moved forward, eyes on the hills.

And then they saw a pale figure, riding on a pony.

His face was unpainted. His chest was bare but for a pebble on a cord, and he had a single hawk's feather at the back of his head. Trotting beside him was a three-legged wolf in a buffalo-wool waistcoat and, sitting upright on his pony's withers, was a small black poodle. She too, had a pebble around her neck and a single hawk's feather at the back of her head.

'It is Crazy Horse,' the agency people whispered.

'Crazy Horse!' one of them shouted aloud.

And then suddenly, they were rushing forward, laughing and shouting and waving their arms.

'Crazy Horse!'

'Crazy Horse!'

Crazy Horse reached the brow of the hill and halted his pony. Riding either side of him were He Dog and Little Big Man, both in all their finery, both holding lances and shields. He caught their eye and, very softly, began to sing. They took his cue and began to sing, too. The song spread. It spread to the Crazy Horse warriors, to the women, children and old folks. It spread all the way down their two-mile long line, and then it spread to the The Red Cloud Agency. The song drifted over the hills and filled the valley below. Soon it seemed that all the world was singing. All the world, with one exception. Maka Mani glanced at Red Cloud. Red Cloud was not singing. Red Cloud was not amused.

The final part of the journey took several hours. As the Crazy Horse people came down from the hills, they were welcomed by the agency Indians and counted by the soldiers. Eight-hundred-and-eighty-nine men, women and children. Their ponies were counted. Seventeen-hundred. Finally, their guns were counted. One-hundred-and-seventeen.

Then the ponies and guns were taken away.

CHAPTER FORTY-SIX

The Red Cloud Agency, Nebraska.
Six weeks later
The end of June, The Moon of Berries, 1877

The Crazy Horse people pitched their village at the farthest end of the agency, six miles from Fort Robinson.

They had many visitors over the next few weeks. Some were friends from the old days, some were just curious to see the famous Crazy Horse. Many were surprised at how slight he was, how modest and shy.

No one was more curious or surprised than the soldiers. Here was the man who'd closed the forts on the trail to the gold fields in Montana. Here was the man who'd given Crook and Miles the runaround. Here was the man who'd routed Crook at The Rosebud and beaten Custer at The Little Big Horn.

The soldiers were fascinated.

They liked Crazy Horse and he liked them.

He couldn't really talk to them. He wasn't a great talker at the best of times, and his English was poor, but they rubbed along as best they could, using hand signals and, occasionally, an interpreter. They quizzed him endlessly, especially about the about the battle at The Little Big Horn. Who had helped him? Nobody. Did he kill Custer? No. So who did? He didn't know. Did he see

248

Custer? He didn't know that, either. Possibly. He didn't think so.

The soldier who visited Crazy Horse the most was Lieutenant 'White Hat' Clark.

White Hat was in charge of the agency, and therefore in charge of making sure that Crazy Horse stayed there. Crazy Horse had no intention of going anywhere. He was in charge of looking after his people. He wanted to make sure they were properly fed and cared for until they could move to the land they'd been promised.

Every time he saw White Hat, he asked about this land.

'I have chosen the place,' he said one day. 'It is beside a creek that enters The Powder River…'

'You will get your land,' White Hat snapped. 'But first you must go to Washington to meet The Great Father.'

'I already have a father,' Crazy Horse replied. 'I do not need yours. I will see your father when I have my land.'

'But *why*?' Buffalo Rabbit asked Legs. 'Why does Crazy Horse have to go to Washington?'

'Because he's a prize catch,' said the wolf. 'The President wants to show him off. He wants Indian haters to see he's been caught, and Indian lovers to see he's alive and well. And *tame*,' he added with a snarl.

White Hat persisted with his plans for the Washington trip, and Crazy Horse began to ask questions. It seemed he was considering a visit to The Great Father, after all.

'How will I get to Washington?' he asked.

'On the train,' White Hat answered.

'On the iron horse,' said the interpreter.

'What is it like to ride, this iron horse?'

'Oh, *I* know that!' squeaked Buffalo Rabbit.

'You do?' Legs was incredulous. 'How come?'

'I went on one once. Ages ago. When I was a puppy.'

'*And*? What *was* it like?'

'Noisy. When it started, it made a hiss. I think that's the steam coming out. And then it went whoosh a bit, and then it went puff. Puff. Puff. The puffs were slow, at first, but then they got faster and louder, like this, *Puff-Puff! Puff-Puff! Puff-Puff!*'

'You're panting, Rabbit.'

'Because that's what it's like. It's just like a panting dog. It got faster and faster. I could feel the wheels going over the tracks. They went clunk-cluck, rattle-rattle, clunk-cluck, rattle-rattle and the carriages swayed from side to side. Then it whistled, *toot-toot! toot-toot!* That made me jump!'

'Would I enjoy my ride on the iron horse?' Crazy Horse wondered.

'No,' Buffalo Rabbit shook her head. 'No, you would not! You'd *hate* it!'

Every morning, Crazy Horse, Buffalo Rabbit and Legs went to check on the people and ask if they needed anything. The answer was usually no. They'd received their government supplies. They had their blankets, flour and bolts of cloth. Friends had brought more things. They had these things, but they had nothing to do. The warriors had no need to choose fletchings, make arrows or mend bows. They couldn't hunt without ponies, and anyway, there was no wildlife. The women had no fresh kills with which to deal. No meat to dry, no wasna to make, no stores to prepare. No skins to scrape, stretch, cure and soften. No travois to pack for the move to new grazing, no camp to set up, no ponies to water. No ponies. No more gentle snorts in camp. No stamping of hooves and swishing of tails. No washing in streams and plaiting of manes. No soft ears to bend back, no muzzles to snuffle the hand, no hooves to pick out. There was no racing, no competing to spin and turn, no sweeping up of fallen arrows, no practise for the buffalo hunt. There were no ponies. The people missed their ponies. They missed their work. They were bored.

Legs and Buffalo Rabbit were bored, too, but at least they had their freedom. No one was spying on *them* from the back of an army horse. No one was following *their* every move. Sometimes they'd wander out of camp, sit on a bluff and watch the world go by. Other times, they'd go for a walk through the agency.

One day, they stumbled into the Bad Face camp.

'Turn around,' Buffalo Rabbit suddenly hissed.

'What?'

'Turn around. Walk with me.'

'Why? What's the matter?'

'Black Buffalo,' whispered Buffalo Rabbit. 'I just saw Black Buffalo!'

'Where?' Legs looked over his shoulder.

'Don't do that! She'll see us!'

'So what if she does? She must know we're here in

the agency. Where is she?'

'Over there.'

Sure enough, Crazy Horse's one time love was sitting under a nearby tree. Next to her was a little girl. The girl was about six-years-old, and her hair, which Black Buffalo was combing, was unusually fair, as was her skin.

'You don't think?'

'That she's Crazy Horse's child? Probably.'

'Ooh,' Buffalo Rabbit cooed. 'I wonder what No Water thinks about that!'

'Not our business,' said the wolf. 'Let's move on.'

Deeper into the Bad Face camp, the poodle and the wolf came upon a huddle of men. They were seated cross-legged on the ground, smoking pipes and whispering. One of these men was Red Cloud. Next to him was No Water.

'Let's eavesdrop,' said Legs. 'Quick. Duck behind that cactus.'

'Crazy Horse has agreed to meet with The Great Father,' said Red Cloud. 'Now White Hat will reward him with a buffalo hunt. Crazy Horse will be given guns and ponies and allowed to go north and hunt!'

'This is not good,' said No Water. 'Why, I would not be surprised if Crazy Horse took his guns and ponies and never came back. He could start the fight all over again…'

'No,' Buffalo Rabbit hissed. 'He wouldn't do that.'

'The soldiers at Fort Robinson should be told,' said a slimy voice. 'We should tell them that Crazy Horse is planning to fight them again.'

'Don't you dare,' Legs growled.

The slimy voice belonged to Woman's Dress, a slippery sort and gossip who was always sucking up to people, especially the officers at Fort Robinson.

'White Hat has also promised a feast,' added a man named Red Dog. 'If Crazy Horse goes to Washington, the agency will hold a feast!'

'Ah, yes,' growled Red Cloud. 'The feast. And do you know where this feast will be held? In the Crazy Horse camp!'

'That was the idea of Young Man Afraid,' grumbled No Water. 'He told White Hat that Crazy Horse should host the feast. Crazy Horse is new to this place, but already White Hat wishes to please him.'

'This Crazy Horse has many friends,' said Woman's Dress. 'Many friends and many followers. They are saying now that The Great Father will make him head of all the Lakota.'

'Pah!' Red Cloud spat above the crack of something breaking.

'He's snapped his pipe!' giggled Buffalo Rabbit. 'Red Cloud's so furious he's snapped his pipe!'

'We must stop Crazy Horse's trip to Washington!' Red Cloud ranted. 'We must stop the hunt and stop the feast! Most of all, we must stop Crazy Horse from having his own land!'

'He must stay here,' No Water agreed. 'He must not have his own land and his own agency.'

'He must not be made head of all the Lakota,' added Woman's Dress. 'No one can be that. But Red Cloud must be head of the agencies. Only Red Cloud.'

'Toady,' Legs snarled.

'We must start a rumour,' said Red Cloud. 'Crazy Horse must hear that The Great Father plans to send him far away and lock him in an iron room. That will stop him wanting to go to Washington!'

'His hunt will be cancelled,' No Water nodded gleefully.

'But so will the feast,' blustered Red Dog. 'I was looking forward to the feast.'

'Forget about the feast!' Red Cloud snapped. 'We will start a second rumour. The soldiers must hear that Crazy Horse plans to fight them again.'

'That will stop his hunt!'

'Yes. It may even stop this land of his.'

'HOYE!'

'Well, one thing's for sure,' said Buffalo Rabbit as she and Legs slipped away from the cactus.

'What's that?' asked Legs.

'Red Cloud's rumours. They'll spread like grassfire in this place. Everybody gossips.'

'I know,' said the wolf. 'It's partly because they're so bored. But a lot of them are jealous of Crazy Horse. They always have been, but it seems worse than ever, now. They don't like the attention he's getting.'

'Nor does he,' said Buffalo Rabbit. 'He'd rather be left alone.'

'Yes, well, I don't think that's going to happen.'

'Let's get out of here,' Buffalo Rabbit quickened her pace. '*I* don't like this Bad Face camp. Those women are pointing at us and sniggering.'

'I don't like it either,' said Legs. 'In fact, I don't like this whole agency.'

'So why don't we escape? We could run away, just the three of us. You, me and our master. Maka Mani could come too. We could live together in the wild. We can find food. We can all hunt. It wouldn't be a problem.'

'Hunt?' Legs laughed out loud. 'You've never hunted in your life!'

'I could learn.'

'Of course you could,' the wolf said kindly. 'And if you couldn't, I'd do your hunting for you. Leaving is a very nice thought, but Crazy Horse won't leave his people. Not until he gets his own land. When *that* happens, we'll *all* leave.'

CHAPTER FORTY-SEVEN
The Red Cloud Agency, Nebraska.
Two months later
The end of August, The Moon of Ripe Plums, 1877

The first of Red Cloud's rumours worked well. Crazy Horse heard that his visit to Washington was a trap. He told White Hat he'd changed his mind about going there, and the buffalo hunt and the feast were cancelled.

The second rumour was less successful. The soldiers didn't believe that Crazy Horse was planning to fight them again. They knew he wouldn't risk losing his promised land. And anyway, if Crazy Horse was going to run off and cause trouble, he'd have done it by now. His pony had been returned to him and he'd been given a gun. Crazy Horse had become an agency policeman.

He'd taken some persuading. He didn't want to wear a blue soldier coat. But then He Dog had become a policeman, and he and Young Man Afraid had said that being a policeman wasn't any different from being an akicita. All Crazy Horse need do was help keep the peace, just as he'd always done. For that, he'd be able to ride again. He wouldn't be so *bored*. So Crazy Horse had signed up as a policeman, been given a gun, a blue soldier coat and the thing he'd most wanted - his pony.

Meanwhile, way up north, a tribe called the Nez Percés, or Pierced Noses, had left their agency in Idaho and crossed into Montana and The Big Horn Country. Now they were causing havoc and running the army ragged.

Three Stars Crook was furious, until he had an idea. The Crazy Horse warriors were captives and still fighting-fit. No one knew the Big Horn Country better than them, and no Indian had fought there more recently. With their help, Crook could crush the Nez Percés.

He decided to enlist Crazy Horse's warriors into the U.S. Army. In exchange, they would be given ponies, guns and ammunition. A few signed up immediately. Others wavered. Most said they would not fight unless Crazy Horse was at their side.

Crazy Horse refused. He didn't want to help Three Stars Crook and he didn't believe the story about the Nez Percés. He thought he was being tricked into hunting down his old friend Sitting Bull. In the old days, Indian signals would have told him that the story about the Nez Percés was true. They would also have told him that Sitting Bull was safely in Canada. But these were not the old days. The Indian signals had been shut down. Crazy Horse was convinced that Three Stars' true target was Sitting Bull.

'No,' he told White Hat. 'I will not fight. You got me to come here. You said it was for peace. You can keep me here if you want to, but you cannot make me go where I do not want to go.'

White Hat kept trying.

Day after day, he and his interpreter came to Crazy Horse's tipi. Day after day, they badgered him.

Finally, Crazy Horse snapped.

'All right!' he shouted in Lakota. 'I will fight. I will fight until every Nez Percés is dead!'

'What did he say?' White Hat asked the interpreter.

'That he will fight until every white man is dead.'

'No, he didn't,' Legs leapt to his feet. 'He did not say that! Take that back!'

'Take it back!' Buffalo Rabbit barked.

'Translate properly, you stupid, stupid man!' screeched Maka Mani.

Legs snarled, sprang at the interpreter, knocked him sideways and pinned him to the ground.

'What is the matter?' Crazy Horse asked.

'He's trying to get you into trouble, master,' said Buffalo Rabbit. 'He's telling lies to get you into trouble.'

'Get this animal off me!' gurgled the interpreter in English.

'I can't do that,' White Hat replied, his face as white as his hat. 'Only Crazy Horse can do that.'

'Then shoot it!' said the interpreter.

His eyes were squeezed tight shut and his neck was turning purple.

'I can't,' said White Hat. 'I came here to talk. I didn't bring my gun.'

'My wolf does not attack without reason,' said Crazy Horse.

'Good reason! Good reason!' squawked Maka Mani.

'Then why's he doing it?' asked White Hat.

'Open your eyes,' Crazy Horse told the interpreter in Lakota.

258

The interpreter did as he was told.

Legs' jaws were within inches of his face. The black lips were curled back, gums exposed, yellow teeth snapping.

'Those jaws can crush the bones of a buffalo,' said Crazy Horse slowly. 'They can snap you in two as the elk snaps the willow. Remember that. Now translate again. Tell White Hat what I said. I said I will fight until every Nez Percés is dead. Translate it!'

'He says he will fight until every Nez Percés is dead,' said the interpreter in English.

'Nez Percés?' White Hat repeated. 'That's not what you said before. You said every *white man*.'

'I know. I was wrong. It's Nez Percés.'

'Definitely?'

'Definitely.'

'That's more like it,' Legs growled.

The muddle had been cleared up, but the damage had been done. A seed had been planted in White Hat's mind.

CHAPTER FORTY-EIGHT

The Red Cloud Agency, Nebraska.
A few days later
2nd September, The Moon of the Black Calf, 1877

On 2nd September, Three Stars Crook arrived at Fort Robinson to collect his new soldiers and meet with the Indians at The Red Cloud Agency.

Crazy Horse stayed in his tipi. He didn't want to be a part of this meeting. He didn't want to listen to Three Stars droning on in English. He didn't want to hear Red Cloud and others speak in Lakota and most likely be mistranslated. He was sick of the whole damn thing. His people were sick of it, too, but Three Stars might have good things to tell them. He'd promised to speak to The Great Father about their food. They were already living on soup, and now winter was coming. They wanted to hear what Three Stars had to say.

As the people wandered to the meeting place, Three Stars Crook and White Hat Clark set out from Fort Robinson in a horse-drawn carriage accompanied by mounted soldiers. Maka Mani flew alongside them until, halfway to the meeting, Woman's Dress suddenly charged in on a pony and rode up to Three Stars.

'Oh, oh,' chattered the raven. 'Here comes trouble.'

The raven swooped and landed on Woman's Dress' shoulder.

'What is it?' Three Stars asked impatiently.

'Information,' said Woman's Dress greasily. 'I have information.'

'I don't have time for this,' replied Three Stars.

'No, wait,' said Woman's Dress. 'Do not go to the meeting. If you do, you will die! Crazy Horse will kill you, and his warriors will kill your soldiers.'

'Lies! All lies!' Maka Mani screeched.

'We should turn around,' said White Hat.

'Turn around? I never turn around!' barked Three Stars.

But then he seemed to think again.

'Who is this man?' he asked with a nod to Woman's Dress. 'Can we trust him?'

'No!' Maka Mani squawked. 'No, you can't! No one can trust Woman's Dress. He's a meddler and a gossip! Just a pawn in Red Cloud's game!'

'Yes, we can trust him,' said White Hat. 'He is one of our informants. Whatever he tells us will be good and true. We should turn around. Crazy Horse will not hesitate to kill you. He killed Custer, remember?'

'Ugh!' Maka Mani despaired.

'Turn the horses!' Three Stars ordered the carriage driver. 'Turn the horses. We're going back to the fort. No. Wait!'

He gestured to two of his soldiers.

'Go to the meeting place,' he told them in a low voice. 'Say that I cannot attend. Say I am called away on urgent business. Then ask the following Indians to come immediately to Fort Robinson...'

Maka Mani didn't wait to hear who these Indians were. He didn't need to. He flapped his wings and prepared to take off. Before he did, he pierced Woman's Dress' soldier coat with his talons.

'Take that!' he screeched as he raked the Indian's flesh.

CHAPTER FORTY-NINE
Fort Robinson, Nebraska.
A little later

Maka Mani followed Three Stars and White Hat back to Fort Robinson. When they got down from their carriage and strode towards one of the fort's buildings, he flitted past its windows until he spotted them again, taking seats inside an office. They were joined by an interpreter and Lieutenant Colonel Bradley, commander of the fort.

Maka Mani landed on the windowsill. By then, the hand-picked Indians whom Three Stars had summoned were beginning to arrive. The raven watched them take their place, cross-legged on the floor.

'Ah, as I thought,' he cawed. 'The usual suspects. Red Cloud, Red Dog, No Water, Woman's Dress, various Indian headmen, a few agency police.'

Three Stars Crook opened his secret meeting by asking Woman's Dress to repeat what he'd told him. Woman's Dress did this in English. The interpreter translated, but it was hardly necessary. Most of the Indians present spoke good English, and even those who didn't had understood the words 'Crazy Horse' 'die' and 'kill'. They nodded knowingly and made tut-tutting noises.

Three Stars then asked White Hat to tell everyone what Crazy Horse had said to *him*. White Hat replied that Crazy Horse had told him he would fight until every last white man was dead. He left out the bit about the mistranslation.

'So you see,' Three Stars addressed his audience. 'This Crazy Horse is a dangerous man. He is not a peace lover, like you. He is out to make trouble. He will make trouble for all the Lakota.'

Three Stars paused to scan the Indian faces and gauge their reaction.

'I want to help you,' he sighed. 'I want to help you to stop this dangerous man, this Crazy Horse. For that, I will need *your* help. I want you to catch Crazy Horse.'

'*What*?' Maka Mani pranced on the windowsill.

The Indians huddled together in earnest whispers. Maka Mani craned his neck. He wanted to hear what was being said, but he was afraid to fly right into the room. White Hat would see his ankle bracelet and White Hat could not be trusted. He might decide that a pet of Crazy Horse was a trophy worth having. So Maka Mani stayed where he was, straining to hear the hushed and muddled whispers. Finally, the Indians seemed to reach a conclusion. Red Cloud spoke for them.

'You say that Crazy Horse is dangerous,' he said. 'You are right. You say that he will make trouble. You are right. And so we say, let us not just catch him. Let us kill him!'

Maka Mani was stunned. At first he couldn't move, he was so shocked. But then the life rushed back to his legs and wings, and he pranced and screeched and flapped in a fury.

'Traitors! Traitors!'

Three Stars shot him a look. Maka Mani feared he might order that the window be closed, but he soon returned to the matter in hand.

'That will not be necessary,' he told the Indians. 'I do not want you to kill Crazy Horse, just arrest him.'

He turned to Colonel Bradley.

'Give them guns and ponies,' he added. 'And give them the 3rd Cavalry. Eight companies should be enough.'

'*Enough*?' Maka Mani cawed in disbelief. 'I should say so. Eight companies is almost five-hundred men! That's more than Custer had at The Little Big Horn.'

Three Stars rose from his chair.

'Make sure it is done,' he told Colonel Bradley. 'When you have him, put him on a train to Omaha. From there he will go to the Dry Tortugas.'

'NO!' Maka Mani screamed. 'You cannot send him there! Even the ravens don't go there!'

Three Stars swept out of the room.

When he'd gone, White Hat spoke.

'I will give two-hundreds of the dollars to the man who arrests Crazy Horse,' he said.

'Hoye!' the Indians chorused.

'HOYE!' shouted a single voice.

No Water was up on his feet.

'He can hardly wait,' the raven sighed. 'He's so desperate to get at Crazy Horse, he'd probably pay White Hat!'

'SIT DOWN!' barked Colonel Bradley.

No Water sat, reluctantly, and Colonel Bradley raised a hand and turned to the interpreter.

'I want you to translate this,' he said. 'I want the Indians to understand what I am about to say. There must be no mistake. Now, listen to me,' he told the Indians. 'General Crook is my senior officer. I cannot overrule him. So. Crazy Horse must be caught and arrested. But I am commander of this fort and I can give my own orders. Those orders are that you are *not*, I repeat *not*, to arrest Crazy Horse tonight or any other night. He will be arrested in daylight and he will *only* be arrested. I do not want a hair on his head to be harmed.'

He waited for the interpreter to translate.

'Is that understood?' he asked the Indians.

'Hau.'

CHAPTER FIFTY

The Crazy Horse camp, The Red Cloud Agency.
Three days later
5th September, The Moon of the Black Calf, 1877

On the morning of 5th September, eight companies of The United States 3rd Cavalry mustered at Fort Robinson. The five-hundred troopers climbed onto their horses, adjusted their sabres, picked up their reins and rode out of the fort. They were joined by four-hundred mounted warriors and policemen, many with guns. At the very front, and jostling to stay there, were Red Cloud and No Water. Amongst the others were Little Big Man, American Horse, Young Man Afraid and He Dog. There was no sign of White Hat or Woman's Dress.

Maka Mani landed on Young Man Afraid's pony.

'Don't worry,' said Young Man Afraid. 'I am here. He Dog is here. We cannot stop this. But we *can* make sure your master is not harmed. Go now, bird. Try to warn him what is coming.'

'I *have* tried,' the raven gaped his beak. 'I've been trying for two whole days! I've drummed against his tipi and pranced on his floor. I even grabbed his hair at one point. He knows they mean to arrest him but he also knows he's innocent. He thinks that's enough, that things will turn out right.'

The raven stared at the nine-hundred horsemen.

'He has no idea,' Young Man Afraid added sadly. 'Go, bird. Fly quickly to him.'

It was a full six miles from Fort Robinson to the Crazy Horse camp. Flying at top speed, Maka Mani could cover the distance in ten minutes. Assuming the horses and ponies followed at a steady trot, it would take them three times that long. Maka Mani had twenty minutes in hand.

As he approached the Crazy Horse village, he spotted a pony. It was galloping ahead of him, flat-out, neck stretched, tail streaming out behind it. On board was a young Lakota warrior. His name was Red Feather, and he was Black Shawl's little brother.

Maka Mani and Red Feather reached Crazy Horse's tipi at exactly the same moment. Legs and Buffalo Rabbit were standing outside. They barked, but Crazy Horse had already heard the beating wings and skidding hooves.

'They are coming!' Red Feather leapt from his pony.

'How many?' asked Crazy Horse.

'Nearly ten hundreds.'

'*Ten hundreds*!' Legs and Buffalo Rabbit growled.

'*Ten hundreds*?' Crazy Horse was amazed. 'But I am only one man!'

'I know,' Red Feather nodded. 'But now you must run. Run! Take my sister and run!'

'Yes!' Maka Mani squawked. 'You must run! Don't stay here. If you do, you'll be put on an iron horse to

Omaha, then sent to the Dry Tortugas! Do you know about the Dry Tortugas? They are islands. Flat, arid and surrounded by sea. There is nothing on the Dry Tortugas. Nothing except for a prison.'

'I cannot leave my people,' said Crazy Horse. 'I have done nothing wrong. I will talk to Colonel Bradley. He will listen to me. He will know I speak the truth. What is it, Rabbit?'

The poodle was pawing at her master's legs.

'Look,' she whimpered. 'Look over there.'

A cloud of dust was rolling in from the west.

Crazy Horse ducked into his tipi and quickly returned with Black Shawl and his policeman's gun.

'Take this,' he said, handing the gun to Red Feather.

'No. Keep it,' said Red Feather. 'You may need it.'

'I do not want it,' Crazy Horse replied. 'Take it.'

He put an arm around Black Shawl's waist and drew her close to him. Then he lifted his blanket from his shoulders and placed it over both their heads. It was a sign that he wanted some private time with his wife.

Red Feather backed away on his pony, but Maka Mani, Legs and Buffalo Rabbit were not so polite.

The raven craned his neck from his perch on the pony. The wolf and the poodle sat up on their haunches and peered into blanket's shadows.

'You cannot stay here,' Crazy Horse whispered to Black Shawl. 'You must go with Red Feather. Let him take you somewhere safe. I will not be long. I will explain it all to Colonel Bradley and then I will come and find you. Hush, now. Do not cry.'

'Don't cry, Black Shawl,' repeated Buffalo Rabbit.

'Cante chante sica yaun sai ye. Don't have a sad heart.'

'Heyah nolotancila,' sobbed Black Shawl.

'I love you too,' said Crazy Horse.

He kissed his wife and slid the blanket away.

'Now go,' he said. 'Quick!'

Red Feather reached out a hand and Black Shawl grasped it and leapt up behind him. She didn't look back. As she and Red Feather cantered away, the sound of their pony's hooves was replaced by the thunder of four-thousand more.

Crazy Horse was escorted back to Fort Robinson.

He was allowed to ride his own pony. Buffalo Rabbit sat on its withers. Her master's hands were on either side of her, one holding the reins, the other resting on his thigh. Buffalo Rabbit could see them trembling. She could see Legs' long, silver body moving along beside her, Maka Mani's wings shimmering above her, and Young Man Afraid riding close and keeping watch. Further out, maintaining a distance, were the Crazy Horse warriors. They whooped and shouted and jeered at the soldiers, but they couldn't do much more. They were unhorsed, unarmed and heavily outnumbered.

Nearer to Fort Robinson, He Dog trotted up and laid a hand on Crazy Horse's shoulder.

'Hau, old friend,' Crazy Horse forced a smile.

'Be careful,' He Dog smiled back. 'I will stay with you as long as I can. When we get to the fort, watch your step. It is a dangerous place.'

'Dangerous...'

Buffalo Rabbit remembered something.

She whipped her head round and glanced at her master's chest. It was completely bare. She raised her eyes and scanned his hair. It was flowing freely.

'PEBBLES!' she barked to Legs. 'He's not wearing his pebbles!'

'*What*?' the wolf barked back. 'Are you *sure*?'

'Yes, I'm sure.'

'Crows,' Legs swore. 'Should I go back for them? I don't know what to do! What should I do, Rabbit?'

'Go back. Please go back.'

'It'll take me almost an hour...' the wolf pondered. 'We're nearly at Fort Robinson. Shouldn't I stay with Crazy Horse?'

'NO!' Rabbit squealed. 'Go and get the pebbles! What the..?'

Maka Mani had swept low over Legs and raked his fur with his talons. Now he was twirling and spinning at the wolf's feet. 'This is no time for dancing, bird!'

'He's trying to tell you something,' said Buffalo Rabbit.

'I know that,' Legs replied. 'I wish I understood what he's saying, but I don't. I'm going back to the tipi,' he added as he turned away. 'I'll see you as soon as I can.'

Buffalo Rabbit watched the wolf go. He was running fast with his lop-sided gait. For a while, Maka Mani stayed with him, but then the raven flipped in the air and shot off like a bullet.

'He's gone to fetch the pebbles!' Buffalo Rabbit suddenly realised. 'Maka Mani's gone to fetch the pebbles!'

Just outside the entrance to Fort Robinson, Little Big Man came alongside Crazy Horse, and Buffalo Rabbit smiled.

'Good,' she muttered to herself. 'Little Big Man speaks good English. He can help Crazy Horse. He can explain all the jealousies and rumours, clear up the misunderstandings. I haven't always liked him, and it's true he can be rash. He's got himself in plenty of trouble over the years. He's got Crazy Horse in trouble too, especially on the day of the No Water shooting. He caught my master by the arm and held him back, but Crazy Horse said he was only trying to prevent a fight. Yes,' thought Buffalo Rabbit. 'It's good that Little Big Man's here.'

Inside the gates to the fort, Crazy Horse was told to dismount from his pony. He did this quickly, handed his reins to He Dog, and set Buffalo Rabbit on the ground. Soldiers and Indians were pouring up behind him, then dividing to face each other. Some of the Indians were restless and noisy. Their ponies were snorting and pawing the ground. The soldiers raised their rifles and the Indians fell silent. An officer emerged from one of the fort's buildings and strode up to Crazy Horse.

'Captain Kennington,' the officer introduced himself.

'Good day,' Crazy Horse replied in English. 'Good meet with you. I wish see Colonel Bradley.'

'Then I will take you to him,' Kennington smiled.

He nodded to Little Big Man who got down from his pony and took Crazy Horse by the arm.

'Don't let him do that!' Buffalo Rabbit barked.

She stood on her hind legs and pawed at her master.

'Don't let *anyone* do that! Remember your vision. No one must take you by the arm.'

'It is all right, Rabbit,' Crazy Horse replied. 'We are only going to Colonel Bradley. Come. Walk beside me.'

'Follow me,' said Kennington.

Kennington and Little Big Man led Crazy Horse towards a doorway. Buffalo Rabbit followed. When she reached the threshold, she paused and glanced back. The soldiers' guns were still raised. She scanned the Indians' faces. Red Cloud and No Water, standing at the front. American Horse, wearing his blue soldier coat and his grizzly bear necklace. He Dog and Young Man Afraid, so close to each other that their ponies' sides were touching. Around them, the Crazy Horse warriors, the men who'd stayed loyal, who'd never gossiped or spread nasty rumours, who hadn't gone with Three Stars to fight the Nez Percés. There was no sign of White Hat or Woman's Dress.

Inside the building, Crazy Horse again asked to see Colonel Bradley.

'It is too late today,' Kennington replied. 'You will see him tomorrow. This way, please.'

They walked down a corridor, Kennington, Crazy Horse and Little Big Man all in a row, Buffalo Rabbit behind them.

Buffalo Rabbit raised her nose and sniffed the air. It smelled bad and it was getting worse with every step. An acrid cocktail of sweat, urine, faeces, rotting food; the odour of cockroach, the stench of rat, the mustiness of maggot.

They came to a door. To the right of it was a soldier. He was holding his rifle diagonally. The barrel was resting on his left shoulder. Slotted onto it was a long, razor-sharp blade, a bayonet.

The soldier clicked his heels, unlocked the door and pulled at it. It was heavy and slow-moving but, as it groaned open, the smells beyond it rushed forward, and so did other groans. Buffalo Rabbit steadied herself against the stench and tried to decipher these groans. They sounded almost human. She pushed between her master and Kennington and saw a row of cages. There were men inside these cages. Some were soldiers, most were Indians. All were chained to the floor by their ankles.

'NO!' she yelped.

'NO!' Crazy Horse roared.

He tried to shake himself free but Little Big Man held on fast. Crazy Horse reached to his belt and pulled out a knife.

'Let me go!' he roared again.

Buffalo Rabbit crouched, ears back, tail tucked in, teeth bared.

'Let him go!' she snarled.

Crazy Horse slashed with the knife, cutting wildly through the thick air until the blade found purchase and Little Big Man was bleeding.

'Stab him!' hollered Little Big Man.

'Stab him!' echoed Kennington.

The soldier at the door lowered his bayonet and

plunged it into Crazy Horse's stomach.

'NO!' screamed Buffalo Rabbit.

'NO!' came a screech.

Buffalo Rabbit whipped round.

Maka Mani's vast wings were hurtling towards her, filling the corridor with blackness. The raven's right foot was stretched, iron-hard talons ready to rake. His left foot was curled. Grasped between the scaly toes were two leather cords.

'The pebbles!' Buffalo Rabbit squealed. 'Quick! Give them to…'

The soldier withdrew his bayonet and plunged again.

Crazy Horse screamed and flung out an arm to save himself from falling. As he did so, Maka Mani swept overhead, opened his talons and dropped the pebble necklace. For a moment, the necklace seemed to float in slow motion, as though searching for its master. Its cord spanned out, formed a perfect circle and hovered. The soldier plunged again and Crazy Horse crashed sideways and slumped against the wall. Blood was pouring from his stomach. He clenched his teeth against the pain and reached out for the necklace. It fell, bounced once, then rolled away from him. Buffalo Rabbit charged forward to grab it but Little Big Man got there first. He scooped the necklace up and closed his fist around it.

'Mine!' he sneered. 'All mine!'

'The other one!' Buffalo Rabbit screamed at Maka Mani. 'Give Crazy Horse the other pebble! Give him the one he wears in his hair!'

'No,' cawed Maka Mani. 'We must save that for later.

Kennington's gone for the army surgeon, and I must fetch Worm. Stay here, Rabbit.'

'Don't go!' Buffalo whimpered. 'Don't leave us!'

'Stay there!' the raven repeated from over his shoulder. 'Friends are coming! I can see them! Stay there!'

Buffalo Rabbit returned to her master. He was quiet, now. His twisted body was pressed against the wall, half sitting, half lying. His hands were clasped across his stomach but they couldn't stop the flow of blood. It streamed between his long brown fingers, seeped into his leggings and dripped to the floor. Buffalo Rabbit growled a warning to Little Big Man and the soldier.

'Stand back. Leave me alone. Let me go to him.'

They didn't try to stop her.

They allowed her to lay her head on her master's arm, nuzzle his hand and lick his fingers.

The friends that Maka Mani had seen were Legs and He Dog. They came haring up the corridor, but the soldier and Little Big Man didn't stop them, either. They knew better than to mess with Legs, and He Dog had his policeman's rifle.

'What happened?' panted Legs. 'No, don't tell me. I can see what they've done.'

'It's bad Legs,' Buffalo Rabbit whispered. 'It's very bad.'

'Did Maka Mani bring the pebbles? He got to the tipi before me. I saw him fly back with them.'

'Yes,' said Buffalo Rabbit. 'He brought them, but he couldn't get them to Crazy Horse.'

'So where are they?'

'*He's* got one,' Buffalo Rabbit snarled at Little Big Man. 'The other one's still with Maka Mani. He flew away with it.'

'Gone for Worm, I imagine,' the wolf surmised.

'There was an officer here,' said Buffalo Rabbit. 'Kennington. I think he's gone to get the army surgeon. We'll have the army surgeon *and* Worm.'

She glanced at her master's face. The eyes were closed, the skin was grey.

'Will it be enough?' she asked.

'I don't know,' said the wolf. 'I really don't know. He Dog will help in the meantime. Step back, Rabbit. Let him do what he can.'

He Dog removed his blanket and used it to bind Crazy Horse's stomach. Soon after that, the army surgeon arrived, and so did Maka Mani and Worm.

'Son, I am here,' said Worm.

The surgeon unravelled the blanket. When he saw the terrible wounds, he caught Worm's eye and shook his head.

'Let me take him home,' said Worm shakily. 'Will someone please ask Colonel Bradley? I want to take him home.'

The surgeon nodded.

'I will go,' said He Dog. 'I will go to Bradley.'

Kennington and the surgeon carried Crazy Horse out of the cold, dark corridor and into an office. The sun had gone down, and the room and its windows were stark and bare, but at least there was an oil lamp. The surgeon worked by its pale orange light. He rebound the wounds then poured a measure of liquid and held it to Crazy Horse's lips.

'What's that?' asked Legs suspiciously.

'Morphine, I think,' said Buffalo Rabbit, sniffing the air. 'Yes. That's morphine, all right. Mr Irvine had it once. It's a painkiller.'

'So is this,' Maka Mani cawed.

He hopped forward and carefully placed the remaining pebble on Crazy Horse's chest.

'We cannot take him home,' said He Dog from the doorway. 'Colonel Bradley said no.'

'Then we will stay here,' Worm replied. 'We will all stay here.'

Towards midnight, Crazy Horse opened his eyes.

Legs' head was resting on his shoulder, Maka Mani was perched beside him, and Buffalo Rabbit was curled against his chest. Worm took his hand and leant over him.

'I am bad hurt,' Crazy Horse whispered. 'Tell the people it is no use to depend on me now.'

He ruffled the wolf's deep silver fur and stroked the raven's silky black throat. He ran his hands over the poodle's soft, curly coat and whispered again.

'Cante chante sica yaun sai ye,' he said. 'Don't have a sad heart. Heyah nolotancila. I love you.'

Then he closed his eyes and died.

"A robin redbreast in a cage
Puts all heaven in a rage."

'That was written by a famous poet, William Blake,' said Cavendish.

'Well, Mr Blake was right,' answered Bo. 'You can't keep a robin in a cage. Crazy Horse was a robin, and that agency was a cage. He couldn't live that way.'

'No, he couldn't,' Cavendish agreed. 'Actually, it would have been worse than that. If he hadn't died, he'd have been put on a train and sent to a *real* cage. The government planned to send him to the Dry Tortugas and put him in a prison.'

'So Red Cloud's rumour was right...'

'Only by coincidence. The rumour was made-up. It just happened to be true.'

'Then I'm glad Crazy Horse died when he did. His heart was broken enough. Do you think Buffalo Rabbit and Legs would have heard about the government's plans?'

'I'm sure they would,' the spaniel nodded. 'Gossip spread fast in the agency. They'd have heard, eventually.'

'That's good,' Bo smiled to herself. 'It would have

made them feel better, knowing their master was saved from that. They must have missed him terribly, but they already knew he was sad. They knew he'd never be happy. Not in an agency. Not without his own land.'

'The land was a lie,' Cavendish sighed. 'There *was* no land. Three Stars had no right to make that promise. He did it to get Crazy Horse into the agency.'

'I thought as much,' said Bo. 'I think Buffalo Rabbit and Legs thought the same. They knew it in their hearts. They knew it was all a trick. What happened to them? Did they stay together?'

'Yes. They lived with Worm. They were well looked after and very happy. Maka Mani was there too, of course.'

'Of course. I'm glad about that. Legs and Buffalo Rabbit loved that bird. He was so clever...'

Bo caught Cavendish's eye.

'Though not as clever as Legs...' she added.

'Oh?'

'No. Legs was the most clever animal ever!'

'Don't try to flatter me, Bo. I've told you before. I wasn't Legs.'

'But you were there? You must have been there.'

'Yes, I was there. I would never send you back in time on your own. I'm always with you in some form. I have to keep an eye on you. A *beady black* eye...'

Bo looked blank.

'Oh, for heaven's sake!' the spaniel groaned. 'Can't you guess? I was Maka Mani!'

EPILOGUE

'So what were the best bits about being Buffalo Rabbit?' Cavendish asked Bo. 'What will you miss the most?'

'Oh, that's easy,' Bo replied. 'It has to be Crazy Horse. He was amazing. Brave and kind, brilliant and strange. He was the best master that any dog could have. Thank you for choosing him, Cavendish. Thank you for making me Buffalo Rabbit.'

'My pleasure,' the spaniel grinned. 'And you're right. Crazy Horse was an amazing man. What else you will you miss?'

'Loads! Let's see now. Fur. I probably shouldn't say it, but I did enjoy sleeping on fur. The ponies, of course. I love ponies and horses. The food was good, too. Not so exotic as in Cleopatra's time, but good all the same. Arrows. Hunting. I liked hunting. It was scary, sometimes, but very exciting. I liked everything, really…'

Bo tipped her head.

'Come on, then,' she giggled.

'Come on, what?'

'Where are you sending me next? That's why you asked what I'll miss, isn't it? Now I suppose you'll choose somewhere with *none* of those things. Just to annoy me.'

'On the contrary,' the spaniel laughed. 'The place I'm

thinking of has *all* of those things, and more.'

'Ooh!' Bo wagged her tail. 'This sounds good. What's the name of this place?'

'England.'

'*England?*'

'Yes. England in a very special time. A time of danger, skulduggery and a very famous mystery.'

'What sort of mystery?'

'The mystery of two little boys,' said the spaniel. 'They were brothers, both princes. The elder boy was supposed to be king, but his uncle took the crown instead.'

'So?'

'The boys disappeared. No one knows how. They were last seen in The Tower of London. Some people say they were murdered.'

'Murdered! Who's the prime suspect?'

'The uncle, who else? His name was King Richard III, and you are going to be his pet.'

'The pet of a murderer? I don't *think* so! No thank you.'

'Hold up, Bo. Richard is only a *suspect*. One of many. We don't know that he did it. We don't even know that the princes were murdered. We know nothing for sure.'

'So if I agreed to go back, if I got to know this Richard chap…'

'You might be able to shed some light.'

'Yes! I might see what really happened. I could become a *detective* dog! I could try to solve the mystery of The Princes in the Tower! When can I go?'

'Soon,' Cavendish smiled. 'You can go very soon.'

The story of Bo's adventures with Richard III and the
Princes in the Tower will be told in her next book

THORNY ROSES

www.bothepoodle.co.uk

PEOPLE AND PLACES IN IRON HORSES

The dates, descriptions, people and places in this book are based on historical fact. Here's what became of the main characters.

American Horse was born near Paha Sapa in about 1840 and was a lifelong friend of Crazy Horse. He entered The Red Cloud Agency at the same time as Young Man Afraid and, as an agency policeman, received ponies as a sign of Crazy Horse's surrender. American Horse later worked hard for fairer treatment and proper rations for the Lakota. He died at Pine Ridge Indian Reservation in 1908.

The Battle of The Little Big Horn took place on the afternoon of 25th June 1876. The only known survivor of the fight on the high ground was a horse. 'Comanche' was rescued by the army, treated for wounds, and became a mascot of the 7th Cavalry. When he died aged 30 in 1891, he was stuffed. He can be seen at The Natural History Museum, University of Kansas.

Bear Coat, General Nelson A. Miles was an ardent Indian fighter. The day after Crazy Horse surrendered, Miles attacked and defeated a band of Minneconjou, the last free Lakota on the plains. He also captured the chief of the Nez Percés and the Apache leader, Geronimo, and was involved in the Massacre at Wounded Knee. Miles became General-in-Chief of the Army and died in Washington, D.C. in 1925.

Black Buffalo had four children. The youngest, a girl, was born less than a year after Crazy Horse and Black Buffalo eloped, and was unusually fair-skinned. It is not known what happened to Black Buffalo, but the daughter was still living with the Lakota in the 1940's.

The Black Hills became the largest source of gold in the western hemisphere. The single most successful mine, Homestake, was discovered in 1876 and produced over $1 billion in gold before finally closing in 2002. Only one mine remains open today, although gold can still be found in the hills' rivers and streams. In 1980, the U.S. Supreme Court ruled that the Black Hills had been taken illegally and that the Lakota should be paid the original price plus interest. The Lakota refused, saying they wanted the land, not the money. The money remains in a bank account, still earning interest (in 2008 the total amount was over $800 million). The Black Hills has many tourist attractions and visitor centres, including Homestake Gold Mine, The Crazy Horse Monument and the Mount Rushmore carvings of presidents Washington, Jefferson, Roosevelt and Lincoln.

Black Shawl was successfully treated for tuberculosis by the same U.S. Army surgeon who tended Crazy Horse. She died in 1927.

Buffalo are really North American Bison, not buffalo at all. The original plains herds may have numbered up to 50 million animals. By 1870, there were 5 million. By 1900 there were less than 1,000. The buffalo had been slaughtered for meat, skins and sport, and in a deliberate attempt to starve out the Indians. The plains were covered in buffalo bones. These bones were collected, often by Indians, who sold them to be ground into fertiliser. Many of the bones were not buffalo bones at all, but the bones of Indians. The North American Bison is now being reintroduced by private ranchers and conservationists.

Crazy Horse was born at Bear Butte in about 1839 and died of bayonet wounds at Fort Robinson in September 1877. His body was taken away by his parents who later buried his bones and heart near Wounded Knee Creek. No one knows exactly where. The Crazy Horse Memorial, a rock carving of Crazy Horse on a pony, was started in 1948 in The Black Hills. Work goes on to this day.

Custer, George Armstrong was born in Ohio in December 1839 and died at The Battle of The Little Big Horn. He was extremely close to his wife, Libbie, who called him 'Bo'. When Custer's body was recovered from the battlefield, a lock of his hair was sent to Libbie. Custer was buried at the U.S. Military Academy, West Point, New York.

The Dry Tortugas are a series of small islands at the mouth of the Gulf of Mexico, 70 miles west of Key West,

Florida. In Crazy Horse's time they were used as prisons. It was said that no one who went there ever returned.

He Dog was one of Crazy Horse's closest friends. He was born at Bear Butte in 1840 and died at Pine Ridge Indian Reservation in 1936, having become highly respected by both Indians and whites. Much of what we know about Crazy Horse is thanks to interviews with He Dog.

Gall was born in about 1840. He was a huge man and an extraordinary warrior who always fought with a hatchet. Gall joined Sitting Bull in Canada but returned to the United States in 1881, surrendered, and became a farmer at Standing Rock Indian Reservation. Having hated the white man for so long, Gall eventually supported many of their ideas, particularly when it came to schools. Gall got very fat in later life and also had problems with bayonet wounds received in 1865. He died in 1893 after falling out of a wagon.

Indian was the name given to the native people of America and her islands by Christopher Columbus. He 'discovered' them whilst trying to sail to India. Columbus brought two very important things to America, the horse and the wheel. His arrival also decimated the local, Arawak tribes. Hundreds of thousands died in less than ten years. When the English landed in Virginia in 1607, the same thing happened to the Powhatan (Pocahonta's tribe). Over the next three-hundred years, '500 Nations' of Indians were slaughtered, sold into slavery, driven to starvation or sentenced to death from imported European diseases such as measles, smallpox, cholera and tuberculosis. The Shawnee in Indiana, the Seminole in Florida, the Creek in Georgia, the Winnebago in Michigan, the Cherokee in Arkansas; the Apache, Araphoe, Comanche, Cheyenne, Chikasaw, Crow, Delaware, Kiowa, Navaho, Ree, Shoshone, the list goes on and on. This book is about just one of those many tribes. All faced similar problems.

Interpreter The interpreter who mistranslated Crazy Horse's words, 'every last Nez Percés' to 'every last white man' was the experienced guide and frontiersman, Frank 'Grabber' Grouard. He'd been a friend of both Sitting Bull and Crazy Horse, and spoke fluent Lakota, so his mistranslation was almost certainly deliberate. Frank Grouard became famous for his part in the Indian wars and died in St. Louis, Missouri in 1905.

Little Big Man was a fine warrior but also something of a trouble-maker. He became a policeman at The Red Cloud Agency and was always trying to 'get in with' the soldiers. Little Big Man held Crazy Horse back on two occasions - when No Water shot him, and when he struggled at Fort Robinson. Little Big Man died at Pine Ridge Indian Reservation in about 1888.

Lakota - Language is extremely beautiful and musical. In Crazy Horse's time it was only spoken, never written down. It has been written down since, but too few people speak it. The older Lakota are trying to encourage their children to learn it and save it for the future.

Lakota - People are a division of The Sioux Nation (the other divisions are Santee and Yankton). The Lakota consist of seven tribes: Oglala, Sans Arc, Minneconjou, Hunkpapa, Blackfeet, Brulé and Two Kettle.

The Northern Pacific Railroad ran out of money in September 1873. Work re-started four years later. In 1883 the tracks were joined. They ran from Minnesota in the east, to Washington State in the west, and went right through what had been the Crazy Horse country.

The Oregon Trail was the only feasible way to travel from the eastern states of America, over The Rocky Mountains and into the west. The trail was first used in 1836, but the biggest wave was between 1843 and 1868 when more than half a million people made the journey by wagon, on horseback and even on foot. The glory years of the Oregon Trail finally ended in 1869 when The Union Pacific and Central Pacific railroads were joined in Utah, and iron horses could chug right across the country. Actual wagon ruts can still be seen along the route of the Oregon Trail.

No Water was Black Buffalo's husband. He was a possessive, aggressive man, and a heavy drinker of whiskey. He moved to Pine Ridge Indian Reservation in 1877.

Red Cloud was born in 1822. He was a brilliant warrior and played a crucial part in driving the U.S. Army from The Powder River Country in the late 1860's, but his signing of The Fort Laramie Treaty was taken as a victory by the whites and caused resentment and division amongst the Lakota. Red Cloud had a scheming nature, but he understood the white man's world and battled hard for his people. In the end, he lost to both. The whites thought he was difficult, the Lakota thought he gave in too easily. Red Cloud died peacefully, but embittered, at Pine Ridge Indian Reservation in December 1909.

The Red Cloud Agency was disbanded in 1877. The Oglala Lakota were moved to Pine Ridge Indian Reservation, South Dakota. The Hunkpapa went to the Standing Rock Reservation, North Dakota. Other Lakota went to the Rosebud Reservation, South Dakota. The Lakota still live on these reservations, most of them in extreme poverty and with high rates of diabetes, suicide and alcholism.

Red Feather, brother of Black Shawl, warned Crazy Horse that the soldiers and warriors were coming to arrest him. In fact, Crazy Horse and Black Shawl fled to another agency. I left this bit out because it involved people and places not previously mentioned and did not effect the outcome. Crazy Horse was persuaded to return next morning with the promise that he could speak to Colonel Bradley. That is where I pick the story up.

Reno, Major Marcus never recovered from The Battle of The Little Big Horn. Some blamed him for Custer's death. The Army held an inquiry and found Reno innocent, but he was later dismissed for drunken behaviour. Reno died in 1889.

Sitting Bull was Hunkpapa Lakota. This extraordinary man was born around 1831. He was extremely brave and very soft-hearted. He was never a 'chief' (a white man's word), but was highly respected and loved by his people. He was past fighting age at The Battle of The Little Big Horn, but helped with tactics before leading the people to safety. After the battle, Sitting Bull got tired of being chased by soldiers and escaped to Canada. When he returned to America in 1881, he was arrested. He was imprisoned for two years but then allowed to rejoin his people at Standing Rock Indian Reservation. When he protested that they were starving, the conversation went like this:

S.B: 'I wish to say a word.'
Government Officials: 'We do not care to talk to you.'
S.B: 'I would like to speak.'

(Uncannily similar to the words of King Charles I at the end of his trial, as Storm Dogs readers will know!)

Sitting Bull became the star attraction in Buffalo Bill Cody's Wild West Show. He toured America and signed autographs, but his heart lay with his people. He quarrelled with officials at Standing Rock, was arrested again in 1890 and was shot dead by Indian police.

They Are Afraid of Her was Crazy Horse and Black Shawl's daughter. She died very suddenly whilst Crazy Horse was away from home, checking on the Crow. Some reports say that They Are Afraid had cholera, but there was no epidemic in camp, so it seems more likely that she died of childhood diarrhoea and dehydration.

Three Stars, General George Crook, kept up the Indian fighting. He chased the Apaches and their leader, Geronimo, until they surrendered to Bear Coat Miles in 1886. Crook died four years later, in Chicago.

Two Moons and fifty of his Cheyenne surrendered to Bear Coat Miles in 1877. They were eventually moved to the Cheyenne Reservation on The Tongue River, where Two Moons became reservation leader. He visited Washington several times, and died in 1917 aged 70. A monument marks his burial site near Busby, Montana.

White Hat (William H. Clark) was an able soldier who was genuinely interested in Indians and wrote a study of their sign language. White Hat died suddenly in 1884 aged 39.

Wolves used to be found all over North America. In 1630, bounties were offered in Massachusetts for anyone who killed one. Other states soon followed. Between 1870 and 1877 a huge demand for fur meant that more than 10,000 wolves were slaughtered. By the 1930's they were almost extinct in America. Nowadays, wolves are a protected species in certain states. Montana and Wyoming currently have about 500 wolves each.

Woman's Dress had been a childhood friend of Crazy Horse. He remained a scout and informant for the army and died in 1920.

Worm was born in 1810 and moved to the Rosebud Indian Reservation in 1877.

Young Man Afraid was born in 1930. He was a lifelong friend of Crazy Horse and was fiercely protective of Indian rights, whilst still managing to keep peace with the whites. He died at Pine Ridge Indian Reservation in 1900.

The characters on The Oregon Trail, the **Irvine** family, the **MacCauley** brothers and **Spotty**, are made up, but based on various documented, 'real-life' people who travelled the trail.

Legs and **Maka Mani** are also made up, but wolves and ravens would have been everyday sights for Crazy Horse. Indians had a natural affinity with animals, kept many dogs, and often rescued and tamed wild creatures.

they were almost extinct in Amer... Nowadays, are a protected species in certain states. Mont... Wyoming currently have about 5-6 wolves each

LOCAL COLLECTION